MICHAEL FISHWICK

Sacrifices

VINTAGE BOOKS
London

Published by Vintage 2007

2 4 6 8 10 9 7 5 3 1

First published in Great Britain in 2006 by
Jonathan Cape

Vintage
Random House, 20 Vauxhall Bridge Road,
London SW1V 2SA

www.vintage-books.co.uk

Addresses for companies within The Random House Group Limited
can be found at: www.randomhouse.co.uk/offices.htm

The Random House Group Limited Reg. No. 954009

A CIP catalogue record for this book
is available from the British Library

ISBN 9780099285946

Printed and bound in Great Britain by
Bookmarque Ltd, Croydon, Surrey

For Imogen

Acknowledgements

I owe a great many thanks to my literary agent David Godwin for his wonderful insights into this book at crucial moments in its progress, and to my publisher Dan Franklin for his kindness and support; also, for their various welcome contributions, Ellah Allfrey, my editor at Jonathan Cape, Cathryn Summerhayes at DGA, Rachel Holmes, Suzanne Dean, Caroline Michel and Mick Mahoney.

Contents

ALSO BY MICHAEL FISHWICK

Smashing People

Schooling

All of us often go wrong; the man who never says a wrong thing is a perfect character, able to bridle his whole being. If we put bits into horses' mouths to make them obey our will, we can direct their whole body. Or think of ships: large they may be, yet even when driven by strong gales they can be directed by a tiny rudder on whatever course the helmsman chooses. So with the tongue. It is a small member but it can make huge claims.

What an immense stack of timber can be set ablaze by the tiniest spark! And the tongue is in effect a fire.

James 3: 2–6

M Y FATHER WAS an honourable man.
He was, he was.

Steadfast, loyal and kind.

His purposes in life were always for the best. His eyes were fixed ever upon the far horizon, where greatness lay, and I feel he went there, that long journey to discover and disseminate the best, before the end. Well before the end.

And no matter what his detractors say.

But I won't think of them now, even though they are walking with what dignity they can muster up the long dark path towards us as we shiver in the sunshine. The early March air cuts harshly into exposed skin and makes it raw. Mummy looks blue with it. I wonder what she is thinking. I wonder what they are all thinking.

Why am I so absurd? I know exactly what they are thinking.

While the wind chafes, the sun warms. I can feel the pulse of the sun, the first, really, of the year. Over the flooded valleys and over the escarpment the wind swings, unable to let the winter go. Prickles of sweat turn to tiny cold globes. This is the day that a daughter buries her father, and my heart is splintering.

Up they trudge. A slow march. Their black shoes glittering,

3

their black trouser-legs edged like razors. All black cloth and silver buttons and dignified mien.

Getting a bit incoherent. Daddy would not have approved.

'Like mathematics, Anna,' I imagine him saying, 'grammar is the sublime soul of the universe. It's all in the Ancients, if you know where to look.'

Now, I don't know where to look.

Perhaps I should look at them all, one by one. I shall look at them as if with his eyes, reprovingly. They will see him in me, watching them.

We have chosen readings for the select few. Will they guess?

I am too conscious of everything – of the bright green grass, of the dark green yews, of weathered stone inscribed with the records of others going where my father has gone. *His* faith was flintlike. He'll know the truth of it now. And at least he will be beyond the reach of his enemies, of whom there are a number here today, come to pay their last disrespects.

When he retired, not so many years ago, a thousand filled the cathedral, the only place with the capacity to host the throng. He was a wronged hero then, everyone thought so, an honourable victim of rumour and malice. They filled the pews like ball bearings running along a track, clack-clack-clack, the whole city flying the flag for the wounded man.

Not many of them here now.

So who do we have?

We have Alexander Rainsford, headmaster since Daddy retired.

Who spoke to the press first? Was it him?

He's a well-built man. Tall. Floppy dark hair, which he flicks out of his eyes like one much younger. Could wash it more often. He's got a son called Luke somewhere who lives in London and wants to be an actor. He hardly ever sees him. Wide-open pores, skin like a sieve. Not a bad nose, straight, with wide nostrils. Eyebrows like slugs. Huge ears. A sign of intelligence. Full lips but disastrous teeth. Someone really had a go at those. His eyes are downcast, but I know they are a rich peat-coloured brown. That lovely colour you get in streams in the hills. Intelligent clear thoughtful brown.

I think he may have been the one.

Even if he didn't start it, he did enough, I think. Enough to finish off a father, anyway, or to push him to a place where he might *be* finished, which comes to the same thing. And a daughter, if it comes to that. And it may do.

Here they come, loose-limbed or stiff-limbed, vacant-faced, really just ordinary people with their commonplace desires and frustrations and tragedies locked like tiny tree-knots into the spreading rings of their lives. Well advanced in the life business now, most of them.

We have spent the last week plundering literature for plangent rhythms and resounding aperçus, for wisdom dressed up in its glad rags. I have been burying my nose in anthologies and leafing through loved volumes of poetry, not looking for solace, no, not that, because it's all been so busy and solace seems a luxury. Somewhere ahead, above the road I travel, there lies a deep bar of cloud, oppressively black, sweeping across the sky. But I haven't got there yet. So far it is the petty ritual of appointments and decisions and arrangements that concern me. I think I am lucky in this, because the deluge of things that need to be organized make it impossible for me to think about the things I so need to think about.

What would I think about?

There are things I would try not to think about.

The end, mostly. That is a distant region, for now, its borders fiercely protected. I know the way to it, but I choose not to go. I may never go. There was wrongdoing, certainly, a crime, I suppose, and an insane one, but deserved. And it would be misleading of me to suggest there was only one, to be truthful, though the second was of a very different nature. And these are things that someone someday might find out. So for now I leave that dark country with the bristling but ultimately vulnerable frontier to itself, decaying out there in my imagination. Let it fester. I'll go back there soon enough, will be dragged screaming and wrestling and pummelling my abductors as they haul me back into their clouded, low-lying valley, the place of shadow I'm choosing not to illuminate.

What I should be thinking about is the occupant of the oaken box as it sails along, polish flashing in the sunlight. What does sunlight do in the presence of sorrow? It does not animate, it is metallic somehow; I can almost taste the sour, hot glare. The newness of the box from which it glints is the most offensive thing. It's a here-today-gone-tomorrow, mass-produced factory affair, it doesn't look like the one I thought we chose. Someone has put a lot of elbow grease into polishing it, though, and the polish magnifies the grain, brings the curling ruddy-brown lines that crowd in upon each other like the contours of a weather system up to the surface. There are knots in it. It is new, it is now, it gleams like Las Vegas.

To be honest, it is catastrophically vulgar.

It is passing me. It is passing. He is passing. Over the threshold. They all avoid my eye.

Come on, Mummy. Come on. Pretend you care. It's the least you can do. Let's make believe those tears are the real thing. Let's go in now and take our places. Everyone else is there, we shouldn't linger. Up to the front. Why did we wait outside? I'm not sure it's the usual thing to do; were we welcoming him? I am beginning to see that a funeral is really about the triumph of the living. Death is a terrible humiliation. How must it feel to die at another's hand, at another's instigation, knowing they will live and you will be gone?

Perhaps choosing it is a kind of triumph, then. The Japanese writer Yukio Mishima, whom I read with the scholarship class as a distraction from Milton, Donne, Lawrence and the rest, knowing that if they can parachute his name into an interview they will undoubtedly impress the university examiners and their glory will reflect well upon the school, was a great enthusiast for disembowelling oneself and spilling one's own gleaming intestines in sliding heaps upon the floor. The death lust of the self-conqueror. No one shall have power over me, only I over myself.

There am I standing at the border of the dark country again, looking in.

And here is my mother, small and frail and fretful, just like me. Side by side we stare blankly into the future. I am aware, without looking, of the powder on her face; she hasn't got the colour quite right, it's a little too yellow and it streaks across her nose and up into her forehead like a river delta, golden and fissiparous. It gives her a mildly tigerish appearance, absurd since she is more mild than tigerish. It is not that she doesn't care for herself; if anything she does so more than is necessary, though she is prone to such lapses as today's: a little overexcitement leading to carelessness in the application, an unwillingness to gaze more thoughtfully into the mirror.

She often looks a bit of a mess. I think she always did, and I know Daddy thought so too, but he was an extraordinarily exacting man, in a way that I found admirable from my earliest memory of him, when he was a humble housemaster at the

Hall, before we came to Meniston. My god, how the wind howled round the windows and eaves of that place. Thomas Hardy may have glorified upland West Country bleakness but his books are for reading when curled up underneath a mound of bedclothes. One doesn't want the real thing, for any money. The Hall. A clumsy early-nineteenth-century edifice that inflicted lifelong damage on the boys passing through its portals, not because it was architecturally dismal, though that would have been reason enough for anyone of sensibility, but because a regime had been allowed to form there which was repugnant to any right-thinking person. I think Daddy did a lot to help those poor innocent boys. Well, innocent? Not so innocent at all, if you ask me. It takes two to tango, as Daddy would one day learn to his cost.

Which reminds me. Is Daniel here? If he is, I shall be dignified. I don't know whether I shall be able to look *him* in the eye. I am not sure I will recognize him, after all this time. I wonder what he is wearing. A proper suit of mourning, I hope; he could be very slapdash. I hope he has taken the trouble. Now Daddy is gone, perhaps we could be together, just for a little while, maybe for longer. Is that more of my madness? Too much time has elapsed, far too much. Could it be possible after all that has happened, after all I have done? Can I ever be normal again? Can I be forgiven? How I long for him to be here. I hope he is here. He needs someone to look after him, he always did. I should never have let him go. Did I have the choice? Didn't he let me go? Didn't we all let each other go?

THE HALL. I think that is where it began to go wrong for Mummy, though I was too young to see it. What did she expect from Daddy, I wonder? What does anyone expect from anyone? Now that's a question as big as the sky. And I'm sure I don't have the answer to it, though I count myself a shrewd judge of human affairs and affairs of the heart especially. I know people think me finicky and difficult and withdrawn, and something of a curious coughdrop, as Aunt Belinda used to call me, but it's not all simply down to experience.

Daddy was tall, of course, which is always a good thing, and an army man. In the faded photographs in the broken-backed albums that they kept in the old linen box — I could never understand why they didn't keep linen in it but Mummy was like that and probably contrived to lose the linen to avoid having to iron it — they appear comically ill-matched. His own father had survived Dunkirk, came back full of tales of the horror of the beaches, tales I feel I could tell myself with his very own inflections, too, the points where he would stop for reflection or effect. Grandad liked his stories to be prac-tised to the point of perfect familiarity, so they seemed as much a part of him as his old walking stick with the battered brass ferrule and the heavy ivory handle, or his three sports jackets with the frayed elbows that he managed to run a patch over himself (Grandma was no good for that sort of thing, in India she had had servants and still thought she had), or the red velvet slippers with the gold crest he wore. And what stories they were, of the battle-weary swarms of dejected men, patiently awaiting the end, having seen at last the reality of war and the lightning speed of the German advance, which had surprised even Churchill, who like everyone else still thought that the Second World War would be fought like the first. (Grandad would pause here and raise his eyebrows: this was an important point.) They had seen brutality as never before, and what is more it was systematic, carefully planned brutality calculated to strike terror and dismay into the hearts of both civilian and soldier. The gratuitous slaughter of fleeing refugees by the Luftwaffe was intended simply to block the roads to Dunkirk and hold up the Expeditionary Force's retreat, an action the like of which few had ever encountered. I can hear him now. *'That* was terrible!' He told of how he kept the morale of his bedraggled, bleeding men high by singing the popular songs of the time in different accents, Australian, German, Italian, and herded them into the water to climb aboard a fragile rivercraft that looked as if it had last seen service at Henley Regatta, only to see it hit by a stray shell as he waded back to shore to pick up and carry a man with a shattered knee, and the two of them watched as the sea was filled with the torn limbs of their comrades.

And then his eyes would be downcast, and nothing more would be said for some moments.

Mummy's family was very close. They were Quakers and she was the youngest of five sisters. She was outrageous then, from what I can tell. She was not yet out of her teens, he was touching thirty. She took an unhindered joy in life, the kind you see in baby mice or puppies. You would scarcely credit it now. Maybe she will get some of it back, though it has been a long time. Somehow I don't think so. But *then* – it bursts through even the bleached-out colouring of the photographs – she was insouciant, she was brave, she wanted to give the world a good kick and see what happened. The world was an apple tree ripe for picking. I'll have this one and this one and this one.

Daddy didn't approve of her religion. His own father had been of indeterminate faith: he travelled a good deal in later life, and the two of them were not intimate. My grandmother, though, she was staunch Church of England, and would have nothing to do with any variations. She liked her religion as high as she could get it. 'High to the point of being gamey, gamey to the point of being rancid,' I once heard Mummy remark, without obvious bitterness. I can't imagine quaking or shaking or indeed any of that kind of unfettered religiosity was to Granny's taste, and Daddy did take his mother's line on such things. So much so that he forbade Mummy to attend Quaker meetings. I don't think this mattered greatly to her at the time; she was at the age when all things must be questioned, and one's birthright most of all. But it must have clipped her wings a bit.

Daddy went straight into teaching when he left the army. I think it was an occupation he longed for: the years in the army had simply stoked his determination, even if it was not the real reason he had left, had had to leave, as I know now. He knew he would have a life in teaching, and that the passing-on of knowledge was a great calling. History and science were his subjects. Both were to him the most significant studies of the age. The first, because it was, self-evidently, the past that could elucidate and be illuminated by the momentous events of the great wars, one of which had so dominated his early life, and the second because the dropping of the atom bombs in Japan seemed to bring an era to an end. That era began, he would say, with the publication of Max Planck's papers on quantum physics in the early nineteen hundreds. Physics was to be the liberation of mankind, but the splitting of the atom did not, in the context of war, seem to point that way. Physics had become a science of death; the new science of life, following the discovery of the double helix, was genetics.

In the nineteenth century, the writings of Darwin came after faith had already begun to falter. Fossils were a revelation that challenged the Bible, just at a time when such revelations were needed. 'Illumination comes when it is looked for,' as Daddy used to say. 'We are the architects of our own futures.' He would go on. 'And our failures.'

For most of his life, it might be recorded, failure did not come readily to Daddy.

BY THE TIME I was five years old, we had long been settled in at the Hall. I remember the great hill that rose up behind it as you looked from the drive that led to the front door of the main building. When the sky was overcast this hill was at its most terrifying: it was a pure arc, like one of the boys' protractors, and black as ink. It was particularly so in late summer, when the bracken had turned and the slope, sweeping unbroken to the crest, was an impenetrable darkness as the sun set behind it. The boys were sent on long runs over its top, once a term.

Poor darlings, in their billowing vests and black pants and pumps, straining up that implacable hill, its top always, or seemingly always, beyond the brow. Scrawny, pale limbs panting after one another, feet scuffing the turf, perspiration soaking their bodies. We used to stand, Daddy and I, at the starting tape, which was clasped by the gloved hands of the sports master and his callow assistant, whose grey knees shivered in the gale. The boys were herded jostling against the tape, as if they were a flock of newborn lambs, even the most thuggish of them. My heart bled, though I knew it should not, and that the brave should be brave. My grandfather survived Dunkirk, after all. But war seemed far away then; it has come closer since. We lived in a black-and-white world of black-and-white television and black-and-white values. I didn't think this then but I think it now: there was an innocence to be had in an age when nuclear warheads would obliterate us all in moments. The boys as they streamed white and vulnerable in their hundreds down the black shoulders of the ridge to the finishing line were just exhausted boys, at the back some of them walking and at the front small speeding deities, fit beyond all that seemed necessary. Boys didn't need to conquer, any more; the missiles would do it for them. Down the ridge they hurtled, the frontrunners, their frames packed with amazing energy, running, running.

What an effect Daddy had on that school. It was, as I say, a forbidding place, with its blackened stone and the windows darkening as they reflected the sombreness of the moor. Its children were those of prominent West Country businessmen and other dignitaries from the counties round about, who thought that the apogee of life's success was to send their children – the boys, at least – for a private education, and pretty much any private education would do. The farmers thought the same, though of course the really big landowners sent their sons to Marlborough or Eton. The boys that came our way at the Hall were the sons of practical people, not drifters or idealists or the rich. And they were treated as such.

Daddy's arrival caused a small earthquake. No, I'm wrong about that. A proper, relaying-of-the-masonry revolution; that's a better description. He arrived with the intention of turning the school upside down, and that is exactly what he did. The teachers hated him; most of them had been there for many years and cobwebs hung about their ears. There was worse. Beatings were common, humiliation the current coinage. The boys were expected to become practical like their fathers, and anything more elaborate was greatly discouraged. Why Daddy lighted upon the place as the means to his advancement is beyond me. He was terribly ambitious, and I think that when you can see your final destination with blinding clarity, the stations of your advancement may be clear to you, but perhaps not to everyone else. I would put it like this: to arrive at a school of plodding ineptitude, where the mundane is the norm and the pupils leave with no greater understanding of learning in their poor lame noddles than they had to begin with, and to make that school into one where there was some semblance of achievement and self-respect among its benighted scholars, is a sign to the world of real greatness, or at least potential greatness. That is what Daddy sought; but at the Hall he was only a housemaster, and he could do much but not everything. He could lay the founding stones of the fortress, and caulk the first planks of the outgoing vessel bound for glory. And then move on.

He was a gifted teacher. There were few like him in the country at that time, and he was a revelation at the Hall. He longed to implant the secrets of his knowledge in the minds of his pupils; and he had an uncanny sense of their individual capacities for learning. He had no gimmicks, of the kind that teachers who want to be loved and who seek a cheap notoriety have, but he had an intense desire to instil in his pupils the same love of the subject that he had himself. Perhaps a little too intense: more than once a boy would comment on the way in which he felt exhausted by one of Daddy's lessons. He demanded, and received, complete attention, and each lesson, whether it were on the economic underpinnings of the Reform Act of 1832 or on the bloodletting at the Battle of Isandhlwana in the Zulu Wars, whether it were on the mating pattern of the fruit fly or the components of the periodic table, he would drench his rapt listeners in the beautifully delineated principles of the subject.

We could all have benefited from teaching of that kind in our lives. I know I could.

He did love those boys. Love makes the best teacher. In the best kind of way. I, too, have been guilty of loving too much.

As a housemaster he was, I think, not so successful. He was competent; and to how many of us is that given? He was energetic, which is usually sufficient. But it was not his first love. Perhaps it is only those who knew and loved him well who could see this distinction, and I am not at all sure that he himself could see it, for his ambitions told him that house-mastering was a necessary step to take, and that he could accomplish it with his usual ease.

When he stood before an audience of boys, at the end-of-term house play, for instance, or the weekly assemblies, he was diffident, but never tentative. He had views, and was always candid. With parents, however, on those rare occasions on which they deigned to show an interest in their offspring's lamentable development, he could be quite demure. His large hands would flap unhappily, his weighty eyebrows lower with forced concentration, his large ears blush a little, and he would from time to time run the end of his middle finger soothingly along the side of his scalp from the temple to just behind his ear. His whole posture projected an awkward sufferance as his eyes darted anxiously from one questioner to another. With fellow teachers it was a different matter. With them, he tended to use his height, leaning forward on his toes, seemingly on the point of crashing into them should an unfavourable breeze come their way, and exercising his alarming eyebrows, which were just a little too thick and a little too broad not to remind one of those figures of the silent screen, comic males or female beauties with floppy hats and fur stoles. He was intimidating when he wanted to be, and I think he often did want to be, for on the whole he despised them: he always knew that he was a better teacher than any of them, and they knew it too. That was why he was there. What *was* a challenge was facing down those who deeply resented his incursions into their domain. A housemaster had a certain position: enough to chide heads of department about the quality of their own incumbents, and as Daddy was, or quickly became, head of history, with a special role in the teaching of science which seems peculiar now but was not so at all in those days, and certainly not at that school, his remit to interfere gave him considerable leeway for rapierlike probing of the extended guts of the hidebound practioners of learning-by-rote and sneaking-off-for-a-crafty-drag-five-minutes-before-the-end-of-the-lesson who thronged the Hall at that time.

All of which made him unpopular. However, he was also feared, and this mattered a great deal. It mattered to him, who knew the value of fear, and it mattered to Mummy, because his many enemies visited their vengeful feelings upon her *faute de mieux*. She found herself ostracized in a tiny community, and she a girl who had expected a somewhat easier licence in life's sweet course. Fat chance. When they married I wonder whether she expected to serve in the way that Daddy manifestly intended her to do. By 'serve' I don't mean that he wanted her scrubbing steps or washing down blackboards. He did not want her passing around cucumber sandwiches at school open days. He wanted her to serve the interests of the house – his interests, yes, but arguably those of the greater whole – and this meant glad-handing the parents and planning the outings and arranging menus and second-guessing his oversights and taking a view on the new matron. He wanted her to be first mate, best friend and second-in-command. There are many women who know how to fulfil such roles. I could do it myself. I did do it myself. I understand exactly what Daddy wanted of Mummy. But she seemed to be incapable of it. No coaxing of the head of the English department to take charge of the under-11 B league football for her. And yet it would have been so easy. It is so easy. I do it all the time.

So what was she good for? What did she *think* she was good for? I know I am hard on her. It is a long time since we have been close, if we ever were, but, honestly, I don't think we ever were. She and I are not really alike, a point my aunts are often — they are a long-lived lot — happy to emphasize. (Hapless is the niece of a thousand aunts.) Whatever else, she and I certainly have a different conception of the word 'duty'.

I do not mean that Mummy was fly or giddy in any way. She was perhaps a little excitable, that's all. Grandma and Great-Grandmama were freethinking, adventurous souls, with a somewhat florid conception of what life has to offer. I'm sure they encouraged her; in many ways, they encouraged me, they all did, that side of the family. They were intellectuals and artists and philanthropists in the grand tradition; Great-grandfather was one of the first Labour MPs, though he was given his peerage and so sat in the Lords. So Mummy was of course a passionate socialist, yet she married a man committed to private education. Not that this ever seems to have encumbered her with doubts. On the contrary, *au contraire* as darling Daniel always said, finger raised in mock caution, she was — is — a free-booting idealist, whose opinions and artistry were much enjoyed in the early days at the Hall. She has a wonderful, if reedy, voice, and when she chooses plays the piano beautifully. Not just beautifully; she has a gift that allows her to express herself in a way she is rarely able to do in any other way. It is sad how seldom she gives rein to it now, though only yesterday I found her playing as I have not heard her for years; I thought someone had put my prized CD of the early work of Alfred Brendel on, but no, it was Mummy, and the fluidity of her movements, the grandeur of her execution were – curiously, since she and the music were so alive – like ghosts of the time when she had been her real, essential self, so long ago. I came upon her unexpectedly, in the cramped living room of the cottage to which they were reduced ever since everything happened to Daddy, and the billowing exuberance of her playing might have graced the stage of the Albert Hall.

As I say, she was a great success when she arrived, the bohemian wife of a new housemaster, the hippy chick in the bowels of the establishment, wearing tie-dye T-shirts at assembly and her hair long. Imagine the look on the face of the chemistry master, and the lascivious thoughts of the geography master, who was trying to grow his sideboards long and let the hair on the back of his head creep over his collar to impress her. She was the breath of fresh air that galvanises and terrifies. The air of the Seventies was flowing ever faster in the world outside the Hall, but it is the nature of such places to resist change, and Mummy was the exotic, the stray flown in from the tropics on the breath of easterly winds. She played Bach on the organ in the school chapel. She led painting expeditions out on the moor. (Three pupils and two masters' wives accompanied; she usually managed to find a way to fob off the geography master.) She was a soloist in the school choir for a time and I remember her singing as if it were yesterday, and the way her forehead puckered into a tiny furrow when she reached the high notes.

She tried to be part of the school. She tried to be what

Schooling

Daddy wanted her to be. Every morning at chapel, regular as anything, she was there, quietly in a corner, soberly dressed in boots and long skirts and a dark grey headscarf, where no one would notice but of course everyone did; and she would be there on Sunday and at evensong, too, for though she had abandoned her childhood faith she was actively in search of a new allegiance and she was determined to find one. The Hall chapel was not really a good place to find such a thing. The Hall chapel was good for nothing but vacuous teenagers pulling faces at each other over the pews and making boorish statements by sitting upright all the way through prayers, as if they had ever in their short, brutish lives sensibly and properly considered the nature of Christianity, its glories, comforts and certainties. At morning church, three times a week not including Sundays, housemasters would sit with their houses and Mummy and I would sit together, always in the same place three rows from the front and to the left, which was inconvenient for me as I wanted to look around all the time and was strictly forbidden to do so. Near us sat the choirboys in their red cassocks and white surplices, looking bored out of their wits for the most part, in spite of the antics of the organist, who was the assistant head of music and did most of the work. The head of music, Mr Salter, was often ill and eventually had to leave altogether. The assistant, whose name was Bannister, was a terrible show-off, and though his back was turned it was apparent that every movement was directed to the congregation. He would hunch with the tension of a cat about to spring, then he would run his feet over the pedals with the joviality of a Morris dancer and hurl himself upon the keys, elbows akimbo, his grey hair becoming more and more unkempt as he slid a hand through it in dramatic frenzy whenever a hand happened to be spare, which was surprisingly often. When Mr Salter was absent and there was no one to conduct the choir he would attempt to do it himself, which did little for the choir save replace boredom with amusement, but often led to misplayed notes and crashing discords: the whole performance delighted me, and even Mummy, trying so hard to be good, found it hard to keep a straight face. The rest of the time I concentrated on running my finger over the names of boys long since departed which were cut deep into the backs of the pews, names whose edges had softened and blackened with age. Testimony to the everlasting imperviousness of the boyish mind to the word of God. Where had they all gone, I wondered. In the stained glass the beasts symbolizing the four gospel writers ramped over images of Christ feeding the five thousand, John the Baptist making way for the coming of his Lord, the water changed into wine and the figure of Judas black against the light of Christ at His last supper.

She taught a little, English mainly. She occasionally liked to put on plays. In this I am like her, though of course it was not till much later that I was allowed to put on plays myself, which have always been a great delight to me. She had an abiding passion for Shakespeare, not dissimilar to most people, I suppose. Her enthusiasm was not a guarantee of success: I recall an ambitious attempt at *A Midsummer Night's Dream* in the school garden, which had to be abandoned halfway through the first performance because good old Dorset rain put paid to the magical forest, which was made of cardboard and melted under its own soggy weight. I'll say this for Mummy, though; she had a new forest planted out by the following evening.

She could be a great one for entertaining. In her teens she had been to stay with family friends in Provence and had learned all sorts of things like how to bone and stuff a chicken or make a *pissaladière* or – unheard of then – a *salade niçoise*. I don't think Daddy noticed much – food was never a concern to him – but his colleagues treated her cuisine as a matter for suspicion. This meant that Daddy had to ask her to stick with more conventional fare, so Mummy did, and kept her real skills for visiting friends, upon whom she lavished her culinary attentions. These friends visited less and less frequently, however, for we were a long way away from London, and Mummy became more and more disinclined to be at home for the kind of visitors she did get, and she developed a habit of hurriedly concealing herself in the broom cupboard and dragging me in with her hand clamped over my mouth when their shadows darkened the front door. At first I thought this great fun, but after a while it became apparent to the staff that she was in when she was pretending to be out – it is hard to keep up this kind of pretence in a small boarding school – and in a housemaster's wife this is unseemly conduct, and Daddy had to be severe with her. When they had a row, Daddy tended to win, so this was one of their early rows, and there were not many after that. Mummy didn't really have very far to run to. Not easy, the position of housemaster's wife.

As for me, I had no trammel. I was too young for responsibility, and my father was too important for me to be ignored. I was indulged, even caressed, by the staff, and treated, respectfully, as a curiosity by the boys. When the time came, I had my lessons with them, an arrangement which I don't suppose would be condoned now, though it was not uncommon then. I am not in a position to say whether it did me good or ill; not the latter, but not unquestionably the former, either. Boys can be tiresome and slow and dull, but

I never spent much time with my own sex, about whom I know comparatively little, so I don't know about the ghastliness of little girls, though I have heard about it. I can certainly surmise it from some of my colleagues.

My ally, my partner in crime as she used to call herself, was our matron. Her family had been Jewish refugees from Austria, and she still spoke with a thick accent. I never heard her refer to the past save once, when the boys jeered at her and told her to go back where she had come from after she had tried to intervene in a sock fight outside her room, where I was visiting her as I often did. It was as if she had been slapped hard in the face.

'Where I come from,' she said, very slowly, without intonation. 'Where I come from, we were not wanted.'

For a moment, this small comical figure, with her shock of greying fair hair and her high cheekbones and her soft blue eyes and her determined chin, possessed a dignity we had not seen before. Those eyes were moist as she turned to me, and behind her I watched the young warriors slink away. She made me my hot chocolate and added some cold milk at the last minute as she always did because, she said, she was afraid of my tongue being scalded.

'Those boys, those boys!' she cried with her back to me, and I could tell she had recovered herself. Her manner of speech was one of constant exclamation marks, and this was one of her favourite phrases, so much so that the boys themselves never tired of imitating it, very often to her face in richly overexaggerated accents of variable pedigree and questionable origin.

'Those boys, those boys!'

The best time to go knocking at her door was after the business of the day – the endless round of overseeing the washing and ironing of sheets, for a house matron had all that to see to as well as the health of her charges and the administration of the sick room – and before the mêlée of the evening when the boys started going to bed, rushing along corridors and cannoning into each other, surreptitiously prosecuting their feuds and alliances while they thundered in and out of the bathroom leaving taps running and bars of soap on the floor, and above all would be heard her cry of 'Oh, you boys! You *boys*!', which was echoed mercilessly back to her, and she would stand at the door of a devastated bathroom wailing ineffectually, 'Oh! They are such *mucky* pups! *Mucky* pups!'

Between the hard work of the day and the helter-skelter of the evening she would be found with a cup of tea and a plate of biscuits and a ready smile for me.

'You know, it is sad, little one, that you do not have a brother or sister to play with,' she said to me once.

'But I have you, Mrs Boke,' I replied. Her real name was Kobak, but I could never remember it, so I was privileged to be the only person who didn't call her Matron, or Mrs Kopeck, as the postman and the milkman did. It was my secret name for her.

She seemed pleased, and nodded thoughtfully, and went on to talk more about her family. But later she looked at me again and said, 'But you know, it is still a shame.'

We would talk of the doings of the school, what I knew of them in my child's universe, though because the school was its own universe and mine was part of it I did know a lot, and about Daddy, whom matron thought very highly of, and about Mummy, whom she respected. And about those boys: who had fallen out with whom, who was being ganged up on, who had received a food parcel and who had a birthday coming up: matron was very good at birthdays, which was one reason the boys loved her in spite of their mimicry, and she was good at finding out about bullying and getting something done about it. Most of her information I am pleased to say came from me, because although the boys thought I was an oddity and set apart from them, this meant they could either tell me things they did not share with each other, or sometimes hardly noticed I was there when hostilities broke out in earnest. I was a useful little ghost, someone who was there and not there, a listener, a magpie for Mrs Boke.

And then one day it all came to an end.

It was Mrs Boke's fault. She shouldn't have told me what she did, because I knew it already, somewhere in my heart of hearts. Mummy was going mad. Slowly but surely. Matron didn't put it like that exactly: what she said was, after I told her that I had been given the same tea for the last month and how cross it was making me: 'Your mummy's not well, little one. You must be patient.'

'Not well? What sort of not well?'

She made a little gesture, an upward movement of her palm past one ear.

'She is unhappy,' she said.

'She should stop being unhappy.'

Mrs Boke gave me one of her thoughtful looks, which I didn't always like.

'You know, it is not always so easy. But you are too little to know.'

I was even more cross at that, and I didn't go and see her for few days. I thought and thought about what she had said. Mummy seemed to have grown quiet recently, so there was no use talking to her, and however much I loved him, Daddy was always busy, always striding here and there or staying up late, working in his study behind his beautiful mahogany desk, and I resolved to go and see Matron again, and was on the spur of doing so when I received for tea the same Marmite sandwiches I had been given for weeks and weeks and as usual I complained and Mummy simply sat there staring at the table and I decided to do something about it. Picking up the plate and holding it in front of me like an offering for the altar I marched down the hall and went into Daddy's study when he was at work – a thing I had never done before, some madness of my own must have crept into me – and placed it in front of him and told him how annoyed I was.

It was not a warm gaze with which he contemplated me. It was a ferociously tidy study, and not welcoming to the likes of me. Not that there were any likes of me. That was probably the problem, when all is said and done. My problem, his problem, their problem, everybody's problem. There was just me.

He ignored the sandwiches. I panicked and ploughed on.

'She always gives them to me and I'm sick of them. Daddy, is there something wrong with Mummy?'

'Don't be silly, Anna.'

'I think there is. Matron thinks so too. She thinks she's unhappy.'

Daddy straightened himself. I thought he was going to speak, but he stood up and marched round the desk and picked me up and stood me on his desk, so that my feet were close to his papers, whatever he had been working on, and I tried not to get my feet anywhere near them in case they got dirty. I had sandals on, broad at the toe with a rose pattern punched out of them, and a grey cotton shirt like the boys wore, and a black corduroy skirt, because I had been in school that day, and I stood on the polished top of the desk worried about putting scratches into it, and my eyes could look deep into Daddy's, and his anger terrified me. His brows were drawn together like a long black bar of cloud, and I noticed how wide his nostrils were, how his ears curved into his skull, how the veins on his cheeks were crimson, how the light was caught in his eyes like lightning in a storm on the horizon at sea, silent but impending.

'What do you mean? What have you been talking to Matron about?'

'I always talk to Matron. She's my friend. That's how she knows all the things she tells you. I know she does.' I felt confused and my eyes were beginning to prickle.

'I see.' He lowered me to the floor again quickly. 'I see that you are a little busybody who is given to holding opinions she doesn't understand. If I find you talking to Mrs Kobak again I shall teach you a lesson you will find it very hard to forget. You are lucky to be given tea at all and we expect gratitude, not complaint.' He took the plate in his right hand, with a quiet deliberate motion that was a kind of signature note for Daddy at times of crisis. His body seemed to slow, refusing to be rushed, and his slowness seemed to slow the rest of the world, too. It was a barely imperceptible kind of swagger which dared anyone else to move faster, and time seemed to slow, too, or perhaps this was a trick of the memory, for moments like these are always more vivid, more drawn-out. I wondered what he was going to do. It could have been anything. Take the plate back to Mummy, throw it across the room, break it over my head. Instead, he walked over to the wastepaper basket and dropped the sandwiches into it carefully, one by one, each with distaste.

Suddenly I felt desperately hungry and would have given anything to have them back. I would have given anything not to have come, to be back in the kitchen with Mummy's silent stare and with Daddy still working undisturbed in his study, the plate of dull but eatable sandwiches sitting in front of me.

'Go straight to bed. I shall talk to Mrs Kobak tomorrow.'

I never saw her again. She was gone, and I was cast from my little Eden. She left nothing behind. Her replacement was kind and smiling in a breezy way, but it was not the same. And without Mrs Boke the dark windows of the Hall gazing out over the valley towards the distant hills seemed even more oppressive, the black stone more beetling, the boys huddling like sheep for shelter before yet another school run even more wretched than they had been before.

I DON'T SUPPOSE the Hall has changed much over the years, but mercifully we moved on not long after Mrs Kobak's departure, though not far away. Daddy was going to be headmaster at Meniston School, which as everybody knows is one of the most prestigious public schools in the country and certainly the most important in the South-West. And if Mummy did not get much better, she didn't deteriorate any further, and there was this to be said about the move: no one at the new place had witnessed Mummy's decline. Come to think of it, I am not convinced anyone noticed it at the Hall, but everyone there was a troglodyte by comparison with Meniston, where I don't think Mummy's condition could have passed without comment.

It was assumed that my taciturn mother had always been that way. I thought the change might have helped, but it seemed as if whatever had altered in her had come to stay. And I know that Daddy was not an easy man – indeed, in many respects he was quite impossible – but I do think she could have made more of a fist of things than she did. Somewhere inside her something had wilted. I, however, was full of the selfishness of youth and as the years passed and I grew into a teenager Mummy was simply part of the furniture, and Daddy became revered by all, and Meniston went from strength to strength. He was seen as all the more remarkable for enduring that rather strange wife of his.

It is extraordinary how the success of a school really does depend on the character of its headmaster. Meniston's reputation was beyond doubt, but institutions do change and sometimes it is not for the better. For many years the school had been the charge of a gentle giant of a man by the name of Orringer. I say he was a giant; to one of my height the world is disposed to giantism, and when I was a child the problem was acute. But I do believe Mr Orringer towered over his colleagues, indeed I have often heard it from those who were here then, for Daddy allowed quite a number to stay on. He could always see the ability in people, even when they had perhaps not exercised it as well as they might, or had not been allowed to, during Orringer's reign, which appeared to have been an erratic and greatly overlong affair characterized by muddle and drift. There had always been a rule, or at least an understanding, at Meniston that the heads of departments would have tenure for five years at most, and would thereafter be asked to step down, but one or two had been allowed to remain longer than their allotted span, and because of this a dangerous lassitude had crept into things. One could tell this by the exam results, which were suffering. Exam results are the litmus test of a school's character. Have disciplined, inspired, thoughtful and ambitious teachers and you will flourish. Meniston, however, was, at that time, reclining very heavily on its reputation. Extensive grounds, excellent facilities for art and music, a prodigious first eight and the pick of society from the surrounding counties are all very well, and will serve for many decades, but Daddy had greater aspirations for the school, some quite radical. For instance, he established scholarships specifically for boys from the town who came from households of lesser incomes, boys who might normally have left school at sixteen. He encouraged the departure of those formerly eminent staff who, like the school, he deemed to be resting on laurels earned some years previously. They were easily recognizable by the way their teaching began to rely on their own peculiar enthusiasms to flesh out the dry bones of their subjects: the head of history had a love of Macaulay, for instance, and entire lessons and many tutorial classes for the older boys would be taken up with minute dissection of screeds of the great historian's writing, and most points of history would ultimately be referred back to his manner of judgement, sometimes in quite surprising ways. The head of English had made a fetish of certain words and passages which he reckoned to possess literary magic, and would have the boys stand on their desks and recite couplets from Auden or Donne, and even went so far as to inscribe pentagrams within circles in chalk and have the boys stand therein and recite. All of which was well and good and could be interpreted as perhaps an endearing eccentricity, but which, taken together with his frequent revelations of his sexual enlightenments as a young country boy, which were by no means confined to discussion of *Cider with Rosie,* but could be brought into play when studying anything from *Troilus and Cressida* to *Paradise Lost,* led to a standard of achievement that was woefully inadequate.

Having spent my childhood years in my father's school, it seemed only natural, to me at least, that I should go on doing so. To my horror, I overheard my parents discussing plans for me to attend the nearby girls' grammar school one day, and, possessed by unaccountable passion, I stormed into the room and, in a flurry of tears and physical prostration – I literally flung myself headlong on the floor and drummed my heels against the wainscot – I beseeched them to let me stay at the school. This produced in them looks of fearful concern the like of which I had never achieved before, which gave me a great deal of satisfaction. It was the first time I had bewildered Daddy. The grammar school was quietly shelved and I had a mixed bag of teaching: private tutorials with teachers from the school, and subjects like chemistry where I was allowed to join the classes, sitting to one side imagining myself wearing a cloak of invisibility, but dimly aware I was becoming an object of more and more fascination for the boys; not just Aunt Belinda's curious coughdrop, but a girl.

Daddy took a little more notice of me now. He would ask how my lessons had gone, and what we had studied that day. And I, desperately anxious to please, would paint in vivid detail the answers to his questions. I would cleave to precision, would reach into the furthermost recesses of my vocabulary to conjure for him the lessons and their various aspects. In biology, I would tell him of the delicacy of butterfly wings; in maths, of the delights of algebra; in French, I would amuse him with verbatim repetitions of the new constructions I had learned; in English, I would look for those underlying structures, those shapes lurking beneath the surface of the glittering sea of language, the movements and the tropes, the more to interest him and hold his attention. And subtly I would venture comments on the teachers and the coursework, with little asides like, 'I'm sure what Mr Atkins *meant* to say was . . .' and 'We couldn't quite finish the work because Miss Jones had to leave early, I don't know why, and left us some reading to do.' I was careful to praise judiciously, too, and to be sincere in my judgements, but I began to discern how certain things I remarked interested Daddy more than others, that some subjects and teachers engaged his attention more readily. The boys became legitimate topics, too. I was limited in my observations of them because of the paucity of subjects I studied in their company, but I did what I could. And as I became more interesting to the boys, and they to me, I was able to find out more about them, and pass on what I knew to Daddy, and so my earlier experience with Mrs Boke stood me in good stead, and I learned to find out what Daddy wanted to hear, and that way we grew even closer.

One way in which I was able to enter into the life of the school was through its plays. Among its amenities Meniston featured a small theatre. Most schools mount their performances in the school hall, with all that entails of making do and the perpetual roster of putting up lights and taking them down, and all the other activities of the hall – the assemblies, the societies, the indoor games – have to accommodate themselves grumpily to the overbearing presence of the latest set. Not so at Meniston. We gloried in our theatre (how well it sat in the prospectus), and our theatre gloried in me, because I was the only girl. I played Juliet and Desdemona and Cicely (boys can play Lady Bracknell and Miss Prism with remarkable ease). How I loved those parts, loved them as much as they frightened me. I barely had the courage to step onto the stage, but once there, buttressed by the words which were proven and true, and the character, which was not me, before people and lights, not a creature of the shadows nor an anomaly but in a role of my own, I felt transported to a

region of happiness I had never visited, nor even suspected
was there. I was not an oddity. I was special.

My favourite role, though, was not a woman, nor even a
man, but Ariel in *The Tempest*. My Caliban, my victim, was a
dark and hairy boy called Christian, rather perversely, strong
as an ox and with a tendency to overact, so that Caliban could
not open his mouth without grunting or shrieking or
growling. Prospero was tall and spindly, not much given to
movement but possessing a sonorous, mournful voice that
commanded attention. Miranda was one of the prettier
younger boys. I remember an enormous amount of noise in
the production, with booming waves and wrenching timbers
and crashing surf. The rage of Caliban appealed to us,
Christian and me: there was a gleam in his dark brown eyes
I liked and he was always telling blue jokes and getting away
with it because of his smile. Caliban made us rebellious –
'You taught me language, and my profit on't Is, I know how
to curse.' But Ariel's language had the upper hand – 'Those
are pearls that were his eyes: Nothing of him that doth fade,
But doth suffer a sea-change': the lovely balanced strokes of
those last two syllables I could leave hanging in the air and
feel they could go on into eternity. Then the silliness of
Sebastian and Antonio and Gonzalo made us laugh and laugh,
so that rehearsals were times of exquisite, uproarious happiness, when I felt on the threshold of a different world, but
what that world was I could not guess. It was not the play
itself: the play was where the rehearsals led, but it was also,
too quickly, the end of them. The play, the rehearsals, they
were only the green room for the greater play beyond, the
greater happiness. When Prospero addressed his elves and
demi-puppets and we listened spellbound even as he was
abjuring his rough magic, we seemed to be somewhere near

that other world; and as I, his tricksy spirit, sang 'Merrily, merrily, shall I live now, Under the blossom that hangs on the bough,' contemplating my freedom, I felt part of it, that other-worldliness, wherever and whatever it was, or is.

One evening, after we had exhausted ourselves with running about, for it is a very physical play if you want it to be, and we were listening to Prospero intoning his great speech about 'the baseless fabric of this vision', I looked up into the darkness at the top of the bank of raked seating. Spotlights like a row of tiny suns dazzled me and made me squint, but I could make out a figure up there. There was nothing unusual about this, but I shaded my eyes and went on looking. There was a strange familiarity to the features, and I could not place them, and then I was called to do something, and the next time I looked whoever it was had gone. I thought no more about this until a few days later, when glancing upwards I saw the figure had returned and was sitting a little further down the seating ranks towards the stage, and I saw that it was Mummy, and felt a thrill of guilt that I had not recognized her before, and mixed in with that thrill was excitement, something to do with her not being part of that place that was so much part of me, as if I had found somewhere she could not go except anonymously. In the theatre I could be whoever I wanted to be, and Mummy was no one at all.

Yet once it had been her passion, too, though she had shown no interest in drama since the Hall, no interest in anything save the day-to-day affairs of the house and her reading. And here she was, watching, immobile, face cast in darkness, until something made her turn her head and the light glimmered on her cheeks as if they were wet.

I half made to wave at her, but was distracted by the play,

and when I looked again I thought she had gone again. Unaccountably, I felt annoyed. How dare she come and go without telling me? But she had only moved down to the front row, and she could clearly be seen and her cheeks were dry and she smiled at me and I waved back. This time she stayed to the end of the rehearsal, and we walked home together. She was animated and chattering away as I had not seen her before or since. Her smile dispelled her careworn look, and brought back beauty to her face as if that were its rightful place. Her hair was limned with white but was still full of its youthful blondness, which she kept wrapped up in a bun that she unravelled and redid as we talked – she always had trouble keeping the pins in place – and it was like releasing sunlight. I was aware of a different Mummy from some other part of her life, returning like a long-banished spirit of the south for a brief sojourn in its old haunts.

SOONER THAN I liked came the time for me to leave Meniston. It would not be for long; I wanted to become a teacher – what else? – and I needed to spend some time away at a teacher training college. I was unhappy to be going, but I consoled myself I would be back for good when it was over and I was. That is the short of it. The long of it is that that was when I met Daniel. It was silly, really, my head only came up to his chest, we were mismatched from the start.

Only, of course, that's not true. I suppose I only wish it were. And that's not true, either. What do we regret most, the happiness, or the sadness that follows after? So often they are inextricable, so often I have turned these things over and over in my mind, remembering, regretting, not regretting.

The teaching college I will not dwell on: it had nothing

for me, for what did I not know about teaching, or school life? It was a necessary distraction, albeit a painful one. To distract me from the distraction I slipped away to the coast, for long walks along the sands and along the coastal paths as the clouds pressed against the horizon in autumn, and to swim there in summer, when the water was unaffected by the hottest sun and the cold clamped my limbs like a vice. It was in the autumn that I noticed Daniel had begun to take an interest in me, but I continued to walk alone. I had no notion why he was interested: I don't mean I was naive, simply that for some reason I thought he wanted to be friends, and this I emphatically did not want. I was determined to be through that college without touching the sides. My fellow students seemed to me uncouth, their interests trivial and hollow. I did not wish to like them, or be like them, or become involved with them. They, once they realized how I was, were happy to ignore me.

Except for Daniel.

How he irritated me. I never seemed to be able to shake him off. He was there beside me in the canteen, and lo! he came and sat next to me as I addressed my cheese salad. He would comment on my appearance – he liked the way I had my hair cut into bangs, as the Americans call them, he liked my rings (which were my great-grandmother's on my mother's side), he liked my scarf. I dress plainly as a rule, but I do have a fondness for silk scarves, so there was often something new for him to admire. And I would nod and smile and concentrate on my book. One day in February he asked me to go out with him in the evening – I could tell this was momentous for him, and he had probably been urging himself on to ask me for weeks – and I hurriedly invented a prior arrangement. Then, when he did so again, I had to invent another one, and this went on until I had created for myself the most glittering social life you could possibly wish for, one that for a trainee teacher billeted on a small training college in a medium-sized town near the Dorset coast must have seemed quite astonishing. In order to conceal my mendacity I had to stay in my room every night, which I did not enjoy. I did not mind keeping my own company, and I certainly did not want to go near the students in the college bar, but neither did I relish effective imprisonment. In the end I had to capitulate. Then I spent a week wishing I hadn't, and dreamed up countless schemes to get out of it, all of which foundered on impracticality and a feeling that it was fated. This did not obscure such a growing dread that as we entered the snug of a small pub a little distance from the high street, which had the virtue of being seldom frequented by other college students, my legs genuinely shook and my heart was fluttering like a wet flag in a gale. I sat very still trying to preserve my sangfroid until he had fetched drinks from the bar. He placed them on the table, paused to position himself carefully on a small stool and then turned to me smiling and said, smooth as you like:

'So, let's talk about you.'

I'm not sure what I was expecting, but it wasn't that. And as no one had ever said such a thing to me before, I was not sure how to answer. Frankly, I had never talked about myself, not as a topic of conversation, not unless you count Mrs Kobak, and that was more like talking about my world, with me at the centre of it.

I ducked it.

'Why are you so keen to have a drink with me?' It sounded more aggressive than I meant it. I just wanted to change the subject.

'You're different from the others,' he said. 'In fact, you're different from anyone I've ever met.'

'How do you know?'

You've got to admit, it was a good question.

He smiled. He had good teeth, even and neat.

'You mean, because I hardly know you?'

I nodded.

'Well. Because I've been watching you. Do you mind?'

'I'm not sure.'

Actually, I was quite flattered. To my surprise.

'Also, I'm allowed to guess, aren't I? I bet you know a lot about Shakespeare.'

Beginner's luck.

Except that it turned out he had been more sly than I suspected. It also turned out that quite a lot of them knew about me and who I was and where I had come from. In fact, it turned out that I was back to being a curious coughdrop: they ignored me, but that didn't mean they took no notice of me.

Once I had finished talking about Shakespeare, and school, and teaching, and boys, and even me — at which I felt like I was walking on stilts or roller skating for the very first time — I realized two things. First, that Daniel Ellis was a gentle, thoughtful, courteous man and I liked him. Second, that for all my eighteen years, the subject of me could not be made to last quite as long as it really should have done. There wasn't nearly enough to say with confidence.

I became friends with Daniel. It struck me how seldom I had had the opportunity to become friends with someone my own age. Properly friends. I took him swimming with me when the summer came; just him, I didn't want anyone else there. I could tell our friendship was attracting interest from the others. He had a very skimpy, old-fashioned swimming costume which exaggerated his pale body, and he shrieked when he stepped into the sea and would not move for five minutes, pantomiming agony until I was weak from laughter and had to sit down. I looked at my own body, just as scrawny but half the size, and a wild unbidden thought – a funny thought, too – went through my mind that our bodies were rather similar, in their way, and sort of suited each other. Then I flung myself into the water, and gasped at the headache the cold always brought on along with the numbness, then relaxed into the swirling motion of the waves and the way they keep pushing at you as you wade through them and float on them, like indefatigable, overenthusiastic dogs who want you to play. Then I splashed Daniel and he ran screeching back up the beach.

'Excuse me,' I said, when I caught up with him. 'If you're going to be my boyfriend you're going to have to be braver than that.'

He stared at me, halfway through bending for a towel.

'Am I?' he said. A big grin spread quickly across his face, and his eyes fairly turned into soup-plates. '*Am* I?'

'Well,' I said, 'you heard what I said.'

He stood up, still looking at me with that bright smile of his, then sped down the beach again in a foolish knees-up-in-the-air cartoon dash, splashed noisily through the shallows and dived over the nearest wave, bellowing madly. He disappeared, then shot vertically upward out of the water, his arms windmilling.

'Brave?' he called. 'I'm Mighty Mouse!'

'Mickey Mouse, more like!' I called back. And I ran to be with him.

'Boyfriend, is it?' he said as we floated in the rocking,

churning water just beyond where it turns into breakers.
'Would you be after giving us a kiss, then?' he said in his
best roguish manner.

I panicked, but held the line; swimming into his arms, I
shut my eyes and felt his lips half on my mouth, half on my
cheek. I flinched, felt we were both about to go under.

'Help,' I said.

'First time?'

I nodded, wishing this wasn't happening, gamely ploughing
on.

Next thing I knew, his lips were upon mine, soft and warm
and wonderfully vulnerable. I felt myself beginning to
tremble, with shock or something, I suppose. Something.

Well! A sea-change. Something rich and strange.

I started it, I suppose.

Why did I do that? I thought good would come of it. I
think good could have come of it.

To hell with it. We were in love.

We were madly, sweetly, happily in love. I had never felt
anything like it before.

We were happy in a love that had so much to find out
about itself and each other and our place in the world; we
wanted to be with each other all the time; without Daniel,
the rest of the world was grey and savourless; together, we
were absorbed by everything the other did and said, every
joke became a special joke, with its own meaning that made
it ripe for endless repetition, every place we walked to was
placed there specifically for us, all the people we met and
talked to we judged together and always agreed what we
thought (and usually found them wanting). For a few, giddy
months Daniel was everything to me; being with him was
like cramming one's mouth with fruit you could never get

enough of, it was something you couldn't resist, something you did deliberately, something you chose every moment of the day.

I couldn't wait to make love. I had always been a bit wary of it, as something not particularly to do with me. I didn't feel afraid: I knew that Daniel would be gentle, and he was. It turned out he had little more experience than I had, for all his early bravado. He had had a girlfriend before, but they had broken up before they ever got so far as sex, and I think he was, after her recalcitrance, surprised and pleased by my eagerness: not that we hurried into it, but when I have made up my mind, which took me a month or so in this instance, I don't like to dawdle. We agreed on a time and place, which was my room one Saturday evening, and I bought some flowers and Daniel bought a bottle of real champagne, and we took all our clothes off and kissed for a while as our bodies and the bedclothes generated a stable temperature, and I began to feel him hard against me and I fought back waves of terror and tried to encourage the waves of excitement and a positive sense of adventurousness about it all, so that when Daniel asked, 'Are you sure you want to do this?' I was able to nod confidently. I turned on my back and drew him into me and it hurt like hell but I kept on with my positive attitude.

We got better with practice, and we got in a lot of practice, too, even in the woods on one of our walks; twigs were sticking into my back so I went on top and we did it that way. The things you get up to.

While all this was going on Meniston drifted away in my thoughts, yet it was still there, of course, and my life had changed and this meant that Meniston had changed too for me, in a way that perplexed me. For if I had feared leaving, now I feared returning. I didn't think of it as fear at the time, but I think I sensed, knew even, that my something rich and strange might not necessarily pass through the gates of my old life.

Yet there could be no question that I would not go back. I tried to entertain it briefly, but it was hopeless. I could not imagine living away from Daddy; how devoid of meaning my life would be. He brought out the best in me, and I like to think I did something of the same for him. He had his weaknesses, I know, but even they were the necessary shortcomings of his virtues. So I told myself. Nevertheless, I was confused, for the first time, and thankfully for the last.

Daniel was a sensitive boy, but how was he to know what was going through my mind, when I hardly knew myself? For him, it was different. There was nothing more he wanted than an excuse not to return home. He didn't mind going back to see his mum and dad, he said, just so long as he didn't have to live there. No, Daniel had a better idea.

'If my results are good enough, I'm going to apply for a post at Meniston,' he said. 'Maybe you could mention me to your father. Then we could still be together.'

What a turbulent outpouring of joy and dread there was in my heart, then. Of course it was a solution; it had all the inevitable sense of something that should have been obvious from the start. Perhaps I had been parking it in a shady part of my mind and pretending it wasn't there. What would Mummy think? What would Daddy think? What was I doing even thinking of it?

I looked him full in the face. He had freckles now from the summer sun. His eyes had the puzzling warmth that hazel has. I reached to stroke one of his ears, which stuck out just ever so much more than is normal.

'All right. Could we . . .' How could I say this without hurting him. 'We needn't tell them we are . . . we don't have to . . .'

'Why not? We are, aren't we?'

'You don't understand, it's not like that.'

'How is it like, then?' He frowned slightly, then shrugged. 'Well, maybe I *will* understand. When I'm there. If I get there. When I've been there a while. You're probably right anyway. It wouldn't be good to arrive in one's first job as the head-master's daughter's boyfriend. People might doubt my brilliant teaching skills and uncanny understanding of the child's mind.'

'We'll keep it secret.'

'It sounds that way.'

'And I'll talk to Daddy.'

It felt like a trade-off, a kind of treachery. He wasn't happy with these arrangements, not one little bit, and we were sullen with each other, for the first time ever, for some time afterwards. Yet no progress without crisis. Daniel came to Meniston to teach history in the Michaelmas term of that year.

It goes without saying that I was happy to see him, but though I thought I had successfully circumnavigated a sign-post whose every direction would have led to unhappiness, with his presence my turmoil became acute. My relief at being back with Daddy again had been immense, so much so that I had been quite distracted from my journey of discovery and my chancing upon Daniel Ellis Island (I liked this conceit enough to tell Daniel about it). When I thought of Daniel it was with an obscure sense of betrayal, but I was no longer sure whether I was betraying Daddy or Daniel. My intelligence told me that having two men in my life to love should present me with no problems, but I wondered if Daddy's love wasn't more exclusive than I had realized, in a way that Daniel's was not. And I must have realized some of this, otherwise I would not have insisted on not declaring an interest (as if he were a business proposition) in Daniel to Daddy. What would happen if Daddy found out? And if he never did, how could I see Daniel as I longed to do? The bliss of the summer turned with the leaves into autumn wretchedness.

It could have gone on for years. Daniel was popular with the boys and staff: his height gave him an air of reassurance, as height does, and the boys I think felt comfortable around him. And Daddy liked him: my recommendation was good enough to secure that. What I had not bargained for, something which had a significant effect on both Daddy and me, was Daniel's effect on Mummy.

There was something about the pair of them right from the start. Every beginning of the school year Daddy brought all the staff, old and new, together for sherry after church on the first Sunday.

'This friend of yours, this Mr Ellis,' Mummy had said a few days previously, 'you must make sure that you introduce me to him.'

'Ye-es, of course, Mummy,' I replied. She rarely showed interest in new teachers. She rarely showed interest in anything.

'Did you have many other friends at . . .'

I didn't like her drift. There was life in the old witch yet.

'Not many. A few.'

'Well, I am looking forward to meeting him.'

When she did so, she clutched at his hand as she shook it and pulled him closer.

'It's so lovely to meet any friend of Anna's,' she said to him softly.

Well, she knew as well as any that you could count my friends on the fingers of one hand.

'It's such a pleasure to meet you. I've heard a lot about you,' said Daniel. *Such* good manners. The perfect gentleman. Naturally, I had scarcely mentioned Mummy to him.

Her gaze rested on his face. It was the first time I had seen him in a suit, his Sunday best, and he looked, I thought, adorable. I wanted to put him in my pocket and run away with him there and then.

'And I about you,' she said earnestly.

This made me a little uncomfortable, and I could see it did the same for Daniel. Just a few words out of place can give you away.

Then she smiled sweetly at him, which, as I said to Daniel later, was unusual enough.

'She must like you,' I mused.

'Do you think she has any idea?'

'Oh, no.'

But I wasn't sure.

And that smile would return whenever she set eyes on him again; she would often make sure she talked to him, and he was unfailingly kind to her and talked back to her.

'Do you know your mother has read all the Russians? Even Lermontov?' he asked, once.

'I didn't, no.'

'What's wrong with you and her? She's all right.'

'She is with you.'

'I see.'

Maybe he did. I wasn't going to rake all that stuff up now for his benefit or anyone else's.

Daddy could see it, too. At least, I think he could; he certainly knew, because I remember talking to him about it.

Or did I tell him? Was it that I told him? Perhaps I did.

It was very taxing for both Daniel and me. We found it hard to find time alone together. For him that was the crux of it; for me, it was not just that, but the ever-present eyes of the school on me, and not wanting to let Daddy down, and being utterly unable to contemplate the idea of Daddy knowing that I had a new allegiance, and yet there he was, every day, in the school. And wondering what Mummy saw. If I told Daniel to keep away from her she would have all the more reason to suspect. The more they talked the more opportunity there would be for him to let something slip. He was just being his lovely, generous, conscientious self — he would be a fine teacher one day — but every moment I was swollen with worry.

Daddy did find out, though. In the end, he had to. We could have kept it secret, but at the expense of never going near each other, never acknowledging each other's presence. If you are desperate to touch someone every moment, that's simply impossible. Our desire was fanned to insanity by our enforced separation. We would, when we could, make off in his barely legal old Austin Maxi into the country, there to make love at lightning speed in ditches and behind hedges: such stolen moments, though they were often nearly farcical, had infinite preciousness, enhanced by the spreading black waters of fear that made me inarticulate with apprehension.

He found out. Don't ask me how. I never discovered. I suppose, on reflection, that a man who likes to listen to his daughter to find out useful things about his school may not speak to her alone. There, I've said it. It's a brave thought for me to think, for it means I was not the only one. And the pain of that thought has dogged me all these years. I can't believe it was Mummy. If she knew, she approved, and I never knew her inflict suffering on anyone. She comes out of all this whiter than white.

And when he found out, he never said anything. I could just tell, from the way he was. I know he didn't like it, not one little bit. And I knew, with dreadful finality, that it would have to be Daniel or him, and that it would be him. And the drop of morphine that helped me endure this was the knowledge I had that Daddy wanted me to himself. And I wanted the same.

I suppose that much is obvious.

I struggled, I really did struggle. But you can't break the habit of a lifetime.

AND THEN I got pregnant.

There was hell to pay.

There usually is, I believe.

Not usually the kind of hell I went through, though.

The day I realized my period was late I didn't panic. I was never entirely regular. I don't think I even noticed until a week had gone by, but then I began to wonder. The doctor, when she confirmed my suspicions, said sometimes the pill didn't work, there was always some slight risk. She looked over her desk at me with some compassion. She knew my circumstances well enough.

'I'm afraid you're one of the unlucky ones.'

I was emptied of feeling, it was all just flushed out of me by the result.

'I'm going to have a baby.'

She smiled.

'That's a good thing, isn't it?' I went on.

'Yes. That's a good thing.'

'So I'm not unlucky.'

'Of course, I didn't mean it in that way. Just a manner of speech. One of the *lucky* ones, perhaps I should have said.'

I could tell she was not telling the truth, and that she knew I knew that. I had just lost control of my life.

'It's exciting, isn't it?'

She looked at me thoughtfully. 'Yes.'

Can one be a cauldron of emotion and yet feel nothing identifiable at all? Can there be emotions flying round at such a rate that one doesn't know how one feels, aware that new unknown emotions, dark, thick black ones and shiny metallic ones and soupy green ones are being churned up – and still have a part of one, the room of one's consciousness, perfectly empty save perhaps one bare light hanging from the ceiling, in which one experiences everything in precise detail quite clearly, seeing dispassionately the edges of things, even one's own thoughts? Is that some kind of insanity or is that dealing with it? Is there in that cold-seeming room a black silhouette on the other side of the light?

Whatever, that's how it was for me as I trailed back to the school to find Daniel and suggest we go for a drive, knowing what I had to tell him and knowing I had to wait until the afternoon, and all the while feeling the tremendous pressure building up, and beginning to find that I and the world around were subtly not quite synchronized or in tune or even quite contiguous: little gaps were opening up between me and my words and the people I talked to and the surfaces I touched and the time that elapsed until we found ourselves driving among fields and stopping by a gate that overlooked a long valley. It would have been beautiful, it always had been when we had been there before, but now I didn't notice.

'I've got something to tell you,' I said.

Something in my voice made him look apprehensive. Poor boy, what a thing to spring on him.

And yet he might have, he could have, said yes.

'I'm going to have a baby. I found out this morning.'

It took one simple second for me to see how he felt: one simple second of nothingness, of no movement, no response. In that one second I knew.

Then tears came like a seizure, like they had battered in the windows of the clean, bare room and it was full of whirling wet leaves messing everything up. He put his arms around me fiercely. He wanted to protect me, but I didn't need protection. I needed him to be ready, and he wasn't going to be. One day, but not now. And now was when I needed him.

Of course, we talked. Oh, we talked. What a soul-searching and a heartfelt pleading and a rigorous examination of all the available options there was. Then and afterwards. But during that one second something had shrivelled up and died and lay there lifeless between us, making all our frenzied, anxious talk irrelevant. Whatever he said, I knew it was going to be all down to me.

So it was me who went to Mummy, alone. And after the tears and the smiles and the fretful realization, it was I and Mummy who went to see Daddy. Mummy did the talking. Just think of that. After all those years. Both of us knew the enormity of it. My deepest fear was what would happen between Daddy and me. Was it? Was it? Was it my deepest fear? I knew Daddy. I didn't know the baby. Some of this I never understood.

He listened intently, without stirring. When Mummy had finished he rose and crossed the room and stood by the arm of my chair. Behind him the sunlight winked in the French windows. The room was peaceful.

'Anna,' he said, and took my hand. 'I need hardly tell you how serious this is.'

Of course it is, Daddy. I'm not a fool.

I'm sorry, Daddy, I'm sorry.

'I had some slight suspicion about this young man.'

Whatever happened, they were never going to be best of friends.

'Do you have plans?'

'You mean, will we be together?'

'I mean, will you get married?'

'Not just yet.'

'Might you?'

'No. No, I don't think we will.'

'Then I think he must leave the school. It would be intolerable for him to remain here, in view of what has happened. It would also, I fear, be intolerable for you to keep your baby.'

My mother and I cried out at the same time. He held up his hands.

'I do not mean you must have an abortion. I emphatically do not believe in abortions. I believe, however, that you cannot stay here with your baby. There are alternatives. You must choose between staying here at the school, and the very excellent prospects you can look forward to, or life elsewhere. As, as I think the term is, a single mother.'

He got up, put his hands behind his back in characteristic pose, and stood in the middle of the room, head back as if addressing the school assembly on the agenda for the coming week.

'I am profoundly shocked, Anna. Profoundly shocked.'

And with that he left the room.

And where did that leave me, and poor benighted Mummy, and terrified spineless Daniel, and someone not yet born.

I did give that baby away, and Daniel did leave and never came back, and though he pleaded with me to come with him I knew he was no father-to-be and I concluded that I was no mother-to-be either, and I'm not the first nor the last, though that's of no great solace. And though I convinced myself it was the right thing to do then I'm not sure it was; but it's easy enough to know what one should have done, looking back. The images that come to me are of Daniel's arm raised in farewell at the railway station, and of the last time I saw my baby, but there are no images possible for the way I felt then. Daniel never saw his son, nor asked after him. Someone else's problem, now, I thought, as he was taken away. The birth had not been easy, and I'm ashamed of that thought. I'm ashamed of the whole thing, really.

WHICH BRINGS ME to the present, for nothing much of note happened in-between. I'm not going to be having any more babies, that's for certain. I am burying my dear, bewildered father, and on the order of service are some of the readings we began to choose together, he and I, each one for particular members of the congregation, not omitting one for himself, in the last few precious hours we had together. There is one for him, one for Alex Rainsford, the one we always suspected, and one for Meadows the MP, whom we knew would turn up, and he has. The gall of the man. And one for Mummy, and one for the hounds, the *soi-disant* gentlemen of the press, and one I chose for myself for Daniel, if he comes. I did write. I thought it might be appropriate, and why not after all this time, now that Daddy has gone, maybe to look at the past again. What is there to be done about the past? Well, he's not here, so either he didn't get the letter, or he chose not to come, or he's late. It wouldn't be for the first time.

It's not so bad a turnout, after all. He always had popular support, even through the worst times. Daddy always denied writing the letter, but people spread vile rumours before that, as we found out, though they were softly spoken ones. When I saw it in the end even I thought it looked remarkably like Daddy's handwriting, and he died before the police could fingerprint it and test the tearstains for DNA and do all the sorts of things to it that they do, but he's dead now and beyond caring. After all, he chose, we chose, the manner and time of his going, retrieving some dignity in our own minds, if nobody else's. There's just Mummy and I left to face the residual music.

My only worry is what they might discover about Jonathan. I think they'll have difficulty. They'll have to find him, to begin with. Why suspect a retired headmaster, even a forcibly retired one, even one that had been let down repeatedly to the point where he was driven, *driven* to take extreme measures in the madness that came upon him? And if they do suspect Daddy, there's no reason for them to think I was involved, however much I was by his side. By his side in all things, and in the last madness more than ever. We all go mad from time to time, especially as we get older. We all do go mad.

Was Daddy mad when he decided to go the way he did? It was a clean way; he was happy for people to know he had taken his own life. He could stand no more. The letter was with the police, they had had it for so long without doing anything. Not that I believe he wrote it. Not that I believe he did any of the things that were imputed to him, never, never. Except the one, the one I found out at the end, which showed me something I did not know about Daddy, and it was not the thing itself that hurt, simply that something had been concealed from me, that there was a part of my father I did not know, and part of my love for him was betrayed. Another thing for me not to think about, there's so much.

I was with him to the last. 'I want you there,' he said, all the fire gone out of him. 'One last thing, darling.' He had never called me that before. And when he could not go through with it, he made me do it for him, my last act of submission, but there was something else there, too, something that made me able to help, some great darkness that rose in a flurry of wings as I slid the needle he had long prepared into his vein and slipped away, peeling off my gloves and treading lightly through the door, tripping down the lane from the front door in the darkness and wet with a song in my heart, Daddy, and not feeling guilty, not feeling guilty at all.

Boy

Oh, that 'twere possible,
After long grief and pain,
To find the arms of my true love,
Round me once again!

Alfred, Lord Tennyson, *Maud*

'DAD?'
   'Son.'
   'Are you going to the high street today?'
   'I could be.'
   'Well, are you? I don't want to know what you *could* be doing. You *could* be doing anything.'
   'True. But on a scale of one to ten, I'd give going to the supermarket about a nine. Verging on a ten.'
   'Can I come with you?'
   'You mean, can you come with me, or can I drop you off at your favourite shop while I go and buy the week's supplies?'
   'Dad, you know, somehow I think you know what I mean.'
   'Somehow, I think I do.'
   'Great.' The boy hunches into the armchair, their only armchair. Its leather is flaking and parched. His long limbs gather together like a distressed spider, his body concentrated on the GameBoy in his hands. Tunes dreamed up far away in a toy laboratory's marketing department jingle horribly and repetitively, but there are only two people listening, and one is too intensely focused to hear them, and the other too amused and in love to care.
   Look at him. A broad band of freckles over his nose, his hair a deep copper, wiry but long enough to flop over his

brow, jug-handle ears, obviously genes of his forebears. Skin pale not because of too much ancestry but because of too much boy life, maybe too much single-boy life, without brothers and sisters, just the ever-present attention of his besotted father. Boy life of miniaturized games and Play Station. Maybe that's why he likes to get out to his favourite shop. At least it's not the arcade, though he does like the arcade, and his dad is worried about that. He talks to the boy's mother about it now and then: he knows he should share these things, though he wants to keep the anxieties to himself as well as everything else. He is lucky to have him, he knows that.

'Right.'

He gets up – he has had breakfast now, a couple of slices of toast and a bowl of cereal. Everything in the flat is cheap: the crockery is from the local hardware store, the furniture all second-hand. After the separation, which is not yet a divorce, they haven't got round to that yet, he moved out of their two-bedroom flat and took an even smaller one. White Formica cupboards, linoleum everywhere. It's not wonderful, it's never going to be that, but maybe life never was; it didn't start out that way.

'Time to go.'

The boy takes no notice, and he is used to this.

'Jason, my mouse, my Mickey Mouse.'

'OK, Dad.' The voice is slow, he is *so* connected to the game.

He stacks the crockery and begins to wash, methodically running a brush round the rims of the plates and cups. Last night's washing is still to be done, and he feels a bit guilty. Guilty to no one in particular, but guilty all the same. He has a good supply of guilt.

Outside, it's not so bad. The flat they live in is quintes-sential old seaside town, the whole South Coast is like this. The furnishings are diabolical, but the buildings themselves are grand: dilapidated, the whitewash despoiled and the white stucco eroded, but at the front there are broad steps to walk down with balustrades and stone balls of imposing majesty on either side. You can feel like a king as you descend those steps; and beyond, the sea, always the same, always reliable. In its bad moods, or in the sweet ones, roaring or simpering, there's only one thing it does. It rolls up the beach and collapses, like a faithful old dog, one that's been in the family a long time, with a bit of a temper on it on difficult days.

So they walk down those broad steps, hand in hand. They no longer have a car. That had to go with the general decline. He can't and wouldn't complain about all that: Sally was pretty good about it really, and it is only because she had taken a job as a nurse in Edinburgh, and because she didn't really want to have Jason in the first place, that he got to keep him. And he hadn't wanted a child either, that's how he explained to himself what had happened when he first had the opportunity, but when he arrived he found that he did want him, very much, and that was the saving of him, but not of her. What she wanted was still, and is still, a mystery to him, and it may be to her also, but he is content to keep things as they are, as long as he can keep Jason from sliding off down the bucking, unruly roads of youth he once followed himself (starting with the arcade prob-ably). It's an unusual situation, but, he reflects, what is life if not full of unusual situations? What is life if not, in itself, an unusual situation?

'Bills?' he asks himself, pausing by the hallway door, where the mail is left. 'Letters?' Jason tugs at his hand. 'Come *on*, Dad!' One is written in black ink, in a hand he still recognizes. 'Daniel Ellis, Flat 6a, South Parade.' How has she found him here? On second thoughts, he is in the phone book, has nothing to hide any more, she knows all he has. She could probably have found him on the internet or something. The envelope is thick, stippled, creamy, old-fashioned. He hasn't been sent anything like it ever before. Curious, he runs his forefinger down the inside of its flap, breaking its spine. The paper is soft like card and gives easily. Inside is an invitation. 'Dear Daniel,' it begins. He reads it through and sees her signature and for some moments is aware of nothing else. A buried past is being buried. The day after tomorrow. And here it is coming back to life. 'I do hope you will be able to attend,' says the letter, politely, tonelessly. Does it say it would be nice to see him again? Perhaps it wouldn't be nice. He can scarcely comprehend what it would be.

So the old man is dead. Well, he deserved everything that happened to him. Daniel had read the details in the papers with exultant fascination, but he hasn't heard about his death, which must have been a paragraph in some news round-up somewhere. Not like the minor headlines of salacious opprobrium that carried accounts of his downfall. You couldn't get away from those. Nobody mentioned any of it at the school where he taught, though. His school was not interested in that kind of school, thank god.

The mystery of it had been how good a teacher Christopher Hughes was (he had always made a point of being a teaching headmaster, which was rare and praiseworthy). It was as if terrorizing the adult world, sending colleagues quaking from his presence and causing a hush to descend upon the staff room when he entered gave him one kind of delight, whereas coaxing the best from even the most recalcitrant boy gave him another, equally powerful pleasure. Not that the boys were less than awed by him, Daniel recalls. But he seemed to be able to make them love him; old boys were glowing in their references to him, and their recollections of their time there always centred on their experience of the towering headmaster, crowlike in his black gown, whose frightening demeanour concealed a warm interest in their own welfare.

Quite how warm, of course, was what all the fuss had been about.

And he destroyed the lives of his wife and daughter, no question about that. Unless Anna had found someone new, in which case she would have had to have left, surely. He cannot imagine a competitor for her affections being tolerated by Christopher.

But he doesn't need to think about this now, and Jason is tugging at his hand.

'*On* we go!'

They dance down the steps like comedians, they always do it this way. Arms akimbo, legs splayed out, hopping on one leg, then the other. 'Da-*dah*-da-*dah*-da-DAH-da!' Then along the seafront. They can't dance here, the press of people is too strong on a Saturday even this early in the year. They flock here with the flimsiest of excuses: a pale watery sun will do it, even rain won't deter them. They want an airing, they want the arcades, they want the shopping and the pleasant *bijouteries*, if they can find them open out of season. There's enough to do. There are treasure-hunters out with their Geiger counters, sweeping the beaches at low tide in hope of seaspoil, their headphones clamped to their ears under baseball caps, hoovering the shore and relieving it of its secrets if they can. Jason and his dad lean against the chapped white railings, Jason standing on the bottom rung to be the same height as his dad, almost, and watch the little lines of purple people clinging to the cliffs as they make their way in search of fossils, the last of which had been found some seven years previously, by a professional, who hung precariously from the clifftops above and found a small sea creature of the Pleistocene no bigger than a fist, in a place no one else could reach. They watch the sea haul itself over the dull grey shingle, rustling the skirts of the beach and tickling its extremities like a lecherous uncle at a wedding, and Jason says, 'Dad, are you in there?' and his dad says, yes, he is, and he has always loved the sea, and Jason says, well, he knows that, he always says that when they stand where they are standing, and can they get on to the shops now. Please.

'Why *do* you like the sea, Dad?'

He hesitates. He wants to get the answer right, because he wants his son to understand. They have the same conversation almost every time they stand here watching the business of the sands, the children building irrigation systems and dams to catch the river which spreads among the rocks making furrows in the gleaming flats, the middle-aged and elderly prone in their rented deckchairs. He wants to get the answer right, and he hasn't done so yet.

'I'm drawn to it,' he says, which is what he always says, and he knows Jason has already lost interest, because he knows what he's going to hear, and his dad hasn't come up with anything new. But Jason still doesn't understand why they stay here, in this marginal place, between elements, where sand and water meet and people enjoy the simplest pleasures. His eyes are drawn to the tankers, broad and long and low down on the horizon. That's where he'd like to be. Going somewhere.

'You know, I met your mum here.'

Jason raises his eyes.

'I know *that*, Dad. But did you keep her here?'

'No. Well, no. She has a very promising career, by the way. You'll be seeing her soon.'

Jason turns his head to lean his cheek on the backs of his father's hands, which he has laid horizontally on the peeling top bar of the railings, each middle finger touching the tip of the other as if for continuity. He squints into the sun.

'But what about you, Dad?'

'What about me?'

'Well, you know. When are you going to get a career like Mum? I mean, are you going to be a teacher for ever? Don't you get to be a headmaster, or something?'

'I think I'm a way off that.'

'Why?'

'Don't be aggravating, now. I'm happy enough. We're happy enough. Aren't we?'

Jason knows better than to worry his dad too much. And his dad resists pointing out that his mum's a nurse, not a brain surgeon.

'Come on.'

The favourite shop lies halfway up the road that runs steeply from the front to where the grand hotels are. Inside it is toy heaven: like a ramshackle seaside Harrods, Stratton's has everything that can be bought or can get it for you. People come from all over the county. It sells bicycles and Barbie dolls and board games and kites and all manner of die-cast models, some at staggering prices, which goes for the hand-painted soldiery too, collector's pieces locked in glass cabinets. There are jigsaw puzzles of up to five thousand pieces imported from Germany, a comprehensive assortment of practical jokes including realistic canine faeces for posting to enemies, a wall of Airfix kits and another wall of Hornby trains, one aisle of cheap gadgets that fall apart within minutes of being unpacked, beach games, and an entire room devoted to war games: this draws Jason like a magnet. Armies of dwarves, Arthurian knights and grotesque, misshapen ogres from a fantastical far-distant future are ranged over the battle-field, while at a small table some boys Jason knows are painting black matt undercoats onto a fresh batch of orcs. The table is littered with brushes and paints with names like Bogey Green and Sick Brown: painting the armies is part of the ritual. The air is heavy with the acrid tang of saturated young male perspiration, and everyone is wearing different shades of black.

Daniel watches his son practise a carefully nuanced saunter over to the table. He can tell Jason is not quite sure of his ground yet; there are a lot of older boys here, and some-times they get stupid. Usually they are serious wargamers, but you never know. Once he gets to the table he will be able to talk to Phil and Adam, he's met them a few times and they're a bit older, both of them go to his school and Adam gets taught by Daniel, which is a bit uncomfortable for Jason but he's used to that kind of thing and it does get you a bit of extra protection. Daniel knows Jason won't want him hanging around.

Phil is small and puny with a nose too pronounced for his face and big brown eyes and long hair the same colour. Adam isn't much bigger and has a rectangular face with freckles and bottle-brush hair and an attentive, thoughtful manner. Both are listening to a fat boy of about seventeen who already has three chins and the beginnings of a moustache.

'The thing about the balrog, right,' he is saying, applying

a brushful of Pitch Black with loving finesse, 'is that it has wings, or does it, right? 'Cos this does, but in the film it doesn't, and then again, if you read the books, it's not really clear, is it? You've all *read* the books, haven't you?'

They all nod knowingly. Of course they have.

'Phil,' says Jason. This is hello. The merest acknowledgement of the other's presence.

'Hi, Jace.'

Relief floods Jason's face. He is acknowledged in turn. He stands watching the activities with benign approval.

'What it says in the book is the balrog has shadows that unfurl like wings but that doesn't mean it *had* wings,' continues the fat boy. Jason has seen him here before and thinks his name might be Robbie.

'So . . .' ventures Phil. 'Does that mean these are wrong, then?'

'Well, it's controversial. I mean, some people think it means it has wings and some people think it doesn't.'

'I think it looks better with wings,' puts in Adam.

'Yeah, but should it have them?' This is Jason, and to his pleased astonishment Robbie looks at him and jerks his head back with a mock squint to signify recognition of an intellectual brother.

'Is anyone going to see Satrap on Friday?' asks Phil.

'At the Shipwrights'?' says Robbie. He lays his hand patronizingly on Phil's arm. 'You're too young, ain'tcha?'

'Hey, stop touching me. So what?'

''Ow old are you, then?'

'Fifteen.'

Robbie looks doubtful.

'Are you? Can't see you bein' let in.'

'I went to see Condition X.'

'Wiv yer dad?'

'Well, yeah, actually.'

'Anyway, they're not really hardcore, are they?'

'They are actually, well, pretty hardcore.'

'I thought they'd broken up,' says Adam.

'They have,' says Robbie, knowingly. 'The guitarist is trying to re-form.'

'And didn't their drummer die in a car crash?' asks Jason.

No one seems to hear him. He remembers that he's thinking of another band, one his dad had been talking about.

'I think I'd better go and see where my dad is,' he mutters. Again, no one takes any notice. I'm too young for this lot, he thinks, bitterly. Go and see where my dad is. Why did I say that?

'See ya, Phil, Adam.' He hasn't got the nerve to say 'Robbie'. He's still not sure he's got the name right. They turn slightly to acknowledge his departure. The distance to the door feels like a million miles.

He'll be back, though. He will, though it feels like a desert to cross every time. And he feels faint inside at the prospect.

He knows where his dad'll be. Through a small square archway is a part of the shop that has a different feel to it. There's a lady behind the low counter, talking to Dad. Tony is there, too, who knows everything. The shelves are packed with old clockwork railway from a time almost before Dad was around, and most of it looks it, lying about all over the place, rusted and twisted and no use to anyone. There's something really depressing about second-hand stuff, Jason thinks. It's what people don't love any more. It's dirty and scruffy and the shine has come off. In the rest of the shop everything glitters; here the rows of old books have their spines peeling, the railway carriages and the steam engines are lustreless; most of the metal cars and trucks have lost their paint, and the dolls look rubbish, but then Jason thinks dolls rubbish on principle. There is a military section filled with tanks and plastic soldiers and Action Men. There are plastic farm animals set in a model farmyard that looks as if it were made a hundred years ago, for models much bigger than the little black-and-white cows that cluster around its gate. What anyone could see in all this is beyond him.

Three small cars are sitting on the counter. A man in a dark red shirt and pale blue jeans is holding a large brown paper bag.

'I'll give you five pounds for that,' he says, pointing to an orange Aston Martin. All its bits are in place, which makes it unusual.

The lady, who is tanned and healthy-looking and wears a lot of rings and a silver necklace with a heart-shaped locket, smiles thoughtfully, gives herself time to reply.

'No,' she says, 'I couldn't let you have it for that.'

She sees Jason and says to his dad, 'Danny, Jason's here. How are you, Jason, everything all right?' She raises her eyebrows at Dad and sort of points them at Jason, as if to say, he's here and that's where he is. Jason thinks she's a bit bossy. His dad always knows where he is. Obscurely, he is annoyed, especially as Dad doesn't seem to mind, but then Dad likes Alice, and says she has a tragic past.

'You know, it's very rare, that. They only made a few of them in orange. They're normally blue. Dark blue. There was one year they made them silver. You don't often see those in orange.'

The customer with the paper bag is unimpressed. He has someone with him, a Chinese woman who laughs easily.

'What do you think about this, then?' he says, fishing a

creamy white vehicle out of the bag. It looks like some kind of plump, sleek armoured car, and Jason recognizes an SPV (Spectrum Patrol Vehicle) from *Captain Scarlet*. They're showing the series again.

'Have you got the rockets?' asks Tony.

'All three.'

'Let's have a look.'

'Don't drop them,' the man says, producing them with a flourish. The Chinese woman laughs. They are bright red, and bound together with Sellotape.

'Red,' says Tony, sounding disappointed. 'There's usually four of them. There should be four.'

Tony is very thin and wears a white cord jacket with jeans that don't quite come down to his old baseball boots, and has hair that sits so neatly on his scalp that it is either very carefully combed or a wig. He looks a bit like the child catcher in *Chitty Chitty Bang Bang*, but he's all right really. His nose is a bit bungier than the child catcher's and there's a kind light in his slightly watery eyes, but there's a ferrety look to him, too, which may come from the endless poking around in people's attics and junk shops that he does.

'Well, there's three,' says the man, flatly, and the woman laughs again.

'It's in good nick, actually. All the Spectrum colours still there,' says Tony.

'Let's see,' says Alice.

She reaches out her hand. Jason doesn't like the length of her fingernails.

'I used to have one of those,' says his dad.

Alice examines it carefully, turning it this way and that. Finally she puts it down on the counter.

'Swap the Aston Martin for it, and I won't make anything

on the deal. Don't know why I'm in this business, really.'

At this both the man with the bag and the Chinese woman laugh.

'You can have it for the Aston Martin *and* that,' he says, pointing to another car, a deep red Mercedes with its boot and doors and bonnet open. It still has its gloss finish.

'Lovely, that,' says Tony. 'They didn't make many of those. Not in that colour. Black, mostly, and blue. Never seen one that colour.' He leans over hungrily.

Alice winks at his dad.

'I can't let them go for that,' she says. 'I just can't.'

The Chinese woman says, 'Why you making face at him? I saw you, going like this.' And she does an imitation.

For a moment Alice is disconcerted.

'I'm fond of him,' she says. 'That's his boy,' she adds, doing her trick with the eyebrows. 'I'm fond of him, too. Aren't I, Jace?'

Jason grins stupidly and feels angry with himself.

'All three for the SPV and ten quid,' says the man with the bag.

'I couldn't let them go for that,' says Alice. 'I just couldn't. What are you doing for lunch, Danny? Do you and Jace want to come to the Beach Street with me?'

The Beach Street café is small and organic and Jason hates it. It even has organic tomato sauce, which he thinks somehow tastes like petrol.

'No, Dad,' he says quietly.

'Sorry, Alice,' says his dad. 'Jason's not keen on that stuff. Nor am I, really,' he adds, loyally.

'Suit yourself. Or we could go to Sweeney's.' She gives Jason the full eyebrow treatment, with mocking wide-open eyes.

Sweeney's is his favourite. Sweeney's is everyone's favourite. They make their own burgers with lots of cheese and bacon, and dreamy chocolate milkshakes. If he had his way they would eat there every lunchtime out of term time, and evenings, too, but Dad says they can't afford this and anyway it would be bad for him. 'What kind of bad, Dad?' he asks, and sometimes it's his teeth, and sometimes his weight, and sometimes his skin. There's always something.

'You'll turn into a hamburger one day,' his dad says.

Alice knows his weaknesses. He wonders whether she meant it about the Beach Street. It could all be a ruse. There was something a bit staged about the way she suggested Sweeney's.

'Yes, Dad,' he says, in exactly the same way he had said 'No, Dad,' to the Beach Street suggestion. His dad smiles.

'Fifteen quid, then,' says the man with the paper bag, his face screwed up as if he has been wrestling with his sense of justice. 'And that's my final offer.' The Chinese woman looks solemn.

'Twenty,' says Alice. 'Sweeney's ain't cheap.'

'It's not your treat, Alice,' says Dad. 'We're taking you. It's your birthday, remember.'

'It's still twenty quid,' says Alice, baring her teeth in her friendly but implacable smile. And the man hands it over.

'You see,' she says a little later, watching Jason's eyes pop as the waitress brings the plate with his burger on it, 'I'm a trader, basically, that's what I am. You can't be soft on anyone. Hard graft is what it is. 'Course, if it were children wanting the stuff it would be more difficult. But they never want it. It's the collectors that do all the business. That bloke would have had a customer in mind and was just adding in his mark-up and working out what he was going ask him for it.' She peers at her salad. 'Anyone want mushrooms? I can't eat them.'

Jason stares at the locket that hangs brightly against her accentuated tan just below her throat, as he munches his way stolidly through his burger and puts his hand up for mushrooms. Food does this to him: puts him in a kind of mild trance as it placates his hunger.

'What you looking at, face?' asks Alice. 'Jace face?'

'He gets like that,' says his dad.

'Do you want to see?' she asks. Before either of them can say anything she presses a catch and the locket opens. Inside there is a picture.

'Is that — ?' asks Dad. She nods.

'Want to see?' she repeats. Gingerly, he turns it towards him. Jason stares uncomprehendingly. He sees the eager look she is giving his dad, her smile's uncertainty and the wetness at the corners of her eyes.

His dad's mouth twists and he lets the locket swing back against her skin. Her fingers clutch for and close around it.

'How long is it now? he asks. 'Ten years?'

'Nine years, five months and twelve days,' she says quickly. Jason isn't sure what to make of this version of Alice. He concentrates hard on his burger and is dismayed to find it is almost finished. He doesn't see her smiling at him frowning at his plate, nor how she catches Dad's eye, but he does hear her say, 'He's a good kid, isn't he?' and it makes him feel embarrassed. He knows his dad will be looking at him, too, and he hates being the centre of attention. Also, he doesn't like being patronized. On the whole he doesn't want to be thought of as a good kid. Good kids don't go anywhere.

A bit later she says, 'I'd better be getting back. Don't want Tony wearing himself out.'

'Bit soft, is he?' asks Dad.

'Soft? No, not him. The opposite. If I left him to it we'd never do any business at all.'

She seems to have recovered herself. Dad has some bits of business to see to so Jason goes back with Alice to the shop.

'He's nice, your dad,' she says.

Jason nods slowly. He has the feeling that there's more she wants to say, or something she wants to ask, and he has an equally strong feeling that he doesn't want to know what it is.

DANIEL LETS THE silk slip between his fingers, feels its coolness. It's a long time since he touched anything like it. He only ever bought a silk scarf once; he didn't have the money for it then and he doesn't really have it now.

'Can I help at all?'

'Just looking.' He smiles weakly at the assistant.

'It's a beautiful scarf, that.' Her eyes interrogate his face blandly, trying to work out how likely he is to buy it. Eighty-twenty against, she thinks. 'Is it for someone special?'

'Yes. Kind of.' He notices she is wearing one of the dresses from the rack. It's a smart shop this, the only one in town. It's this or Marks & Sparks. Maybe he should be more sensible.

'I always think these are lovely.' She is small and scrappy, like lots of girls round here, and she has overcompensated with the make-up. Twirling the stand she neatly fishes out silk after silk, maroons and cobalt blues and primrose yellow.

'I'm not sure . . .' begins Daniel, and stops.

'These are very popular,' she says, holding up a heavily stylized blue peacock design on a muted beige background.

'I'm sure they are,' says Daniel politely.

'How much are you looking to spend?'

Well, he shouldn't be looking to spend anything.

'I wish I knew,' he says, mostly to himself.

There he stands, a stringy schoolteacher in mid life and slightly faded jeans, wondering if he can afford a present which he doesn't need to give to a person he barely knows, and also how to answer this question, which is not far from 'How cheap *are* you?' Even the vanity of one who wears the comfortable clothes of a single father in a seaside town with not much of a social life can be stung.

And why does he want to do this? He only knows Alice because she runs that second-hand toyshop and Jason treats Stratton's as a second home, and there is a condition he has privately christened toyshop tedium which afflicts parents in certain life-situations and leads directly to a compulsion to enter into conversation with the nearest available adult on the premises. Alice is quite a bit older than him, but she looks after herself, as they say, so you can't really tell. He thinks he doesn't know her, and he doesn't, not very well, but they have evolved a friendship over the last year or so, made out of asides and wry jokes about children, especially Jason, and snippets of conversation about old toys and local matters and how her house move was going and the visits to Jason's mother and life at school and the children he teaches who are often in the shop. It is not necessarily a shallow friendship.

'You might like these. Not quite so expensive, but ladies love them, you see, because they can be worn in all sorts of different ways' – she begins to demonstrate – 'so they're very versatile. I've got a whole drawerful of them, wear them all the time.'

They all have a polka dot pattern, but in different colours. He glances surreptitiously at the price and is relieved. He can satisfy his vanity, his pocket and his interest in elevating a casual friendship to something a little more than that. He is moderately sure Alice will be happy about the last bit. He chooses turquoise and spends the next hour as he visits the bank and the shops fretting that he has chosen the wrong colour – he hasn't – and about what Jason will think if he finds out. He reasons to himself that Jason doesn't have to know, but dismisses this. They never have secrets from each other. He could say it is her birthday, but this is not reason enough, and it is a kind of lie, a subtle emotional untruth, and they don't have lies either. Not deliberate ones.

Alice seems safe. She seems to like him. There hasn't been anybody since Sally. He doesn't want to go through anything like that again. He knows how much he owes Sally; she could see it was going to break him up not to have Jason, and he was pretty far gone as it was, and keeping Jason was not just the saving, but the making of him, and he has been very careful about drink for years now and hopes – somewhere there's a tiny bright coal that refuses to go out – that one day she might come back. Sometimes she says she hasn't absolutely made up her mind, but friends tell him that's only because she is trying to be kind, and he says, well, if she is being kind, maybe she still likes me, and they give him simpatico smiles and talk about something else without feeling very guilty, because it has been going on like this for a very long time.

He knows he is an object of curiosity at the school, chiefly among the staff, and sometimes the pupils ask him if he's got a girlfriend, and when he says no there are long pauses and then some of them ask if he's going to get one. 'Maybe,' he says. Some of the staff are quite solicitous, especially the women: he loathes the idea of being mothered, loathes it with a passion. Perhaps, though, that's what Alice is about. Perhaps you can't deny yourself forever, whatever has happened. It's not the need to be mothered, just the need. But he still resents the idea that he is to be pitied, that he is the stricken deer that left the herd, as the English teacher for Year 8 told him, quoting Cowper's poem, one evening when she had drunk too much following her victory in the PTA tennis tournament. He hasn't left the herd, at all, he is not stricken in any way, he is holding on magnificently. And he is a good dad. He doesn't agree with a lot of people's opinions about him, but he is happy with that one.

He is learning a great deal about other people. When he got married and had a child he felt he had entered a new, exclusive milieu, and had left the old life behind. Then, when everything fell sickeningly into cataclysm and he was left on his own again, he discovered that everyone assumed him, paradoxically, to have profound knowledge of all the myriad ways, both dark and light, of the human heart. He has lost count of the numbers – men and women but mostly men (he guesses Sally experiences this the other way round) – who have taken him out to the pub to pour out their troubles. He is beginning to wonder whether there are any people who have normal, happy, faithful, sexually fulfilled lives.

John Meacher, geography teacher to the upper years, has found himself in love again, not with his wife but with an old girlfriend, and he thinks his wife suspects.

'But what can I do, Daniel?' he moans. 'I don't want it to end. It's the best thing I've got.'

'Why did you split up in the first place?'

He makes a face. He is a large man, and the jowls of middle age are well developed under what used to be his chin.

'Don't ask,' he replies.

Daniel reflects moodily that not only does he not particularly want to ask, he did not want to ask in the first place, didn't want this drink, is paying a babysitter through the nose for the privilege and is getting really hacked off with being a human echo chamber for the woes of his friends and colleagues. But duty is duty.

'Tell me about it,' he says.

Sometimes he finds himself interested, in spite of his irritation. He can, however, be mischievous.

'Marital aids,' he says to Terry Parfitt, the PE teacher, who has sex with his wife twice a year on sufferance (hers). Terry is startled.

'Have you – I mean, did you ever try them?' he asks.

Daniel concedes that he never has.

'But I have heard,' he enthuses, 'they can be very effective.'

Terry shakes his head gloomily.

'Can't imagine Moira going for them,' he says.

Perhaps all these tales of emotional and sexual misery have helped keep him straight and single and reasonably well-behaved. He feels lonely often, he feels there's a whole side to him, and not simply – not even remotely – the sexual one, that is unused. But he finds himself in no hurry to take the plunge again. Until, perhaps, now. Consider a silk scarf given a toe wetted in the water.

'Oh, Danny,' she says, as he gives her the crisp little brown paper bag with its looping handles and the shop's logo on the side. 'What's this for?' Inside, the tissue paper rustles. 'You shouldn't have, really, you shouldn't. Oh, my goodness,' she breathes, as her fingers unfold the wrapping paper to reveal the silk. 'It's beautiful. Beautiful. My favourite colours. How did you know? Oh, look at it. It's just me, isn't it, just my kind of thing. You *are* clever.' There is a slight catch in her voice as she says this, and she leans close to the scarf as if to inspect it. Everything seems to pause. Then she straightens and laughs, and comes round the counter and puts her arms round him. It is half a public, well-meaning hug, half a glad, I-like-you, private hug. Her eyes are wet and shining. She laughs again, shrugs and wipes her eyes.

'Sorry,' she says. 'Silly old me.'

Daniel had not expected this.

'Jace,' she says to Jason, who has just come through the door looking pleased with himself. 'Look what your dad's just given me.' She unfurls the scarf like a flag.

'Cool,' says Jason. 'You've got good taste, Dad.' Daniel thinks he can detect mockery in this remark, but before he can reply Jason continues. 'Hey, Dad, if you're in the mood for buying things, there's this wicked warrior pack that's only thirty pounds.'

'It's not your birthday, Jason,' says Daniel, reasonably enough. 'But show it to me and I'll think about it for when it *is* your birthday.' He is glad of any excuse to distract his son.

THE WAR GAME room has scarcely changed since the morning, though once more Daniel can sense Jason changing the moment he walks in. He sets his shoulders back a little and walks warily like a boxer entering the ring, only a boxer affects a slow intimidating swagger and Jason is too nervous for that. His movements are too quick, too awkward, and his poise evaporates. He wants to be one of the boys, but he doesn't know how. He does know that showing off is not going to get him where he wants to be; showing off is *verboten*. He is back in a world where every move or word or attitude or opinion can spell disaster, where you find yourself ostracized without ever knowing what it was you did or said. This is boy learning zone, with its subtle negotiation of shibboleths and its quite medieval chain of being. The rich man is in his castle – in this case he is on the far side of the room, small but packed with attitude, surrounded by admirers, his army, naturally, the best there is. He is the king lad. And the poor man is at his gate; he doesn't even notice Jason when he comes in, though Daniel merits a glance of amused scorn. Jason, feeling like a rookie gunslinger, looks up at Daniel and wishes he were elsewhere, without the slightest awareness of betrayal. Daniel is almost oblivious to all this, but not entirely. He knows from Jason's look that he has just become surplus to his son's requirements; worse, that he has become a liability.

'Jason,' he says, 'you wanted me to come in here and look at something, didn't you?' He is nettled, in spite of himself.

'Yeah, but, well,' says Jason. Robbie, if that was his name, is still there. He looks round for Phil, but he seems to have disappeared.

'Well, what do you want to show me?' Daniel continues, obstinately, then catches sight of Adam and manages a weak smile and a hurried half-gesture of recognition. He hates it when he meets pupils outside school, though it happens all the time and he should have got used to it by now. In this short interval of distraction, Jason slips away to join the other boy, standing just behind him. Adam has moved on to another game and is sitting watching as the others roll the dice and make their moves. A gang of observers surrounds every game.

There is something about Adam that Jason likes; he often talks about him, though he doesn't know him very well. He has a strawberry birthmark on his cheek, and Daniel wonders whether this has anything to do with Jason's fascination. 'Why do birthmarks happen, Dad?' he came out with once in the middle of his homework as Daniel was making him his tea, and Daniel had to tell him that he didn't know. He didn't like not knowing things, so he looked it up in the school medical dictionary the next day and then he could explain it to Jason. Daniel likes explaining things, and he is proud of the way Jason takes an interest in the world and wants to know about things he doesn't understand. Most of his pupils seem to endure rather than enjoy his teaching, eager only for the end of the lesson, the end of term, and in the longer run the end of school altogether. Before the year was out half of them would be getting themselves jobs. They would be postmen, shop assistants, labourers. The other half, the ones that matter to him, the percentage he is always trying and failing to increase, will stay on for their AS levels. And *then* they will go on to be postmen and shop assistants, but at least their writing skills will have improved. And every year a small number, who are regarded by most of the pupils with suspicion, will go on to a university. Adam is one for whom Daniel entertains hopes, but he is a frustrating child whose attitude is mentioned more often than it should be in his school reports. His family are not local and moved into the area only a few years ago, and Daniel wonders if he hasn't really settled. He doesn't seem to have many friends, certainly not close ones, and Daniel wishes he had because he might be more stable in his approach to his school life if he did. Daniel takes a paternal interest in his pupils, especially the ones with potential.

So, in a way, it is good to find Adam here; maybe his social-ization skills are more advanced than he had thought, though Daniel notices that he is concentrating hard on the game and there's no immediate evidence of him joining in the conver-sation. Perhaps it's just shyness. But in class he's like that too, a little bit oblivious of those around him, capable of real concentration but easily distracted if something more inter-esting comes up.

Once he noticed him staring fixedly out of the window.

'Something out there, Adam?' he asked.

There was a long pause as Adam's mind returned to his body.

'I think I've just been watching a flying saucer, sir.'

'A flying saucer?'

'Yes, sir. Over the sea, sir. A long, silver thing; it was dead still for a while, then it flew off and shrank and disappeared. Sir.'

For a few moments Daniel assumed this was a wind-up and felt his anger rising as the class began to laugh. He was about to administer a stinging rebuke and an appropriate penalty when something about the look on Adam's face stopped him. There was a closed off, introverted air to it, as if he were impervious to the opinions of others on this or any other subject, and there was, too, something about the rectangular features and the small frame and the messed-up eyebrows and the bottle-brush hair that Daniel, well, liked. Just as Jason did. He changed tack.

'Some may not believe you, Adam,' he said, 'but I am not one of them. It's very possible that you saw a flying saucer. Flying saucers are everywhere these days. They're getting to be quite a nuisance.' And he turned to the blackboard, pleased with the stunned silence that had just fallen over the classroom.

Perhaps he should have been harder on the boy. It would get about, he knew it would, and someone in the staff room would undoubtedly crack a joke at his expense. And he would be thought of as soft, and eccentric, neither of which were much help to discipline. So why had he done it? Obscurely, he saw that Adam, something about him, had slipped under his skin. He would be careful not to let anything like it happen again. But he wanted Adam to succeed, and it vexed him when he didn't apply himself.

'What did you say to Adam Parker last week, Dad?' Jason had asked him. 'Did you tell him you'd seen a flying saucer? Have you? You didn't tell me.'

'Not exactly. Why? Who's talking?'

'Oh, *everybody*,' Jason had returned gloomily.

WHEN THEY GET home neither of them is in the best of tempers. Jason did not want to leave, and Daniel did not want to stay. He now thinks he should not have given Alice the scarf, that their friendship, which is really an advanced acquaintanceship, has a new shape, and it's one he's not sure of. He shouldn't have done it, he tells himself, though it was only a present. 'Just kind of for being so nice to Jason,' he said to her. She gave him a kiss, on the cheek, and a hug, which was nice, very nice. It is a long time since he has had a single woman that close to him, save at the Christmas staff party where a few had pressed against him, but he knew that was just out of sympathy and he could smell the pity on them. And she tried to catch his eye just as eagerly as he avoided looking at her and he ended up staring stupidly at the tatty lino floor. It was such an expensive scarf, too. Not good for the household budget. And it looked expensive, so it looked as if it were supposed to mean something, and not just be for being nice to Jason. And of course it was meant to mean something, only now he isn't sure he wants it to. He has been on his own for a long time and he doesn't need anyone else. He is managing and he doesn't need change.

He let Jason stay for a while and didn't go back to Alice, but read a paper over coffee in a café across the road. The time that elapsed wouldn't be nearly enough for Jason but it couldn't be helped. He wasn't going to hang around all day for him, worrying about what Alice expected and what he expected. After all, what if Sally came back, even if it wasn't very likely. Once he started thinking about Sally, which was somewhere around the newspaper's foreign pages, he grew more certain that the scarf had been a mistake. Sally would never come back if he had moved on. The whole of the last four years had been about not moving on, about keeping everything steady and ready and showing her that he wasn't like he used to be. He hadn't managed to hold on to her, as Jason had pointed out, and one rule he had was never to respond badly when Jason said things like that. It was an important rule: it held things together. He hadn't held on to Sally, but Jason didn't know or had forgotten what he had been like. He sometimes wonders whether marriage was to blame; they were perfectly happy before they were married. After all, that's why they *got* married; that and the imminent arrival of Jason. But getting married seemed to set ghosts loose in him, and he had begun thinking about things that he had forgotten about or ignored for years. It was as if marriage made it safe for them to come out. They sent him into rages with himself as he remembered what he had done and what he had not done and what he had lost with Anna, and the baby, the boy. Here he was on the verge of new life and the old life wouldn't let him alone. Maybe marriage made him feel strong enough to look back, but it proved a mistake. Let the past stay buried. But he hadn't, and it didn't, and to quell the turmoil he drank, and black moods overtook him and he needed to drink more, and he railed at Sally for not understanding him and what he was going through, but how could she since he had never told her anything. He didn't even want to tell her, the agony of loss was no subject for a newly married couple with a baby on the way, and the shame of it was too great to bear, it was insupportable – and so the drinking went on. The miracle was his work didn't suffer. At first, Sally said it was all his parents' fault, who lived in the small blackened terrace house in Oldham they had always lived in and who hated the immigrants, as they called them when they were on best behaviour, which they were when Sally was there. Sally didn't like Daniel's parents much. And now she thought she saw their meanness and hatred coming through in Daniel. But that wasn't it.

They struggled on together for a while, but Sally was a practical woman and saw she had been sold damaged goods and she knew she didn't want them. And in the end it was not her leaving that brought Daniel round, but the prospect of losing Jason, just as once before it was not so much, or not altogether, losing Anna that made him despair, but losing the baby he never saw. Around Jason, Daniel hovered like an angel. He prepared the milk and gave it to him, he changed the nappies, he got up in the middle of the night and swung him in his arms until he went back to sleep and he was never happier than when buying a new toy for the bath and taking it home and playing with it as he bathed his boy, or buying new kinds of vegetable goo and spooning it into his mouth and catching it as it came out again and spooning it back. He would lie for hours on the floor dangling toys over him and watching him make his first tentative attempts to touch them. He became obsessively protective and double-locked the front door every night and double- and triple-checked the baby seat in their battered Fiesta on every journey and insisted on carrying the baby sling himself everywhere. Lots of mothers said to Sally how lucky she was, and being a practical woman, she allowed Daniel his way, though it did seem to her that he was as unbalanced about Jason as he was about everything else. But he never told her about Anna, or any of that. So all she knew was that she appeared to have married a madman, and she wasn't having that. She didn't leave in one single flourish, but would go away for a while at a time, knowing that, at any rate, her son was in good hands even if she was not, and over a period of years the stays away would lengthen and their frequency increase. And in parallel, or in response, or to compensate, Daniel pulled himself together again, and saw what was happening to him, and his protectiveness of Jason became a protectiveness of the home that his wife was in the process of leaving, so that by the time she was away more than she was at home, and so by definition, so far as he could see, had left him, he was as model a husband as she could have wished for, had she not moved on to other things. She had moved on, but Daniel stubbornly refused to follow suit. He was staying put.

And now Sally seems to be settling down, too. For years she has worked here and there, at different hospitals, mostly near where her parents live; she's never strayed far away from home. She's done a bit of maternity cover, some stints in old people's homes, some visiting. Sometimes she has been living at home, sometimes flatsharing. Now she is renting a house with the new man in her life, quite a nice house by all accounts, about twenty miles up the coast.

'She's got a new place,' he'd been telling Alice. 'She sounds really pleased with it. It's got a garden with swings and a slide.'

'That'll be nice for Jace.'

'Yes. And it's got four bedrooms and a fitted kitchen and a garage.'

'Sounds quite a palace.'

'Well, it's more than she's used to.'

'Who's the money?'

'What, you mean who's he?'

'Well, yes.'

'He sounds very nice.'

He had picked up a small armoured car with peeling green paint and started turning it round in his hand.

'What does he do?'

'A surveyor, I think. Runs his own company. Sally says they're thinking of buying somewhere.'

It's not something Daniel's likely to be doing in a hurry.

'Well, it'll be good for Jason.'

'Oh, it'll be very good for him.'

What Daniel was thinking, has been thinking for some time, is that it might not be so good for Daniel. He tries not to look at it this way. He knows he shouldn't. But he is used to being the reliable centre of Jason's life. He actually enjoys being a bit boringly reliable. It makes him feel solid. He knows Jason gets impatient with him, but that's the point. That's part of things staying put, of being grounded. He is the way he is because of Jason, and he stays that way for Jason's sake. He wants to keep Jason, every bit of him. Still, he's running ahead of himself. Having his mum more solid too would definitely be good for Jason. Definitely.

When they go back Jason's irritability bubbles over. He is not a boy to let his moods go unannounced, and he has done nothing but glower all the way home.

'Come on, Jace,' says Daniel, attempting to put his arm around his son's shoulder and draw him close for a hug, but Jason pulls away, scowling.

'Don't call me that.' He puts the television on and folds his arms and crosses his legs and lets his chin sink to touch his chest.

'Why not? It's your name, isn't it?' There is amusement in Daniel's voice, which Jason catches.

'Don't *laugh* at me,' he shouts, without looking up. 'It's not *funny.*'

'I didn't say it was.'

'But you think it is. I can hear you.'

'Well, it *is* your name.'

'No, it's not.'

'Yes, it is. Lots of people call you that.'

'No, they don't. *You* don't. Only Alice does.'

Daniel doesn't reply. His own anger with himself over Alice is enough to make him wary. He tries to think back. He knows people use the name Jace. He does it himself, but not, he must admit, that often.

'Don't your friends ever call you Jace?'

'Not if they want to live.'

Daniel smiles.

'What about those boys at the shop? What does Adam Parker call you?'

'Jason.'

So that was it.

'Fair enough. So don't you like Alice?'

'She's all right.'

Change the subject.

'You know I couldn't leave you all day at Stratton's.'

'Why not?'

'When you're older, maybe.'

'I'm not a *kid*, Dad.'

'To me you are.'

'Well, that's the thing, isn't it? To *you* I am, but I am *not*
. . . *a* . . . *kid*.' He emphasizes each word, and begins flicking
channels.

Daniel has been sitting on the arm of their ancient
armchair. It creaks as he stands up, stretches and yawns.

'OK, Jason. OK, OK, OK, OK.' He looks in the fridge,
which is in the kitchen half of the big single room they live
in. There is one bedroom, which he shares with Jason, a bed
each in opposite corners, and a small hallway. 'What do you
want for tea?'

Jason doesn't reply.

'Omelette? Bacon omelette? With potato cakes?'

Jason shifts his position to get more comfortable. He has
started watching a children's programme.

'OK, Dad,' he says, his voice suddenly free from fury.

Daniel takes the rubbish downstairs to the big wheelie bin
and picks up the letters lying on the table by the front door.
One looks like a circular, offering him the freedom to spend
a large sum of money against an outrageous interest rate
spread over the next ten years. The other is from his bank
manager, with whom he is not on familiar terms because
every time he rings he gets a different voice, though the
message in the letters the bank sends him is always the same,
and has to do with overdraft facilities. Daniel gets both kinds
of letter and he tends to think they cancel each other out.
He doesn't open any of them. Daniel is not a great letter

opener; he allows them to lie around for days and sometimes weeks, collecting them together from time to time and making neat unopened stacks, and eventually sliding them into the bin if they look unimportant enough. And then there is the third, the one he's already opened.

He goes to the fridge, and notices that Jason has been re-arranging the magnetic words so that they read in long snail-trails across the white metal, little caravans of almost- meaning-something. 'FlowerDadWindButterflySongMusicDangerLight BirthdaySheMorningMagicMixNearCastleHappy'. He takes four eggs from inside the fridge door, then replaces them because if he puts them on the counter they will roll around and might fall on the floor and break, takes down a small bowl and arranges them in it. Their old frying pan has become so battered the non-stick surface has mostly been scraped off so he has bought a new one that day and is keen to try it out. How were omelettes made before non-stick frying pans? It's impossible. Everything gets stuck to the bottom and you have to slide the spatula between the omelette and the pan and it won't go and tears the omelette instead and the whole thing comes out more like burnt scrambled egg. He's got a new spatula, too. He slips potato cakes out of their frost-encrusted bright red packets and puts them under the grill. He breaks two eggs on the rim of a glass measuring jug and drops them into the jug, watching the heavy yolks coil together, then pours in the milk and watches it form a lake inside the whites. He adds butter to the pan and it glides quickly over the new surface. The centre of the pan is slightly raised – he should have bought the more expensive one, that was flat – and the butter pools round the outside of it. It's not going to stick, not this time. Then he remembers the bacon and turns off the pan and begins to chop the bacon finely across the cut to get long thin strips which he knows Jason likes. He likes cutting meat, the way the blade slices and the flesh falls apart on either side. When he's done with the bacon he puts the gas back on and the butter begins to bubble and spit.

'What are you watching, Jason?' he calls.

Jason doesn't answer.

Daniel remembers something.

'You don't like pepper, do you?'

Still no response.

'Jason!'

Jason mimes a cartoon, his body twisting round and his eyes big with instant mock-surprise.

'Yes, Dad? Were you talking to me?'

'Is there anyone else in here?'

Jason strokes his chin with his finger, frowning at the ceiling, gets up to look under the chair and behind the curtains, sits down again.

'You *could* have been on the phone.'

'All I want to know is if you like pepper.'

'No. Hate it.' He snaps back to the television.

Daniel looks at the chopped bacon and remembers he needs to grill it. He sighs. He's not usually like this. When the bacon is cooked he empties the omelette mixture into the pan and watches the big pale bubbles rise above the thickening liquid with its veins of shiny egg white. As he pops them with the spatula they hiss. He angles the pan and whips the egg up its slope to let the uncooked egg run down to the exposed surface of the pan, then when it is solid and the bacon in place he bends the spatula under one side and flips it triumphantly over the other. He slides it onto a plate, adds the potato cakes and hands it proudly to Jason, who accepts it without taking his eyes off the television screen or uttering a word.

'Thanks,' says Daniel.

'Thanks, Dad,' says Jason, without looking up.

'Don't mention it,' says Daniel.

'I wasn't going to,' says Jason.

Daniel makes himself his own omelette with the leftover bacon and the other two eggs and pops a beer from the fridge. He sits down at the table – he likes to keep some formality going, even if it means he eats alone. He watches Jason's programme out of the corner of his eye, then picks up the post and carefully sets two envelopes to one side. The third contains Anna's invitation – his first to a funeral, he reflects – and he reads it several times over, trying to decipher it, to make it reveal its secret messages about what had happened to them, and what has happened since. Soon he makes a grab for his beer can, finds it empty and takes another from the fridge without noticing what he's doing.

He could go. Someone else could take his lessons, and it isn't so very far away. He could be back in time to pick up Jason. He discovers he is quietly hungry to know how it has all turned out, to hear the end of a story in which he once had a part. He wonders what Anna is like now, whether she met anyone else. She could have done, though they would have to be a paragon to come between her and her father. He would see her pathetic, crushed mother again, terminally punctured by the causticity of her husband's tongue, his manifest contempt for her every utterance. It was all or nothing with him, he required unquestioning obedience and loyalty, and if he lost patience, that was the end of it, and the end of you.

And the inevitable question arises. If Anna has someone,

is married, has children, does Daniel want to see her? Does he, if he is honest with himself, want to see her happy?

Surely all that should be over by now. He should be able to go and see how the story ended. Perhaps she would even know what had happened to the baby. He finds it hard to think of it as their child, or his baby. But then thinking of that time summons forth a fog of irreconcilable emotion, of almost unrecognizable feelings which churn him up and have driven him under before now. He doesn't think he wants to tangle with them again.

His feelings for Anna have been stewed so much in anger and resentment and guilt that they resemble the bitter hatred he harbours for her father. He is trying not to allow his feelings for Sally to go the same way. He is trying, for Jason's sake, and he's done okay so far.

'Bedtime soon, Jason,' he says. The familiar routine kicks in early.

The back of Jason's head disappears as he slumps into the armchair in disgust.

'I'll run you a bath in a minute,' he continues.

'Dad,' Jason mutters plaintively.

Star Trek is on.

'Is that the series or the movie or the video or the DVD?' asks Daniel.

'It's the DVD.' Then, 'Dad?'

'Yes?'

'Can we get the new Ali G DVD out? Adam says it's brilliant.'

'What rating is it?'

'PG, I think.'

'Is it? I'd have thought it was a bit older myself.'

'No, I think it's PG.'

'Well, if it's 15, you can't, can you? Take it out, I mean. I don't suppose your mother would be too keen on you seeing a 15. Wouldn't be too pleased with me,' he finishes quietly to himself.

'When are we seeing Mum again?'

'Well, tomorrow, I thought we could go over and see her, see her new place.'

'Have you arranged it?' Jason is aware of a tendency to vagueness in his parents' lives.

'Yes, I have, actually. Just hadn't got round to telling you.'

'When did you arrange it? Why didn't you tell me?' Jason wonders if the vagueness isn't sometimes deliberate.

'Today, while you were in Stratton's. She rang my mobile.'

'Anyway, can I get the Ali G out?'

Daniel wonders if Adam Parker is going to prove a pernicious influence.

'What else does Adam like?'

'Don't know really.'

Daniel can sense the coyness, just like when he asks Jason after school what he's been doing all day, and it seems from the distant look on Jason's face that the events of only a few hours earlier have vanished into the dawn before time began.

'OK, Jason,' he laughs when this happens, 'it's your world. But you must remember something about today. Who did you play with at break?'

'Eddie. A bit. And Ali Eliot.'

'And what lessons did you have?'

'Well . . . maths. We had maths.'

'Did you enjoy it?'

'Yes. I think so. Actually, I'm not sure. Ask me a different question. I like Mrs Saunders.'

'She's nice, isn't she? I like her, too.'

'Yeah.' Jason responds warily. He isn't quite sure how he feels about being in the same school his dad teaches in. His dad teaches the older children, so he doesn't see him that often, and it's nice to know he's there, but he kind of feels his dad is on his patch a bit. But they agree about Mrs Saunders.

Daniel doesn't want to give up on Adam Parker.

'Come on, Jason, you must know a bit about him. I mean, he talks to you at school, doesn't he? I've seen you. What do you talk about?'

'War game stuff.' This is the kind of thing about being at school with Dad that Jason *really* hates. He doesn't like being spied on.

Daniel senses he's gone too far. Also, he is constantly aware that Jason is the only child of a single father. He needs other people in his life. People of his own age. Adam is older, but maybe he is like an older brother. Maybe Daniel should be encouraging them to be friends. But he doesn't know a whole lot about Adam, save that he thinks he sees flying saucers out of schoolroom windows. Assuming it wasn't a wind-up, which he doesn't think it was. Pretty weird if it wasn't.

But what if he was interested in Jason because, you know. What if he was. And what if Sally found out about it?

Well, there was nothing wrong in Jason meeting gay people. In fact, maybe he should be encouraged to. It would be an important part of his education. After all, Jason might turn out to be gay, and how would Daniel deal with that? (He would be fine about it, he knows he would.) Maybe the problem with this town is that, so far as he knows, there is no gay population of any sort. One or two of the teachers, yes. But not the sort of gay culture really that Jason should know about. On the other hand, sexuality isn't like travelling to foreign countries, not something just to be inquisitive about. But people are, aren't they, everyone is, all the time.

The whole sexuality thing is going to be a minefield. Girls are going to be bad enough.

Anyway, he doesn't want Sally to have any more reason than she does to start taking a greater interest in Jason's welfare.

'What are his parents like?'

'Dad, I don't know him that well, I hardly know him at all. Anyway, he's adopted.'

'That's quite a lot to know about someone. Did he tell you?'

'I just kind of know. People know about things like that.'

'What, you mean you can just tell?'

'No.'

'What *do* you mean, then?'

'People know.' His voice had an obstinate note.

'What, and they talk about it?'

'Yeah.'

'Has he got brothers or sisters?'

'Think so. Brothers. Maybe a sister.'

'Where do they live?'

'Elmhurst Park.' This is a tired-looking housing estate on the outskirts of town. It provides much of the school's intake.

'Do you see him a lot at school?'

Jason has begun to stop listening. Daniel repeats himself.

'Yes. No.' says Jason.

Daniel leaves it. His eyes return to Anna's letter. Perhaps he should have opened up to Sally, but how could he be honest with her about what he did, when he finds it hard enough to be honest with himself? And he can't talk to anyone else about it, so he won't find anyone to tell him he'd behaved perfectly understandably, and he wouldn't believe them if they did, because he hadn't, and he can't, and will never be able to, forgive himself. There is only one person who can.

Perhaps this letter is a sign of forgiveness.

She wants to see me, doesn't she?

I don't want to go back there, though.

Here he is trying to set a good example to children, to his own son, and what kind of man is he?

His own son, but not his only son.

But Jason is warm and alive and here, and the happiness of his own life depends on him.

He can't go back there.

'Bath time, Jason.'

He should screw the letter into a tight ball and fling it in the waste bin. But he doesn't.

It stays on the table, and he goes on wondering what to do.

It is a nice house. It wears its newness a little heavily, but it is definitely nice and Jason definitely likes it. He especially likes the computer that Sally's new feller, whose name is Roger, has fixed up in the spare room. Once he discovers it, they don't see him for quite a long time, because Roger and Sally have thoughtfully provided *Doom Star III*, which is the newest thing out. Jason has been begging Daniel for it for weeks, and Daniel has done nothing about it because he knows it will cause their ancient computer to have a seizure, and he has been putting off buying a new computer for the usual reason.

The house is very, very neat. It's a brand new home, and it's as if no one has yet dared unwrap the packaging. Outside the lawn is newly laid and the beds are free of weeds. Some of the houses aren't finished, so the road peters out into a clutter of cement mixers and piles of unlaid bricks, but inside No. 5 you won't find a hair out of place. Daniel has tea with Sally and Roger in the kitchen and takes great care not to spill any sugar.

'It's a lovely house,' he says for the tenth time, after they have finished showing him round. Everything is new: the standard lamps, the bedside tables, the duvet covers, the armchairs, the rugs, the mugs, the enormous wide-screen television. Sally never had much clobber, and it doesn't look as if Roger has, either. What isn't tidied away is arranged as precisely as if positioned with a ruler. Daniel is conscious of an enormity of emptiness so powerfully present in the house you can touch it. This is the house where space lives.

'It's very neat,' says Daniel.

'We're proud of it,' says Sally. She throws the emphasis onto the first word, a little defensively.

'You should be,' he says.

Roger smiles at him. He's friendly. He's divorced but didn't get to keep the children. Daniel overcomes his natural sense of rivalry with a little quiet triumphalism. At least he has Jason. He is impressed, though, that Roger can fund two homes. He seems unassuming enough, and defers to Sally in everything, which is not something Daniel did much.

'Do your children come and stay often?'

Roger laughs. He has a pleasant, rueful chuckle.

'They will do, I hope. They're both away at school at the moment.'

Boarding school, too.

'Where are they?'

'Meniston. It's not far away.'

Daniel takes a breath.

'Sally says you were a teacher there once.'

'Yes,' he says simply.

The emptiness amplifies a sense of expectancy. But he doesn't want to add anything. He doesn't want to think about it; he did enough of that yesterday.

'It wasn't a very happy time for him,' says Sally.

Roger looks embarrassed.

'Sorry,' he says.

'It was a long time ago.'

Roger's hair, which he keeps cropped, has receded quite a bit; you wouldn't call him bald, but it's certainly not the full thatch. He has a pronounced nose which droops at the end, echoing curiously the way his eyes narrow and turn down at the sides. He looks as if he has spent a lot of time in very bright sunlight; there's a scrunched-up look to his face. He is wearing a black polo neck and jeans. They make an attractive couple.

'Anyway,' Roger goes on, 'they'll come for some of the holidays.'

'What are they, boy, girl?'

'I've got Anthony, who's eleven, he's the youngest, and Jeremy, who's fifteen,' says Roger.

'They're lovely boys,' says Sally.

He smiles at her happily.

'Anthony can be a bit wild,' he says.

'We thought he and Jason might like each other,' says Sally.

'I'm sure they will,' says Roger.

'And it will be good for Jason to have an older boy around, too. I don't think it's good for him, being an only child. He needs to socialize with people who aren't his own age, too. He doesn't know anyone who isn't in his class or his own age.'

'No,' says Daniel, 'he doesn't.'

He wonders uneasily where this is going.

'In fact, we thought –' begins Roger, at the same time as Sally begins to say something, and they both stop and look at each other and say, 'Go on,' 'No, you go on' and when they have sorted themselves out Roger says, 'We were wondering if Jason would like to stay here tonight,' and Sally looks at Daniel eagerly, which is touching, really, because she *is* Jason's mother, but still it's hard.

'Yes,' he finds himself saying. 'Yes, if he'd like to. I'm sure he would. If he'd like to, of course he can.'

But he doesn't want this to happen, not at all.

'Jason,' calls Sally.

She goes over to the kitchen door to call again – predictably, there is no response from upstairs – and Daniel watches her and thinks of how well he has known that slight body and the wide, pretty face and the small ears that would never really bear earrings and the baby blonde hair that is now flecked with white as if she has been standing face to a wind which has begun to scrape away her colouring, at the same time carving out the tiny wrinkles at the corners of her eyes and between her nose and mouth.

'Yes, Mum?' Jason calls back.

In an almost coquettish manner she looks down at the floor, her hands stroke the doorframe and she puts one foot behind her so it rests on its toe. She smiles as she asks: 'We were wondering if you would like to stay here tonight?'

There is a yell. 'Oh, yes, *please*! Can I stay on the computer?'

Sally looks meaningfully at Roger.

'Mum?'

'Yes?'

'Can you send Dad up? I want to show him something.'

But he doesn't want to show him anything. When Daniel finds him sitting in front of the screen Jason is waiting with an anxious look on his face.

'Dad, do you *mind* if I stay?'

'No,' says Daniel. 'Yes. No. Of course I do. I'll miss you. But – Roger seems OK, doesn't he?'

'Yeah.'

'And this is a nice house.'

'Nice, yeah.' He begins to turn back to the screen. 'Bit tidy, though. Not like our home.'

Daniel loves him so much for that.

'No, not like our home.'

Jason laughs to himself as he returns to the computer, pulls a face.

'And you know which *I* prefer.'

'Yes, but –' Daniel knows this is what will happen so he might as well say it – 'Mummy might want you to come here a bit more now.'

Jason looks at him.

'Would you be OK with that, Dad?'

'Well, I don't know, to be honest.'

Daniel finds he is not ready for this conversation, after all.

'We'll talk about it another time,' he says.

THE QUIETNESS IN the flat that evening is different. Outside the sea sounds restless and there is a strong wind that makes the sash windows rattle. There is nothing unusual about rough weather on the South Coast, and there is nothing particularly unusual about Jason going to stay with Sally, but Daniel is troubled, even frightened. He thinks this is because of Roger, and wonders why, because, as he said to Alice, Roger is a perfectly acceptable human being. Sally has, to his surprise, done well for herself; her previous boyfriends have tended to be lost causes. And this is the point: she is at last ready for her son. Obviously she has changed her ways. He has been a lost soul himself in his time, and could be again, so he'd better watch it. Almost instinctively he looks in the fridge for another beer and finds them all gone. He should be marking classwork. He looks at his watch. He pulls out the paperwork and pours himself a large whisky. It may be drink, but it will steady his nerves and tide him through the agonizing process of trying to see how his pupils might be encouraged to improve. Part of the solution is spotting the ones who want to improve. Some of the staff have given up doing even that. He watches himself with the whisky, takes a small sip, tries to make it last. It's a single malt and dear, too. When he drank for England he drank own brands, which are cheap, but since he has levelled out he buys the expensive stuff and ramps up the pain of consumption.

He comes to Adam's work and reads it with pleasure and approval. Adam can be a little eccentric, but, on the other hand, he's an original. He has a natural inquisitiveness, takes the work seriously. The more he has got to know him the more he has enjoyed his company. He has a way of looking at you that requires your attention, and he always has something interesting to say, though not usually as interesting as flying saucers glimpsed through the windows in lesson time. Daniel still doesn't know what to make of that remark. Adam has the air of someone who lives in their own skin a great deal. He doesn't seem to need people, and he is titchy and has a half-finished air yet seems not to notice it. He doesn't seem overawed by anything much. Daniel wonders how he had felt when he found out he was adopted. In his experience adopted children take it in their stride, but sometimes they also take it into their heads to seek out their natural parents, which must mean it's not always that easy for them. But then a lot of people wish they had parents other than the ones they do have, so it works both ways. Funny. He didn't know Adam was adopted, but others seemed to, including Jason. He thinks back, does a swift mental calculation. Yes, he could even be the same age. His eyes slide to the letter he has left on the side table. Maybe he will go tomorrow. Sally will take Jason to school anyway, so he could. It wouldn't be difficult. And maybe, just maybe, he might find out something about what happened to his first-born.

The tension in the room is almost gone now, and so is half the whisky. So what has been bothering him? It wasn't Roger, was it? It was brothers. The need for brothers. Older brothers. Socialization. Sally was right about that. He had been wanting to tell her about Adam, but then that seemed silly. Jason hardly knew him, after all.

His life is changing, he knows.

It was something to do with the stillness in that house. The precise arrangement of objects. It was to do with the suffocating emptiness that filled the house up and pressed hard against its surfaces. But this was not, he sees, because he and Jason were naturally antipathetic to conditions of neatness. Quite the opposite. This was a house wanting to become a home. The breathlessness was expectant. The space was waiting to be filled. It all wanted messing up. It all wanted Jason.

It was probably getting a little bit untidy already.

Going On

See you now,
Your bait of falsehood takes this carp of truth,
And thus do we of wisdom and of reach,
With windlasses and with assays of bias,
By indirections find directions out.

William Shakespeare, *Hamlet*

ALWAYS I HAVE had a dreadful problem with supermarket queues, and let me tell you why. The facts are simply these. *Every* time I am standing in the queue, I make a decision. A very little decision. A very little guess. Imagine how it is. There are usually several queues. It's not so bad in the big supermarkets, though it's pretty bad. But in the little ones, sometimes you don't know which one to go to. It happens in McDonald's, too, but I've only been in one of those two times, such terrible places! I won't be going there again. But these little supermarkets where there are a few queues only, you know, quite close together, I always choose the slowest one. Always the slowest. And that is very strange, because I have thought hard and watched every till attendant, or whatever they are called, until I think I know which one is the fastest, and that's the queue I join, and behold! every time I am wrong, I languish in the wrong queue while all the others race past me on either side, and I peek out round the man in front of me, it's always a man, and a big one at that, and of course I am on the small side myself, and there at the front of my queue is someone small like me looking very puzzled at this little machine, the one that takes the credit cards or the one that gives you the extra points so you can save them up and buy a new toaster or fly to Vladivostok or something, and this little man, little like me, is tapping at his machine nervously, or he is asking someone else the price of something. Imagine! He works all day, every day, in a little supermarket, and he doesn't know the price of something. What else is there for him to know? The other checkout people, whatever they are called, they seem to know, in fact they give him pitying looks when he is being petulant with his machine, his till, as if it has betrayed him. It's always a little man, not a little woman, because I think these men think it is beneath their precious dignity to do this job, and the women, they don't have dignity in the same way these men do, and so they get on quicker. For the women, the little machine is simply part of what they have to do to get through this job and get some money and get home with food for their children and it is not an obstacle for them, but for the men it is an obstacle, it is the job itself, it is what to do with these machines. There is something I have noticed and it is very strange and this is what it is: men invent these machines, and they love these machines, I mean of course machines in general not just the checkout tills, but when they have to use them they are depressed by them when they cannot work them out, and often they can't work them out because they take them so seriously, they mean so much to them. (Then, when they are masters of the machines they are masters of everything, and my god how boring and silly they are. Unbelievable, sometimes.)

Another thing about supermarkets. Actually, another two more things, one of them rather shameful, I must say, so let me get it out of the way quickly. Over the years I have – and it has sidled up on me like the benefits and concessions that I suddenly became aware I was entitled to, and *that* was some time ago, let me tell you, but still a surprise it was, being old just jumps out at you like an ambush when you are not looking, though of course that's what an ambush is, it wouldn't be an ambush if you were half-expecting it – I have occasionally slipped things into my umbrella when walking round the supermarket aisles, just a few things to keep me going, I know it sounds eccentric and of course it is not in every respect a right thing to do but it's something I seem to have slipped into the habit of, though I do pay for everything I put in the trolley, it's just that at my age and after everything that's happened I *can't* help thinking –

Well, anyway, last week I have my half hour or so in the supermarket, the local one I can walk to around the corner, it is very convenient and has suited me well these last few years, I go to this supermarket and take my usual list, which is not so long, but on it I include fish food for my fish, Lenin his name is, what else? At least, I assume it is a he, it might be a she, but what female dictators were there ever in history, and let me tell you that goldfish is a dictator! Then there is catfood for Lisa, who is also a dictator as all pets are, and who is always giving Lenin the greedy eye, the little terrorist. (Only cats can be dictators *and* terrorists.) And courgettes, peas, carrots, baked beans, lamb chops, cornflakes, tuna, mayonnaise especially the light kind I try to use nowadays, ice cream of which there are some very marvellous brands recently on the market, olives with almonds in them which are very difficult to find, breads and jelly babies and coffees and biscuits and light bulbs: you know, one can find a use for almost everything they've got in these stores, I suppose that's why they are so successful. Well, some things I slip into my umbrella, which is very roomy and as I say a little bag of sweets, maybe a packet of salt and vinegar crisps because I like the bright green packets, they all have to be soft and supple, like the salads in plastic bags they do nowadays, or a thin packet of ham or cheese, all these things are possible additions to my umbrella collection and I process through the checkout in a grand fashion, out into the open air and the open street where what do I find but it is raining absolutely cats and dogs, and I lift up my umbrella to open it without thinking and immediately I shower myself with my ill-gotten gains. Catastrophe! All around me lies my supermarket produce, the little peas and the dishcloths, lovely bright blues and yellows and reds, for all these supermarket colours are so buyable and edible and wantable, I want them all! And there they are around me in the dirty puddles, making me look an exhibition, or so I think, but nobody notices, or they pretend they don't and they just splash past me and my umbrella and the shopping, well, not shopping if I didn't pay for it, around my feet as if this happened all the time, which it doesn't, just now and then, and I hope nobody thinks it does, I hope nobody knows anything about it, but there, I show myself up like that and still they don't notice, what does that tell you. It must be a consolation for being as old as I am, they say they don't notice you when you get old and I think that's true, or to make matters worse I think what they do is *make allowances*, which are terrible, terrible words, but I can't deny they have their uses sometimes, we all need allowances made for us, don't we so.

Though some people do not deserve to have allowances.

Does that make me sound stern? But it's true. You can't make allowances all the time, sometimes you have to call a halt to the proceedings and draw a line in the sand, as politicians say, though not Mr Meadows, he hates people saying it. 'Oh, I suppose we'll have to draw a line in the sand, won't we, Mrs K.?' he'll say, in connection with something that was happening in the Houses of Parliament, always something those New Labour people are doing, he does not like Mr Blair and Mr Brown and those other people who seem perfectly nice to me but what do I know about it, it's no use talking about allowances for *them*, I can tell you, whether they deserve them or not, I don't know whether they do deserve them but Mr Meadows thinks they don't and what does it matter? When you've lived as long as I have and seen the things I have seen things don't matter all that much. Most of the time. I used to tell Mr Meadows, 'Most of the time things don't matter all that much,' and he would laugh at me and then say, 'How true, Mrs K.,' but he wasn't listening, of course not, and nowadays he says, '*Really*, Mrs K.?' and laughs even more so I don't say it so often.

Anyway I don't see him so much now, I have far too much to do seeing my friends who think I'm a wise old bird, which is not a bad thing, of course a lot of them are much younger. And there's my nephews and nieces, all beautiful boys and girls except perhaps for Sarah who never did what she was told, her mother was in despair about her, but she died, the poor thing, and before she went she asked me to look after Sarah especially, though Sarah won't believe me, so I do my best but she's impossible. So headstrong. Headstrong is a nice word for what she is. A mule! She's a mule. She's so pigheaded, and she's bringing that girl of hers very plainly up the wrong way. Right from the moment she got her hands on her it's been hands off everyone else, but she fed her the wrong things and she put the wrong clothes on her and sent her to the wrong school and that husband of hers is no good either he just tells me she knows what she's doing when any fool can see that she doesn't, and that they waited a long time for her, until they found the poor little soul they had been looking for some-where in Eastern Europe, they are very secretive about where

she is from, but what is that about, I ask, when who would
know about what it's like to be far from home but me, and
Sarah says she's not a refugee like me but an adopted child and
then she says I don't know how to have a child and bring them
up right any more than she does and I say but Sarah I have
experience, which I do, years of looking after little ones until
that awful man Mr Hughes and that terrible time at the Hall.
And Mr Meadows is just a big baby, even his wife agrees with
that and she doesn't mind me telling him so, after all I looked
after him before she came along, so I should know. Men are
just big boys and boys are just big babies, except for that awful,
awful man, and I don't know what he was.

There's a friend of mine in the village, she has a little café,
it's been there the longest, all the shops are changing hands
nowadays, antique shops, delicatessens, children's clothes
shops, when I came here there was only a post office and a
vegetable shop and a butcher and nothing else, but she's been
here the longest of the newcomers, not that anyone thinks she
and me anything but foreigners. She says she wants to write a
book about me and asks me so many questions, and she gives
me free cups of tea after my first one, which I have to pay for,
about what it was like in the old days before we came here,
to this country, and of course I was very little then and I don't
remember most of it. Do I remember men marching and
shouting and fearful faces? No, we left before all that. I
remember cakes and grandparents and furniture that seemed
enormous because I was so small. She says there aren't many
people like me around here and I wonder how true that is
because you never know everything about everyone, but, yes,
she's right most people like me stayed in London but then
most people like me didn't have my mother to deal with after
my father left us, now all *that* I remember like the minute

before the last one. They say happy people are all the same, but I think sad people are too, it's always the same old story when the man runs away and the women are left behind to console each other and get on with their lives. My friend asks me what we did and I say what did we do, why nothing of course, what was there to do, though this is not quite right, what happened was that we left London to find a place far away from anywhere, and we lived alone and pretended my father was dead and to me he may as well have been for I never saw him again and we never talked about him or the past, though we must have lived off something and it must have been sent to us for my mother never worked, and all she did was wear black as if she were in mourning and sit in her chair in the corner and think of more reasons than can be imagined why I could not go out or see friends or see anyone and we lived in a dark room in a dark house in a street on the outskirts of Oxford and saw no one and I wondered whether it would not have been better to have stayed behind in Austria and maybe died there, yes, maybe died there, sometimes I thought that, but I was young, and my life was a living death, and I was wrong, but how was I to know? Every day I went to school along the wet pavements and the streets that snapped shut around me like boxes and spoke to nobody and nobody spoke to me, and in the classroom I would sit and speak to nobody as Mother had instructed and nobody spoke to me except one girl called Hannah who was thin and ill and her nose always ran and she wore a dirty cardigan which once had been white and she had long hair that was badly cut and a long nose and we became secret friends and she told me how her father beat her and her mother screamed at her and made her sit outside in the cold in winter when she spoke out of turn and I thought my life was not so bad after all, but of course it was bad in its

own way. My friend says misery is a very personal thing with
a sigh and I'm not going to argue with her.

When she asked me about Mr Kobak with that sly and
knowing look of hers it was not as if I had not been expecting
her to ask for after all I still wear my rings, and people always
ask, they have less manners than you would think in a country
that thinks itself so polite. But my friend asked more quickly
than most so I was not altogether prepared and I did not tell
her he had passed away as I usually do, and then I wouldn't
say anything at all and she thought I was being rude, and what
a pickle it was. For the truth is there are things that don't bear
thinking about, and one of them is or maybe was Mr Kobak.

Eventually, you see, I persuaded my mother that I should
go and learn some secretarial skills, some typing and some
shorthand, to bring us in a little extra money, and though she
said we didn't need it in the end she gave in because who can
say no one needs more money, and I went to work, after I had
learned my typing and shorthand, at a solicitors' office in
Queen Street, a very big firm and very serious and important,
they did most of the work in the town then, though it's not
there any more, and there was a young man there who was
from Poland, a refugee like me, and he made glances at me in
the corridor and he was a very attractive man, very dark and
small and his eyes sparkled and he walked with a spring in his
step and I could not keep my own eyes from looking at him
no matter how I tried. And he was called Mr Kobak, and one
thing led to another and we decided after a lot of things
happened that we need not go into that we should get married,
but I could not bring myself to tell my mother so we did it in
secret and then, well, naturally he wanted me to go to live
with him but I still could not tell my mother and then she
became sick and needed me to look after her, and sometimes

Going On

I wondered how very sick she was, but it turned out she was sick with something that took a long time to become what it was so she was sick but not sick and whatever the case I could not leave her and he could not wait, he said, so he left me and went away to work in another city, Manchester, I think, and there I was, a wife and not a wife, married but not married, with a mother who was sick and not sick, but eventually it caught up with her and she died and I put my rings on and called myself Mrs Kobak and for all I know I still am Mrs Kobak for I never heard from him again and if you think that sounds a familiar story, it is just what happened to my mother, that is the other thing that annoys me, not just that he left and by the time my mother died I was getting on a bit, you know you had to start early in those days not like now, so I never met anyone new and in any case how do you divorce someone who is not there? The other thing is this, that it happened to me like it happened to my mother. Just the same. That tells you something, doesn't it? Our fate is in our genes. I think so, anyway. Though I wonder if she knew, really about us, you know how people do know things and they're not exactly sure how they do. I know I could never have told her I was married, I remember the look in her eyes when I went away to work for the first time, it was pure terror, and I was terrified, too, of course, for I had only ever been to school and never to such things as parties and I didn't know anything about people, but I like people, I found out quickly I liked people and I wasn't so bad with them, and they liked me and they still do, but Mother's sickness, that was something, I think often it was not all it seemed and it went on for years and was always bad when I was going out and then I had not to go out and under those circumstances how do you meet people? Well, there were some men, you know, at the solicitors', there were other men, but there I was with my secret marriage and there was Mother with her sickness that was not sickness and somehow nothing ever came of anything until that sickness really turned into something, and then the terror came back into her eyes and it didn't go away.

ANOTHER THING ABOUT supermarkets I've noticed and it is this. As I walk round that big store with its long aisles of delicious things, I always find a terrorist has been at work. Right in the middle of where the cereals are, with their big cartons and big cartoons, there is a big loaf of bread. Then when you get to the soups, all the lovely red labels, there is a bottle of shampoo. It never happens among the vegetables, just on the shelves, especially the tins and the cartons. I have found a packet of fish cakes among the yoghurts. Once there was a cucumber with the French bread. He has a sense of humour, this terrorist. Or she. The shelves with the household goods, the sponges and powders and plastic bags, they always have something there, sometimes it's a camembert, sometimes a packet of crisps. It makes me and my umbrella look very ordinary and tame. Who is this person? Every supermarket has them, I think, I have noticed them often. Why they do it is an interesting question. I feel I know this person. I like their way of looking at things.

Once I told Mr Meadows this and he liked it very much, because he had not seen it, but then he does not really go to supermarkets. He has people like me to do it for him, just like I used to do when I was working here all the time and not just on and off and in emergencies like this one, whatever it is. Twenty-five years and more I looked after Mr Meadows, for twenty of them it was Mrs Meadows, too, and she was a nice girl and good for him, I told him so and I know he was pleased because he always took notice of what I had to say to him. He rescued me, and I took care to rescue him whenever I could, because I have to say he was not very good at looking after himself, all these clever men are like that. Hopeless. Hopeless!

MY FRIEND ASKS me very often about Mr Meadows, everyone does, actually, they all want to know what keeps an important man like that ticking, but I'm not so stupid as to tell them. My friend, though, she is a little different, she looks after me very well in her café, and she introduces me to her friends when they come in, she is good that way, so I don't mind telling her a little now and then. It's nice that café, some people call it a teashop but I call it a café which I think makes it sound more French, more upmarket as they say, though I must admit it is more of a teashop. It has paintings on the wall, which are in my opinion absolutely atrocious, though I have not said this to her of course, and you can buy them if you want, but they are extortionate prices and I would not personally be given one. Seventy-five pounds for a water-colour of some stream in some wood. I despair of my adopted country sometimes, and I used to say this to Mr Meadows in the old days and he would reply that he knew what I meant, though in his Conservative party he should not be saying things like that, but there were many things Mr Meadows thought and did that were not quite in line with his party but I never told anyone about them. Some of them I don't think even Mrs Meadows knew, in fact I'm sure of it. Oh, you should have married me, Mr Meadows, sometimes I said to him, only after he was married to Mrs Meadows of course as a joke, and he said once you know Mrs K., I almost think we are married sometimes, and that made us both laugh. And I must say I did more for him that she did – all the ironing and cleaning and shopping and cooking. I think I knew him and his ways better than she did, better than she ever did, because after they married and she came to live with us, I went on doing it all, and her washing and ironing too, I don't think she ever lifted a finger around the house, she was not practical at all, though very nice of course, and quite pretty, not a beauty, but then you know I don't think Mr Meadows really needed a wife, he was a very independent man and I looked after all the things he really needed, but he had to have a wife for his career, you see that, don't you, in politics and in all walks of life, everyone in the public eye who wants to get on needs a wife, the public don't like it otherwise. And they call themselves broadminded. Narrowminded is what they are, really. Now Mr Meadows is broadminded and when I was *humiliated* by that dreadful man Mr Hughes at that horrible school he was so kind, and not everyone was, because it doesn't look good, how do you explain? Mr Meadows listened, and when I knew he was not like all the other people I had been seeing for jobs, who went cold and frosty when I began to talk to them and tell them what happened, the whole thing came out, and I told him about that poor little girl and her silly mother and her monster of a father, and he didn't say anything except, 'I see,' and 'Go on,' and at the end he just said 'Well,' and looked thoughtful. 'She had no one to look after her or talk to her,' I said to him. 'So it was my *duty*, but I think he was jealous.' 'Jealous of what, Mrs Kobak?' he asked, and I said, 'Well,' and he said, 'Yes?' and I said, 'I think he did not want anyone else to know her well or look after her or be near her or talk to her like a friend,' and he said, 'You were the mother to that little girl that he wouldn't let his own wife be,' and what he said was so very much what I had been feeling, he put my own thoughts into words and because he did so I felt less angry and maddened as I was by it all, and I started to cry, not just tears rolling down but rattling sobs because it was such a relief to find someone who understood my problems. And he lent me his handkerchief, which I didn't need because I had one but it was kind of him, and I noticed how well dressed he was, very well turned out and neat and his shoes well polished and his fingernails clean, which I hadn't noticed before because I was distracted and trying to make a good impression. He then said, with his little amused look when his eyes sparkle and he pinches his lips together, 'I don't think you'll have any problems of that nature in *this* house,' which was his way of telling me he wanted me to work for him, and I could have kissed him.

It was not so very far I moved in the end, though I had wanted to put as many miles as I could between the Hall and Mrs Kobak, and after I had been with Mr Meadows for a little time he told me that Mr Hughes had been appointed headmaster at a big school in his constituency, and I think he did not like him much when he met him, whether because of me or not I don't know, but he was a young MP then and keen to make friends so I am sure he never let it show or said anything, though you can imagine I let him know what *I* thought of him over the years, I could never forget, can never forget the look in Mr Hughes' eyes when he told me I was to leave and never come back, that I had told his daughter a most unpleasant lie and that I should leave without seeing her again. Because it was not a lie, it was the truth, and yet I could not even say goodbye to Anna, whom I loved as my own child.

So when the funny business happened at the school a few years ago after he had finished being headmaster I cannot pretend I was not rejoicing. I could have crowed from the rooftops. And when everyone thought it was unfair and that he was accused unjustly and what a good headmaster he was, I said to Mr Meadows that I was sure there was more rather than less to it than met the eye and he said, 'I wouldn't wonder if you weren't right, Mrs K., but we mustn't prejudge things,' and I thought, well, he prejudged me, and it wasn't long before I was not the only one who thought there was something else there and newspapers began writing things and Mr Meadows became more interested and asked me a lot of things about the school and the people there, so many that I think I ran out of things to remember.

And, you know, it has been a long time, and a great deal of it I remember, but a great deal I forget, too. But Mr Meadows, he wanted to know, and he never stopped asking once he started, he went on and on at me, he must be like this, in the House of Parliament, relentless. He wanted to know about the other masters, and who was there then and what they were like, and whether they had wives and whether they had children, but mostly about Mr Hughes, and about the little one, that little girl, how sad her life was, and his wife and what she was like and how she changed and why she changed, which I don't think she did, I didn't see it, not while I was there, she was always like she was, until in the end I said, Mr Meadows, Mr Meadows, *what* is this all about, and he looked very serious and said the newspapers were looking into things and there had been a letter and a complaint and some other things had come to light and there had beeen rumours and now maybe they were not just rumours and things needed looking into and he peered at me very closely as he sometimes did and he said, 'And you and I, Mrs K., we don't really think a great deal of Mr Hughes, do we?' Of course I most definitely did *not* think a great deal of him, and perhaps it was my opinion that influenced him, and perhaps something else, perhaps something to do with politics, but I know he has been getting terribly involved with it and I hope it is not me to blame, after all, I can't remember everything now so he should not rely too much on what I have to say. And I don't follow the news, but my friends tell me what is going on and they say it is all very public now and that Mr Meadows has made himself more famous for having looked into things, as they say, which from my point of view is a very good thing all round, and that man is now ruined, they say, his reputation is destroyed, and all I can think about is not him but my poor Anna, I wonder how she is and whatever became of her and where she is and I hope she never finds out where I am and what became of me. But there. It was so long ago. Why should I care so much? My friends don't really know about what happened to me then, I don't let on, I keep it hush-hush. It's not hard to explain, not to friends, not like to prospective employers, but I don't like to talk about it. Like my mother, I like to keep little disasters to myself, otherwise they might get out of hand, might become big disasters, maybe. But this one thing I did not think of when I told Mr Meadows what I remembered, and it is about what Anna would think. She is a woman now and I do not know where she is or what she has become, she could be anywhere. But still. He is her father. I did not know why Mr Meadows was asking me these things, what it was all about. And Mr Hughes has had his chips, so I should be pleased, should I not? But, but, but. Still I worry, not about him, but about her, wherever she is.

How quiet she was in that house, and how earnest, and how she would puzzle when she was thinking about things, in that big house, the biggest of them all, in that school with all those boys. I thought her my soulful butterfly, unaware of how strange she was. She would stand in my doorway, hands clasped under her chin, and I could see her wings closing silently behind her as she frowned over a new question she had for me, and sometimes they were quite difficult, those questions, but I always found an answer for her.

Sarah's girl is the same, I think. I was there the other day, I may be seventy but I can still get around, let me tell you, even if Sarah wishes I couldn't, I can tell she doesn't, she's not at all like her mother or her sisters. Well, Ursula, the girl, is very small but she has that very black hair that is rich with some red in it like chestnuts and a very proud face, she is musical, they think. Parents can be so silly about their children. But she is a beauty, nevertheless, this one, and she brought me a sandwich on a plate, very politely, only of course it was made out of plastic because it is part of a set I bought her for her birthday which is a pretend cooking stove, bright red and yellow, with little plastic knives and forks and cups and saucers and pots and pans and hot dogs and fried eggs, which Sarah, who is a vegetarian, said would give her the wrong idea, but she plays with it all the time so who is right, I wonder. And when she comes to tea with me, when I can persuade Sarah to let her come, we make cakes together, though she is too little to be of any real help, and scones, and I know this annoys Sarah who thinks women should not be brought up to cook as if they were unable to do anything else, and I think, well, women can cook and do it better than men and you always need something to fall back on, believe you me. I always cooked for Mr Meadows. Ask Mrs Meadows. I don't think she knew how to cook at all. A perfectly nice woman, though, and we have always got on. After all, here I am now, called in to help for I know not what reason, and it was she who called me saying she was worried about Mr Meadows and she couldn't find him and would I come and help look after things. Mr Meadows is always going off without a moment's notice as I said to her but anyway I said I would come. Couldn't find him! She was always a fretful one, that one. Why, he could have gone anywhere, into town or just on one of his walks around the gardens here, which he is proud of and he is right to be, I think, people come to see them from all over the country on the days they are open to the public.

Sometimes I show my friends round the garden on those days when Mrs Meadows is serving tea and chocolate biscuits, which I used to do but I have too much trouble with my knees to do much standing about now, just walking once round the garden is bad enough, anyway, it is her house so she can do it. It's Mr Meadows who made the gardens, though, just a mud patch they were when I arrived, a great dirty mess with a few trees here and there and some paths that had been left to grow over. Oh, it was terrible. Mr Meadows had not been there very long. His first wife had left him and he wanted to start afresh, he used to say, and I think the garden – not that it *was* a garden – was something he could distract himself with. It is a beautiful old house and he said he wanted to make a garden that was worthy of it, so from the rack and the ruin he made one. He raked up those paths, which had been salted by gardeners in the winter, he told me, so nothing could grow there, the salt prevented them, it was easy to pull the leaf mould off, it came up like giant sticking plaster. And he tore down the ordinary hedges and fences and huts and dug up the tennis court that was falling to bits and cut down the new firs but left the old Scots pines. He cut the yew hedges that had gone wild into shape so they billowed like sails in the wind, and made alleyways out of beech and set pedestals here and there and would come back from London on one of his trips in a state of high old excitement with some new statue or bust or whatever and put them on the pedestals with great care and step back and say, '*There*, Mrs K.! Isn't that fine?' He made the little pond in front of the house much bigger and put enormous goldfish in, great fat lazy things, they are, I think. He made a wonderful rose garden and surrounded it with hedges so it was quiet and private in the summer and it was like sitting inside a great pot pourri it was so scented. And he made such beautiful borders, all blue and yellow, delphiniums and lupins and the great mulleins they grow round here and cardoons that seem to rush out of the ground like geysers. And then he would paint benches and put them here and there and some were wood and those he would always paint white, but the metal ones were black or dark blue or even turquoise. He tended the grass like it was his own child, which is an exaggeration but I think the garden *was* like a child to him, and sometimes I would bring him tea when he was out working on it (and of course an MP has very little time of his own, they are so busy) and I would say the garden is like a child to you, Mr Meadows, and he would smile at me and say, 'That's it, Mrs K.! That's it!' but then sometimes he would look thoughtful, too. And where the grass had got too bare he would lay turf or grow it from seed, and after, oh, many years, it took him a long time, he had made this beautiful garden, and by then there was Mrs Meadows, too, and she brought him two small boys, Arthur and Philip, and that I am sure was also very good for his political career. Beautiful boys they are, they look just like their father.

They were tearaways, though, those two, when they were little. Now, Sarah may say I should not tell her what to do with Ursula – she does not say this openly but I know she thinks it — but there is nothing in the world I know more about than small boys and Mrs Meadows let them run riot. She had no control over them whatsoever. They were in and out of everywhere all night and all day in all weathers, bringing mud into the house and getting their clothes filthy and tearing their shorts while climbing trees and falling into the swimming pool and hitting each other with tennis rackets until they cried. Oh, those boys! Such mucky pups. Arthur came in to tea one afternoon and Philip was not there and I said, Arthur, where is your brother and he looked at me straight in the face and said he thought he had gone to the shops with Mama and it was not until Mrs Meadows came in later on at bedtime from whatever it was she had been doing that I realized Arthur had not been telling the truth and we rushed outside and could hear faint calls from the woods at the bottom of the hill and down we went and there was that poor little boy who had climbed a tree and to get to the first branches which were very high up he had used a ladder and Arthur had pushed the ladder over and run away, it was a wicked thing to do. And when he got down Philip flew at Arthur in a terrible rage and we had to tear him away from his brother, it was impossible. 'You are like Cain and Abel,' I said to them, and pointing to a bruise on Arthur's forehead I said it was the mark of Cain, and then Mrs Meadows said that was going a bit far, but no one knows boys like I do, sometimes you have to shock them a bit. And, yes, were they quiet after I said that. I'm not sure either of them knew what it meant, but they did know it was something very serious.

I suppose you could say that Mr Meadows made a heaven out of hell, and the boys tried to make something the other way round, at least that is what I said to Mr Meadows that evening, but I was only joking, though Mrs Meadows thought

I meant it more than I did, I could see. I think one thing I might say about Mrs Meadows and I have not said it to anyone else is that she thinks Mr Meadows is too kind to me. I think she would have liked to have got rid of me years ago. I was here first, you see. I think he needed me here, though, I think he knew I could take care of the boys. She missed her chance early on, and she didn't insist enough, for I know she wanted me to go, that was clear enough even if I hadn't heard them arguing about it one afternoon; he put up a good fight for me, I'm glad to say, told her I had been there almost as long as he had and I was a treasure. Which I need hardly say I agree with. And then the children came and she was quite helpless; she behaved like a dumbstruck animal with the first and it was I who stayed up at night and rocked him to sleep and after that I think Mr Meadows put two and two together and realized how much he needed me to stay. Look at the place now, a mess, everywhere is a mess. Poor Mr Meadows. Crockery everywhere, unwashed dishes. Yucky, yucky, yucky. Where is she? Out looking for Mr Meadows, I suppose, though I could tell her he's out on one of his walks. Every morning, first thing, regular like clockwork, then last thing at night. The last night walk is the long one, beating the bounds, he calls it, and he doesn't go so far in the morning, but maybe he did today, so she is altogether flummoxed by such a little thing. Sometimes he takes the path through the rose garden and down the walk between the yews, some-times he likes to go beyond to where the woods begin.

There is no one here. The children are long gone. Arthur wanted to join the air force but his eyesight let him down. Philip is studying to be a lawyer in Manchester, he will be the one to follow his father, I think. Arthur said to me if he could not fly planes there was only one thing for it, Mrs K., and that was to go off to the city and make a lot of money, but he's a lazy soul that one, maybe he will, maybe he won't. Mrs Meadows won't hear a word said against him, she was soft on him from the start, a charmer he always was. He comes back home very often, though, children take a long time to grow up nowadays, what an easy time they have. And everything has to be just the way it was, the same food they always had, and at Christmas, my god, everything has to be in its proper place, the right baubles in the right place on the tree, cards hung just so along the walls with the red ribbon just the right shade of red, bright red would not do, it has to be dark red like it always was, and the wreath on the front door has to have fir cones on it and a green and white bow, and they all go to mass on Christmas Eve and they ring up days before and make sure I will be at Christmas lunch, and of course I will be, it is my Christmas cake with the little reindeers and the robins and the snowman and the Santa Claus that will be on the dresser though they don't really like it, it's too stodgy and dark, they'll just polish off the icing, and it will be my mince pies with the special pastry and the very alcoholic brandy butter that they will be wolfing down and my god they do like those, and the goose has to be cooked to a turn. Mrs Meadows cooks it but I know and they know and everyone but Mrs Meadows knows that I need to be around just to remind her how to cook it how they like it. When I was a little girl we kept all the fat from the goose when we had one – and the feathers, too. The feathers went into pillows and eiderdowns and the fat was used for roasting and for rubbing on the chest of my bronchial cousin, Peter, who was lost in the gas chambers with all his family. A long way from a Christian Christmas, but I don't mind being part of these occasions, we like to be part of things, don't we? We refugees.

And I have never been a great one for faiths of one sort or another, though Mr Meadows teases me often and wishes me happy Hanukristmas at Christmas and I say happy Ch-hanukah, Mr M. – another mince pie? And we laugh at that.

The children are gone, and in their place Mrs Meadows socializes and does good deeds. She has her tennis parties and her whist drives and her bridge evenings and we have always had our visiting dignitaries, which I used to cook for but I can't any more, they have someone else these days. It is nice to find the house so quiet in the early morning, without the long preparations and worries and people going in and out. When I lived here I liked it at this time, being high up the house gets lots of sun and the kitchen is always very bright, it falls on the walls here and there and it is quite blinding, the dust glitters and whirls through its beams as I walk by, in and out of existence. Everything outside has a washed and ready-for-use look, cleaned up before the day begins.

The drawing room is in its usual state. Perhaps I should do some tidying. It is the best room, this one, big and long and the roof is high, the rest of the house is very old and built when people were very little, which is not a problem for me but for some it is and they are always knocking their silly heads on the door lintels. They keep their best paintings in here, including the ones of Mr Meadows' family which is very old. I think this room was built later on, it is really quite modern, with big windows, Mr Meadows can play the baron all he likes in here, especially now the boys aren't around to turn it into an absolute shambles, I mean more of a shambles than it is now. Poor Mr Meadows, he is so tidy himself, but he never seemed to mind. I kept my thoughts to myself. Sometimes Mr Meadows would look at me and catch my eye and laugh so perhaps I am more of an open book than I think.

He has been very good to me, Mr M., and I have been very happy here, I think I found my niche, as they say. At the café my friend sometimes says to me as she leans across the counter with her elbows on it and her hands clutching her morning cappuccino, she says, 'No regrets, then, Mrs K.?' And I look at her over my glasses from my favourite table by the window where I can watch the people going by and generally keep an eye on things and I say firmly, 'No regrets, Mrs T.!' I think one should never regret things, for there's nothing you can do about them, whatever they are, wherever you are. I could say, well, there are things that did not happen this way or that way, there are things I wish could have happened and there are things you can bet I wish had *not* happened, but could I have done anything to stop them? I'll tell you what it is. Half the time we can make our lives do what we want, half the time we can have no effect at all, it's all down to Lady Luck or Good Fortune or my god or your god and that's it. That's what I always tell my friends, and we all think the same. But you have to live your life before you learn these things for certain, it's no use to you in the beginning because you never believe anything anyone else tells you in the beginning, you have to find out about it for yourself. If you knew the truth of it, would that help you or not? My father was a clever one, he saw the way things were going, he ran a big department store, too, so he knew a thing or two about the world, but he was lucky because his father's uncle had come here so he had somewhere to go to and family who knew this country. And Mother was clever enough to have married him and lucky to come here but then she could not do anything for herself or for me and that was a terrible time. And I was clever enough to run away, which is what I did, and some things went wrong, and I was unlucky there, and luck really deserted me at the Hall, but then I came here and Mr Meadows put everything right.

The dust on these window frames is atrocious, that new girl they have is no good at all. I made sure they were dusted, because there's always someone who will notice, some guest or political friend or someone from the press, they were always coming in here, nosing about when Mr M. wasn't looking before they did their interviews. I know, I could see them when he was out of the room and I would bring in tea, lemon tea for Mr M. and the usual mucky stuff for them, they always had their nose in a bookshelf or a desk or a pile of papers that was not their business. Here we are! I would say as loudly as I could to see how high I could make them jump, you could tell the more honest ones, they did jump, out of their skins some of them, some of them got very angry, one threw his pen at me but the rascally ones, they didn't move at all, just kept on prying, disgraceful they were, it was as if I did not exist. He would talk to all sorts of riff-raff, Mr M., a lot of them I thought looked very shifty and I don't think they always had respect for Mr Meadows, very rude they could be, not just to him but to me. Do you know the headmaster of Meniston School, one asked two years ago when I was filling in, now that was a lucky shot for him, wasn't it? No, of course I do not, I said. I don't like to lie, and I try not to do it, but what choice did I have? Your boss doesn't seem to like him much, this man says. Mr Macallister was his name. Any idea why not, he goes on and looks at me in the eye which I find very unpleasant. I remember him well, that one. Very well dressed, a gentleman from Scotland, handsome, with hair that was combed very carefully, his eyes were watering and he had red patches on his cheeks as people from Scotland sometimes do, I have noticed. Does he not like gay men, he asked, and

Going On

I said nothing but put down the tea tray on the table before the fireplace and said I thought he should ask Mr Meadows about that and he smiled in a way I did not like, though as I say he was a handsome man and in a way I did like his smile too and so I felt a lot of confusion and he said, Oh, I will, or aye, I will, as they say in Scotland, I'm sure that's how he put it. I like the way they talk in Scotland, it is a very musical sound, like they are singing a baby to sleep, even when like this gentleman they are not altogether saying something nice.

After he had gone I told Mr M. what he had said, and he looked at me for a little while as he does when he is thinking, he will look at you without seeing you, and I could tell he was angry, though not with me. We were sitting on the sofas on either side of the fireplace, and the evening was getting darker, and I had drawn the curtains so the lights of the houses across the valley could not be seen, and a fire was burning, and when he finally spoke he said, I think this man Hughes has been doing terrible things. He told me I had been very helpful, and had helped him to get a clearer idea of his early life, and the character of the man, and his great strengths as well as his weaknesses, and at this point I saw that what he was saying was not just what I had said, because I do not think this was a man who had great strengths of any kind, and it reminded me that Mr M. is a man who listens here and listens there, and takes it all in, and makes his mind up about something and forgets who said what, and in that way he lives in his head like perhaps all important people do, and I wonder do they become important because they live in their head or is it something else? He said I was especially useful when it came to the man's family, which is to say the very least of it, in my opinion. He talked about a letter, and he talked about other things that people had been been saying, and he said some things were coming to light, and that there were stories that might have been seen as innocuous or eccentric but that taken together suggested a quite different pattern of behaviour – those were his words – and he asked me whether the headmaster had his own apartment or flat or set of offices at the Hall and I said he did have several rooms that were close together which were his offices, like a suite, Mr Meadows said and I said yes. Mr Meadows asked me if he could have entertained boys there, which I didn't quite understand as I thought of conjuring tricks which was not quite right, but he said I was not far away from what he was suggesting, and had I heard that he used to ask boys to come and do their prep in their underwear and I said I had never heard this, which made me very cross because I didn't want to help this man, but Mr M. raised his hands from his knees and said that some things were rumours with some truth and some had none at all and that was the most difficult thing of all, but in the end the truth would come out and the cat was now well and truly out of the bag, and this sort of thing must be stamped out wherever it was found, whether on the streets or in the most venerable of institutions. No, he went on, and I was sure this was a rehearsal for a speech he was thinking of making, *especially* in the most venerable of institutions, for children were vulnerable to systematic abuse at every level of society. Those were his words. At which he leaned back and put his hands behind his head and looked into the fire and smiled a little to himself. I think he knew the speech would go well.

Occasionally he would say to me, 'I think we're getting something, Mrs K.,' and I would say, 'What are we getting, Mr M.?' and he would say, 'Results!', and he would wave his finger in the air, he was quite boyish with excitement when things were going well. And one day I was more interested to know what was going on than I usually am, for sometimes thoughts of the past come back to me when I am not ready for them, and I asked Mr Meadows if he thought that the headmaster might one day leave Meniston and he laughed, he put back his head and quite crowed, and he said, 'Resign? Why, Mrs K., you do live in your own world, don't you? He has already resigned, or retired, which is how they put it out, but that doesn't mean we're finished with him.' He was right, maybe I did live in my own world, maybe I didn't live in his world, Mr Meadows' world, one or the other, but I asked him when this had happened and he told me some years ago and I felt very silly and old and angry with myself and I said was that not the end of things for him and Mr Meadows looked very serious and fierce and cunning in a way I did not like to see in him and he said, Oh no, no, not at all, nothing was finished, they weren't at all finished, and I said, but if he was not the headmaster any more, all his wrongdoing was over, and Mr M. said, but he must be called to account, there must be justice, no one would let this drop until the truth was established and the matter had been looked into thoroughly and the public would be satisfied with nothing less, I remember him saying this very vividly, for I had worked here in this house with Mr Meadows and his family for many years and there was something in all this I did not understand and it was something about Mr Meadows that made me unhappy and it made me unhappy about myself, too, because I saw that everything had become much more out of hand than I liked, that I had spent my life keeping out of the way of things, not causing anybody too much trouble, and now this was happening, and some of it was because of what I had said, and suddenly I was part of things, and I did not like it, not at my age when I could never have the time to repair it, and I asked

Mr Meadows where the headmaster, though of course he was no longer the headmaster and had not been for some years as it turned out, was living now, and he seemed very uninterested in my question so I had to ask him again. He told me he was living in a small house near the school and added, 'Reduced circumstances in the circumstances, Mrs. K.,' which I didn't really understand and I thought of Anna and asked if all the family were there and he said he thought so. And I summoned all my strength and I said to him, you know, Mr M., surely, surely he is punished enough, this man, and his family, too. I said it in the voice I use when I expect Mr Meadows to listen to what I am saying. And he leaned forward in his chair so the sunlight fell across his face from the big window in the wall at the end of the drawing room, and his eyes caught the sunlight and looked bright and I could see into them very clearly, and he said he was sorry for the family and especially for the daughter whom he knew I liked, but it was a long time ago for me, but the boys – children, he called them, he doesn't know boys like I do – would suffer for the rest of their lives. So I finished the things I had to do and went home and sat and thought for a long, long time.

I thought about writing to Anna. It was desperation, to do that. I had not seen her for how many years? Thirty, was it, or forty. I could not write now, but then I did not know before what I now knew, I did not see the world rolling towards her bent on crushing what she most loved, what I most hated. And then I thought, well, did I hate him most of all? There were other things to hate in life. The things that made my family come here and that murdered most of those that stayed behind, the ones not lucky or clever enough to get away. People who abandon you. I wrote some letters and tore them all up, and some had tearstains on them and some did not, and I began to feel very foolish and very confused, because of course Mr Meadows was right in his way, and I was used to him being right, he was always right, but for once being right was not such a simple matter, and this I found confusing, and I was ashamed that it had taken me so many years to discover it, and still I did not know the answer.

So that was a very funny time in my life, and it shows that you are never too old to learn something new, but, you know, also the old rules are usually good, simple things to follow, that's why we learned them and that's why they are there, and I am not going to start changing them now. There are ways in which you must behave, and ways in which you must not. But I know this with a little icicle in my heart because of Anna, even though it was so long ago.

My friends saw that I was not myself for a little while, and I said I was taking longer to get over the flu than I had expected, and I never told them what was wrong, and I didn't say anything about it to Mr M. ever again, neither did he to me, we pretended it wasn't there, though sometimes I saw newspaper articles he had left to one side, and they were from the local newspaper, and sometimes from the national ones, and sometimes small, and sometimes much larger, and they would appear now and then for a long time, and though I never spoke to anyone ever again about it, I thought of Anna more and more, more than I ever had before.

I think I saw a little of myself in her aloneness. Now, I don't usually say things like that. I never saw myself as alone even when I suppose I was. You don't know what you are missing if you don't know anything about it. I have always found that. But after Mr Meadows told me what he did, I found a quietness come into me and I saw Anna in my thoughts, which I have said, but I saw her not as a faint, blurry thing from long ago, not as if it was so many years but as if it was yesterday, and she was running up the path that led to her parents' side of the house, the side nearest the road, which was the only place the boys stayed away from so it seemed as if it was not part of the house at all, so I felt as she ran that she was running into another world, where her mother sat quietly, never doing anything unless she was asked to do it, and often not even then. She would be running up the path, she was so small but she ran like the wind, her skirt whipping about her bare little legs and her feet kicking up the brown-black leaves caking the edges of the path. In front of her I see the big lifeless house with the sullen windows, and she runs up the steps to the front door and waits for it to open and she turns back to wave to me and eventually the door opens a little bit as if by itself and she is gone and my heart skips in fear for her.

Oh, he was a devil, that man. The whole school went in terror of him, even the headmaster. Either that or they hated him, and they skulked and whined about him behind his back, but there was something about him, I don't know quite what it was, not just how tall he was for there are plenty of tall people in the world who are not like him; it was to do with the way he held himself, a certain stiffness about it, as if he were so *very* superior to you, and you were jolly lucky to get a moment of his time, it was as if he had the Pope coming to tea. All the other matrons asked me about him, we were all good friends, we had so many things to talk about, we often went shopping together and even on holiday. He didn't like women much, we could all tell that, he put on his extra show of gallantry every now and then and behaved towards us as if we were from Mars or Saturn or somewhere, I suppose in that school women were unusual, there weren't many of us around, that's very sure. And then of course there was *her*, his wife, I thought she let little Anna down very badly indeed but he seemed to have drained all the life out of her, I don't know what he did or how but they told me she had been the most lovely woman, quite exotic, I believe, very beautiful, very interesting, and everyone was, you know, curious about her and she did many things at the school, a little teaching, a little drama, but slowly, slowly she faded and the life went out of her, well, it was obvious to everyone, wasn't it, she was depressed, wasn't she, I would be depressed living with someone like him, he wanted her to do this, he wanted her to do that, he *didn't* want her to do the other, what a tyrant he was. No one could do anything at all, not the smallest thing, without it having to be done exactly the way he wanted it. He was the worst bully I have ever come across in this long life of mine. The trouble was he was a most brilliant teacher, there was no getting away from it. He seemed to hypnotize those boys. Something extraordinary was going on there. And, of course, though he could terrorize you, he could make you feel you were the only person in the world when he wanted to, and not only that but the cleverest, the most interesting person there had ever been. Quite a talent, that, Mr Meadows can be a bit like that, but he doesn't do that other thing, which was to make you feel that you were the only person in the world who *didn't* exist, that you were a frump or a bore or a ninny, which is what he did when he didn't need you. He cannot have done anything similar to those boys, though, for they never had a bad word to say about him, it was only the grown-ups. A strange, strange man.

And my Anna, well, she was his Anna, really, that was the trouble, we all thought that. She was like a marionette to him, it was not at all normal. She was at his side, whenever she could be, when she was little, she held his trouser-leg until she could hold his hand, though he often did not let her do that however much she wanted to, especially when there were other people there, and he made her put her hands by her side. As if he were training a little puppy. At mealtimes she would sit by him, he allowed her to do that, and they had no other child to take his attention away from her, so he wanted always to know where Anna was, and how she was studying when she had schoolwork to do, and what she was eating when she was eating by herself, and who her friends were, and some he did not approve of (and she would then no longer see them), and when she had her birthdays they were tiny little affairs, and most friends she had didn't want to stay long in that gloomy house with her gloomy mother so they didn't stay long whatever he thought of them, and she was only allowed to wear grey school clothes on any day of the week at any time and her hair was to be cut just so and he chose what toys she could play with and they were never the ones that other children were playing with but old-fashioned dolls and never teddy bears, I don't know why, he had some theory about them, and sometimes I thought he was turning Anna into a doll herself, his doll, but she never was aware of it at all, poor little girl, and she would come to my room and be as vivacious and mischievous as anything. And sometimes I thought that he had taken the life from her mother and given it to Anna, who would be the way he wanted her to be, and I wondered what Anna's mother had done to deserve her fate, the living death he seemed to have brought her to, but sometimes I am fanciful. It was not a normal household, it had a very particular atmosphere, and I was glad to get away from it, though unhappy to leave Anna, terribly unhappy, and of course not at all pleased about how I went, but that was a very good example of something, another thing, that was interesting about that man, and that was he had no sense of the truth at all. None. He was a wonderful liar, you could never tell where the truth ended and the lie began. It took me a long time to see it, it takes years to know people's faults, human beings are so very artful, even when they don't really know quite what they are doing. They say the best liars are the ones who believe they are telling the truth, and Mr Meadows is a very good example of that, but I think he does know when he is steering wide of the mark, or at least I hope he does. But Mr Hughes never did. When he came to me, furious, terrifying, biting his lips together and his eyes staring, I had no idea what was the matter, until he told me I was leaving, leaving immediately, no goodbyes, pack my bags, and I said why, what's wrong, and he said I had told Anna her mother had gone mad, well, I never told her that, I would never have thought of telling her that, and I said as much to him and he began to rage at me as if it were he himself who was insane, and his eyes were out on stalks and I was so frightened I did as I was told and I was out that day and never went back and never said goodbye to Anna. What must she have thought? What must he have told her? I had told her that her mother was not happy, but is that so much? How many of us are happy? People tell me I am happy, well, there must be something to keep me going this long. But I was not happy then, no, not at all.

He made this thing up. He made it up. He pretended things were true when they were not. When things were not the way he wanted, he pretended they were. He made a fantasy out of life, a play. Only I saw this, I am sure. Perhaps his wife did too. Perhaps that is what exhausted her.

My god, but she had a temper on her, that child, and I

think he encouraged it, and why did he encourage it, because it was all about him, all her rages were about him, she would just fly off the handle whenever she thought someone was being rude or unfair or not sufficiently respectful, which was not very often, of course, but when it did happen she went absolutely wild. She didn't lose her temper about anything else. She could turn quite vicious, too, I've never seen anything like it. There was one boy she took against, I can't remember his name, Liam, was it, something like that, it's remarkable I can remember it at all, it's not a bad old brain in this head, this boy had said something or other about her father, and Anna heard about it and she went to that boy's bed and she poured shampoo all over the sheets so that when he got into it he had to spend an hour running round getting new ones, I remember that well enough because it was me who had to help him and get the sheets and that would have been bad enough but she didn't stop there, did she, she cut up his pillow so all the feathers came out in an explosion and whirled around the room and settled everywhere, it was like snow had fallen inside, and she did that, she cut up that pillow with a knife which she should not have been using, and another time she put a dead mouse into his bed and this went on and on until the boy became a nervous wreck, poor darling. At first I said nothing about it because it was dear Anna and I thought it strange, but – no, I did say something about that, about the shampoo, to her father, I did, there was one thing she did I didn't tell him about, it was a later thing, the mouse, I think, and I'll say why in a moment – I didn't say anything to anyone else because I didn't want them to think she was a little hooligan, it was hard enough for her to grow up normally there in a school for boys with parents like that, it was no life for a little girl, no way to grow up at all, I wanted to help Anna as much as I could. But the reason I stopped telling her father was because he told me a barefaced lie, he told me that the shampoo had been put there by another boy, and that they had been having a fight that day, and I said how did he know, because it was not at all what I had heard, and I had even said something to Anna and I could tell from the look on her face that I was right and she knew I knew, she found it very difficult to keep secrets from me, and he said Anna had told him. Well, my mouth dropped open at that. Who was more likely to be telling the truth, a grown-up who listens to the boys talking all the time and knows everything that is going on, yes, I knew all of it, *all* of it! Who was more likely, me, or a five-year-old girl? And the next time I told him about the feathers and what a mess had been made, he told me it was another boy, a different boy this time, but he didn't say it was Anna who told him, no, he didn't try that manoeuvre this time, he simply looked me straight in the eye and told me, he said they had been having a, what is the word, not a fight – a feud. I can't remember what the feud was about or what he said it was about, I was so shocked that he said this, and I did not open my mouth again because I could see the way it was. *Then* I could see. But do you know how I *know* he was telling lies? Because he never did anything about it. The boys he said had been feuding and fighting, nothing happened to them. It was all put under the carpet. Well, not even that because I was the only one who knew about it apart from the boys, and what did he care for my opinion. But the boys knew, and they talked about it, and they became very scared of Anna, because of what she had done and what she might do and because she got away with it, and because she went on doing it and I think she only stopped when that little boy's parents complained, I think he may even have left the school after that.

So you see how it was.

I WISH SOMEONE would tell me what I am supposed to be doing here now. I told the taxi to come and pick me up at midday, Mrs Meadows said I would only need to be here for a while, she sounded very distracted but I can't stay here all day, I have to buy a present for Ursula, it's her birthday tomorrow, I'm sure I shall buy something Sarah disapproves of, I am quite certain to. I have managed to do it every other birthday the poor child has had. I suppose my ideas about what a little girl might want are old-fashioned. Perhaps I should pay a visit to the supermarket – without my umbrella – and see what I can see. They have some children's things, I notice, and I don't doubt I shall be looking along the shelves and finding a pot of mustard sitting there, or be looking for a top for her to wear and find a string of garlic. Who is that mad person who does that? In my heart of hearts I wonder if I might have a go myself, but I don't suppose I shall. I shall need to get something for Ursula, though, I don't know why I am finding it all so difficult, the number of different things you can buy now, perhaps that is something to do with it, it's not just dolls and spinning tops and jewellery kits but those terribly complicated computers, I've seen them, but I think they were made for boys, at least I guess boys like to play on them more, I don't know, and the trouble with those super-markets as far as I can see is that there's never anyone there to give you any useful advice. There might be a new shop in the village, though, just past the crossroads, someone told me it was new, and it is all for children, so that is where I shall go, if it's there, I think it is, my friend is very reliable, but all the taxis know where to go, will the driver have heard of it, because I don't know its name and I don't want to wander all around the village looking for it, it could take forever, especially if it's not there. But if it is there I shall ask the assistant what little girls like nowadays, bearing in mind that her mother likes to think of herself as unconventional, which is not to say pigheaded and disagreeable, though that is what I think, but I won't say it, of course, unconventional will have to do, and she doesn't want to bring up her daughter in a conventional way, but the world likes convention, is what I think, and there's enough trouble out there in the world for us not to go and look for problems, but Sarah, she doesn't take any notice of my opinions, but I know her mother would not approve, would *not* approve at all. Last week I said to her, where are you going to send her to school, Sarah, because I have set some money by over the years, and I was going to offer to help if they wanted to send her to a good school, a nice school, instead of that stupid one she's at, and Sarah told me she was not going to send her to school at all, and I said what did she mean and she said she was going to teach her herself at home and I said, how can you do that Sarah, you're not a teacher and anyway in this country all children must go to school, it's against the law not to, and she said, not at all, anyone can teach their own children in their own house, even if they are not a teacher, as long as they have passed some examinations, ordinary examinations themselves, and I was so angry. I said this child has been brought all the way from Romania or wherever and has suffered terrible privations and lost her parents, never even knew her parents, and you can see it all in her face, in the puzzled, faraway look in her eyes, and she is lucky enough to come to this country and have all its advantages to help her grow up properly and she is going to stop her going to a good school and I even said I could help them, which is *not* what she wanted to hear. And she said Ursula was not happy at that school and I said, well, I'm not surprised, all they do is sit around painting pictures all day, what kind of school is that, and Sarah said that was not it at all and told me Ursula was having difficulty making friends because of her experiences where she had come from and I said teaching her at home was not going to help her, there wouldn't be anyone there to be friends *with*, and I could see she could see I was speaking the truth for then it was her turn to get angry and how she shouted. And I shouted back, too, I was *not* going to be spoken to like that. And she said what had this country done for me, and I said, everything. And she shook her head and said it was typical first generation and I felt like shaking her head myself until it fell off. *How* did she become like that? It's her husband, I know, he just makes her worse, thank god he wasn't there. I could tell she knew I was right about that, about Ursula being at home, but the thing about that girl is she always likes to make things more difficult for herself, more difficult than they have to be. She never was content, that one, not even when she was a little child, she could never sit still and be happy.

So I shall go and buy a present for her daughter that she will approve of and we can be friends again, until of course we have our next quarrel. I promised her mother I would look after her and so I will, whether she likes it or not, whether she knows it or not. And I'm not going to let that little girl out of my sights, either, she and I have too much in common, even if Sarah won't admit it. She needs someone to look out for her.

Baggage

. . . I charge thee, fling away ambition:
By that sin fell the angels; how can man then,
The image of his Maker, hope to win by't?
Love thyself last: cherish those hearts that hate thee;
Corruption wins not more than honesty.

William Shakespeare, *Henry VIII*

THE DEPUTY HEADMASTER strode through Trafalgar Square, wading ankle-deep in pigeons as if through fluttering, startled water. He had an almost imperceptible stoop, which suggested that at some time in his life he had been ashamed of his height but had now come to terms with it, and he looked up to the lions and Nelson's column and St Martin-in-the-Fields as one on equal terms. Luke hurried to keep up with him, and thought wistfully about things he might be doing other than lunching at his father's club, which is what they did on his father's rare visits to London.

When he entered the club he felt as if the air were being sucked out of his lungs. The entire weight of the building, its size and smell and massiveness seemed bent not just on excluding him but on extinguishing him, on eliminating the space his body occupied. It was a place where the past was oppressively present, and of course you weren't allowed in without a tie. Had Luke possessed one he would have left it behind, but his father carried a spare on these occasions. The waiters wore white jackets and bow ties, and ancient clergy rustled sleepily in their armchairs. Oil paintings of leading lights from previous centuries thronged the walls. Paper bearing bulletins from the newswire spooled soundlessly onto the floor near the library. In the bar ruby-necked members were joshing over gin.

'They've had another recruitment drive,' said his father, squinting round with disapproval. His eyes lighted on his son as if seeing him for the first time. A small grimace, a tightening of a muscle in one of his cheeks, seemed to pass over his face, but Luke could not see it, for he had not looked at his father properly – that is, by some psychological feint his gaze stopped short about an inch from his father's face – since he was nine and his mother had died, slowly, of cancer. It was as if they silently blamed each other. They had never spoken about it. His father's grief was such that he could barely speak to anyone for several years. Luke bore a striking resemblance to his mother, everyone said so. Perhaps this made it worse. Any money in the family came from her side.

They made efforts to speak to each other, if only for her sake. His father's visits often coincided with some upheaval in his life, and he would engage in a kind of unlikely, fumbled unburdening of his troubles. It was not that he felt Luke would be of use or sympathetic. It was that in times of trouble he felt himself in need of family, and all he had was his son, whose milky skin and surprisingly pale blue eyes and long eyelashes were so like hers. Luke let him do the talking. By the time they reached the lamb chops he had been in full flow for some time.

'The headmaster,' he said, suddenly. Alex Rainsford's eyes moved quickly from one side to the other and back, as if judging the contents of a pair of scales. '. . . is in a spot of trouble,' he went on in a rush. He had called him the headmaster for many years, though once they had been more familiar and on first-name terms. 'I don't know if you were aware . . . I don't know how I can put this . . . Do you . . .' He began to nod his head slightly in frustration. 'He has written a letter.' He fixed his eyes on Luke, as if to hint at something. Luke glanced away, and waited patiently.

'He wrote a letter to one of the boys.'

Luke sipped his red wine thoughtfully.

'Most unfortunate lapse of judgement, I must say, quite uncharacteristic.' There was an ugly undercurrent of satisfaction in his voice. He doesn't need me here, he can talk to himself, Luke thought.

Out loud, he said, 'Uncharacteristic?'

His father frowned, unaccustomed to questions from his son.

'Yes,' he said. 'Well,' he went on. 'He's a family man.' He drawled the vowel of the last word and made it seem insinuating.

'What does the letter say?'

'Implicitly it's a love letter. I say implicitly because he doesn't really come out and say he loves him, in fact he goes out of his way to avoid it, he rather says he is not going to say it, in amongst a lot of admonitions to do with the fact that he is mixing with the wrong set and needs to allow his talents to flower in a more favourable bed. Flowerbed, I think he means, though in context it's an unfortunate metaphor. Anyway, the boy's parents have approached me about this, seems his mother found the letter hidden away somewhere at home. And I'm going to have to do something about it.' His long features assumed an air of probity.

'Why?'

'*Why?*' For an instant he looked at Luke as if he were insane, or stupid, or both. 'Surely that is self-evident.'

'Not to me it isn't.'

'Are you trying to be funny?'

'Maybe he does love him. Maybe the boy loves him back.' Maybe that's the only way they can find love, he thought.

'Of course, this must be taken up with the governors.' Ignoring what Luke had said. 'There has been a complaint.'

'Has there been any —'

'Physical contact? We don't know. We suspect there might have been.'

'*We* don't know.'

'I've had to share this information with one or two others.'

'One or *two*.'

'Lucas, you are beginning to sound as if you are taking the headmaster's side, I can't think why. The headmaster of an important and prestigious school cannot be found to be engaging in this kind of behaviour. And there have been plenty of rumours of similar things in the past, and there was that tiresome, silly man Davies. Poor Deborah. Poor, poor Deborah. Difficult to confirm, of course, and one doesn't want to set about doing so, but it seems our headmaster's predilections are finally about to surface . . .'

His voice, hoarse like a fine sandpaper, trailed away.

'Coffee?' he suggested.

IT WAS A troubled time for Luke, and it was going to become more so. He was living with Tamara then as her lodger, becoming more and more humiliated by his feelings for her, which had taken him so much by surprise. His acting career was floundering, his sexuality confused him, he had no current relationship nor did he seem likely to find one, and he regarded both life and death as equally deserving of scorn. He was a man whose early life had been plunged into emotional catastrophe, and it seemed to him that he had never learned to feel things in right proportion, for if you have not known love how will you recognize it when you see it? He was prey to wild swings of temperament, feelings that would grow tempestuously from nothing and die away again just as swiftly without any observable relevance to the outside world, and surely he should have learned to tame these beasts of anger or shame or desire or anxiety, to recognize and name and be wise to these moods and excitements and inner darknesses as they rolled and swelled and heaved through his body. Surely he should have schooled his heart by now.

And this was before his great performance at Tamara's dinner, when he hijacked her ambitions so shamelessly, and when his headlong flight from himself and his past burst into the public domain, with all its attendant consequences.

Luke met her one unremarkable Sunday afternoon quite by chance, not through friends or at a party, but sitting side by side at the National Gallery, where he went when he felt the need for peace and his own company, though of course he soon began to feel lonely. They were admiring Rembrandt's *A Woman Bathing in a Stream* and the sweet features of the artist's beloved Hendrickje as she hitches up her white shift to brave the icy stillness of the stream. Luke in his baffled way wondered whether he and Hendrickje would have been friends or could have been lovers, and thought probably not lovers, but passionate friends. There she was, beautiful Hendrickje in her moment of vulnerability, her face so lovable and loved, with its wide sensuous lips, warm expanse of forehead, generous nose and cheekbones, hair swept back, on the point of loosening; her sensuality lies in the quietly assured air of unhurried abandonment, the sumptuous robe behind her as rich and generous and warm as she. And there was Luke, and there was Tamara, and Luke noticed her pale olive fragile face with its precisely sculpted features, its nose thinning in the middle through the septum, its mouth that was strong and full but not quite a Hendrickje one, and he noticed the eyes, mostly, which were bold and challenging and a smoky dark gentian-blue. Her hair was short, cut close to the nape of the neck, and a little unkempt, like a boy's after school.

Tamara found herself being looked at by men very often, and would usually move away quickly with a disdainful glance, but something about Luke's expression made her want to laugh instead. It seemed inquisitive rather than hungry.

'Do you understand this picture?' he asked, suddenly. He had thin lips and a ragged goatee and hair whose texture reminded her of a teddy bear she once had.

'I'm passionate about it,' she replied.

He scratched his chin ruminatively, as if he had fleas.

They sat there for some time until Luke, whose attention had begun to stray, asked if she would like a coffee, and Tamara was surprised not only by his impertinence but by the fact that, taken up in the impulsiveness of the moment, she liked the idea, so they ended up not far away in Covent Garden, Luke trying to behave as if he did this all the time and Tamara feeling amused and quite out of character. They discovered they had no mutual acquaintances, not even a shared love of art, for Luke looked at paintings in galleries as a kind of therapy when he felt his life was crowding in upon him, but Tamara was pursuing a scheme of self-improvement which meant that she was frequenting as many galleries and going to as many lunchtime concerts at the Wigmore Hall and seeing as many French and German and Italian films as she could, and also reading Proust.

'Any theatre?' Luke asked.

'As much as I can. The good stuff. Do you go much?'

'Ah, well, that would be a sort of busman's holiday for me.'

'You're an actor?'

'Aspiring.' He said this as he was taking a sip of cappuccino and he looked at her out of the corner of his eye much as he had when they first met, and again she felt like laughing.

'So you're out of work?'

'The polite term is –'

'I know. Resting. I know a lot of actors.' She reeled off a list. Luke shook his head.

'I don't know any of those. Only just started, really.'

Was he auditioning? Yes, he was auditioning. Had he been to RADA or something? He shook his head again.

'No, I didn't do any of that. Which is why,' he said, straightening his back in a stretch and fixing a fierce stare on a nearby mime artist who was painted from head to foot in silver, 'I'm not getting anywhere very fast, I suppose. In fact, I think I'm going to have to ask you to pay for this coffee.' His lips parted into a grin, he closed his eyes and raised his eyebrows in an expression of idiotic innocence. She smiled too.

'When you get your next part, I'll come and watch you,' she said, as she paid the bill and left a tip for the waiter.

'Really?' he asked eagerly. He was touched.

'Yes, really. Here, here's my card.'

'Hmm.' He pulled a face. 'Public relations.' He made it sound like royalty.

'Actually, it's my own company.' She was always proud when she said that.

'You can do my PR when I'm famous.'

'It's mostly fashion at the moment but we can make an exception. I'm thinking of branching out anyway.'

'Into theatre?'

'No, into business, media, design, not so much individuals. The Millennium celebrations gave me some new openings. I won't drop the fashion, though, I like it too much. Have you seen the new Dolce and Gabbana? Knicker-dropping stuff.' She paused. 'I don't suppose you know who they are, do you?'

'Of course I do. The finest ice cream in Florence.'

As they walked towards the Strand Luke said, 'Tamara. That's a beautiful name.'

'It is, isn't it? I chose it myself.'

'Did you? What a stylish thing to do. I need a stage name, I think. Luke Rainsford's not very charismatic, is it?'

'You're wrong there. I think it has dignity.'

'Why Tamara, then?'

'It's better than Mary.'

'Yes, but why Tamara? Why not Cleopatra?'

'It's after Tamara de Lempicka. I had a crush on her when I was a teenager.'

'Did she know?'

'Don't be stupid. She died when I was about six.'

'You're not that old.'

'I'm older than you are.' She stopped and frowned. 'I thought she was the greatest. I still do.' She shook her head. 'Why am I telling you this? I never talk to anyone like this. It's not me at all.'

'I can answer that for you. When I say goodbye, you will never see me again.'

'Do you go introducing yourself to perfect strangers all the time? Is it a habit? You ought to be careful if it is.'

'No, I'm much too shy.'

A distant air seemed to settle over his chalky blue eyes. Tamara liked the way they contrasted with the tints of red in his hair. His skin was like porcelain. Unusual, she thought.

'Sometimes I surprise myself, though,' he went on softly.

'I do constantly,' she said. She hailed a cab. Her head was beginning to fill with thoughts of the week ahead. As she opened its door she turned and said, 'I mean it, if you ever get on stage, I'll come and see you. I'll make sure I laugh in all the wrong places.'

'Tragedy's more my thing,' he said, as he held the door open and she settled herself inside.

'Really? How do you know?'

'And who's Tamara de Lempicka anyway?' he called out as the cab drove off.

As soon as she was gone, she was out of his mind. Luke liked to dwell in the present. He was not an actor of ambition; he did not dream of fame. He loved the little theatres above pubs or in community halls, and the way in which a cast could be assembled from the medley of passing strays who turned up for audition, and how they would have several weeks of intense collusion, and then disperse into the night with feelings of relief and sadness. These places had never been designed for theatre, which gave every play an extra precariousness, requiring an extra bit of involvement from the audience who had to believe that little bit more, so that everyone in the room was party to the illusion. Together they perfected the experience of theatre, though reviewers seldom seemed to agree. But what was the point of being realistic and judgmental about a frail new play being performed for the first and last time above a pool and darts tavern which was only leasing the space for a few extra quid to make ends meet? The point of it was that in the most inauspicious circumstances something new was made every night out of words and movement, the playwright's mind, the company's very varied talents and the kindness of the spectators all conspiring together; there *was* something magical about that, as close as he was going to get. But he hadn't been in anything yet over which some critic had not poured scorn.

He did not forget about Tamara, though, and she did not forget him, but it was by chance once more that she saw his name (not in a very complimentary light) when leafing through the week's listings one day. Fringe theatre was not to her taste, she had little patience for experiment, she liked tried and tested theatre, she loved the experience of it and went as often as she could. She had her own flair for drama; in her work, she strove for effect, for surprise, for the generous gestures, the pleasing sleight-of-hand that delighted her clients. But she didn't care for drama in a minor key, so something else must have made her glance at these pages. She can't have had time on her hands; time was a commodity more precious than jewels. Good time, that is. There was the other kind of time that passed through her fingers like dust. Once, every waking moment had gone into building her business and she felt that all her time was well spent. Now, she sometimes felt she was beginning to disintegrate, as if the demands on her were taking gobbets of her flesh, wearing her away before she reached thirty, so that by the time she got there she would be a skeleton, her body consumed by her clients' ravenous demands, for the better she performed, the more they wanted of her.

Luke, for whom time was not yet a problem nor was likely to be, was happy to be a modest failure and did not mind that the *Hamlet* he was playing in had attracted little or no critical attention. He was happy to be playing Hamlet rather than the minor parts that usually came his way; he did have a zeal to inhabit the great roles. They gave him a larger landscape in which to lose himself.

Baggage

He was quite lucky to get the part, but that was about all. Marcus, the director, had thrown the cast together at the last minute, having had his eye on a run upstairs at the Queen Mary on Upper Street for some time. Its location was just right, and its reputation was good enough to pull in the reviewers. It was the kind of place, however, whose regulars were often more famous stars than the actors putting on the plays, and this play was not going well. When the agonizing moment approached for the bell to go Marcus would loiter by the stairs up to the theatre willing the drinkers, who were scruffy and trendy and looked like natural theatre-goers, to rise as one. He was disappointed every time, even though he had managed to land an actor from one of the soaps for this production. The actor thought he should have played Hamlet, but Marcus was too canny for that: the man's vanity was in inverse proportion to the paucity of his talent. In the soap he played a foolish shopkeeper. In *Hamlet* he was Polonius, and though Polonius is not a fool, Marcus was unable to stop him being played as one. Minor celebrities can be good for productions and are useful to directors who want to get on in the world as Marcus did, but they always know better than the director. The worst ones think they can act, and insist on redrawing the character, and tell the director how he can improve things, and how the other actors should deliver their lines, and are very happy to demonstrate, indeed it is quite difficult to stop them. None of the cast had yet walked out of *Hamlet*, though Rosencrantz and Guildenstern had an increasingly mutinous air, but they were only halfway through the four-week run and anything could happen. It is usually at this juncture that the stresses and strains begin to tell.

There were only two reviews and both had been mixed. Marcus had put a great deal into this play, including a loan on which he was paying a very high rate of interest, and he had plastered half of north London with posters and run up a sizeable mobile-phone bill pestering any and every person of influence he could think of to come, and now the audiences were staying downstairs or at the bars and restaurants that lined the street outside and they were playing at fifty per cent of capacity and the whole thing was frankly galling in every respect. He wondered if he should have got more of a celebrity to play Hamlet, but he couldn't really stretch the money that far and Luke, like the rest of them, was cheap, and good, too, he'd been right about him. His natural distractedness suited Hamlet's brooding abstraction. He wasn't that effective at delivering a sense of menace, but then you couldn't have everything. Not on this budget.

The lack of liquidity was his own fault. He had been searching for a new interpretation of the play and had hit upon the idea of setting it in a television studio, which would give him the opportunity to explore ideas of celebrity and communication and vanity and introspection in a contemporary environment that reflected an underlying theme he wanted to suggest, that of television, with its judgements and inquisitions and courtiers and its difficulty telling itself apart from the real world, being a latter-day royal court. The soap star had fitted well into this conception. Marcus's private fantasy was that if the play was a critical success he might succeed in transferring it to the Royal Court theatre itself, where a better budget would help him bring in a real celebrity and give the whole affair a really splendid superstructure of irony and self-reference, but what was a slim hope in the first place had dwindled swiftly to nothing.

It had, however, seized the imagination of the set designer, who had overspent within days of discovering what Marcus's plans were, and who responded to his remonstrations by shrugging his shoulders and saying that it was all arranged now, and that he could take the equipment back to the hire shop if he wanted, but the play would be a disaster, and he should ask himself if that was what he wanted because that was what he would get, and you couldn't do anything decent on any less money anyway. Marcus's defences collapsed at this appeal to his directorial self-interest, and he was thenceforward engaged in constant war with a set that was packed with TV cameras and wire that threatened to disable the cast every time they tried to make an entrance or exit. It was no good in the end: half the kit had to be returned to the suppliers just to allow the actors to move around the tiny stage, and the designer walked out in a huff. They didn't get money back on the lease of the equipment, and the audiences and critics still stayed away.

It was therefore not hard to spot Tamara the night she came, even though she sat up at the back of the seating that climbed steeply from the stage. Luke was distracted for a moment when he first caught sight of her, then mystified, then pleased.

He found her downstairs in the pub afterwards and they had a drink together and he told her of the production's woes in a way that made her laugh, which was the knack he seemed to have with her, and then they walked down towards the tube station together, but it was closed because of a security alert, so Tamara suggested they share a taxi, and in it he told her how much he hated where he was living, and she said she took lodgers and thought her present one was going to be moving on and if he did she would give him a call, and he said she knew nothing about him and she replied that she knew nothing about most of her lodgers but it had been all right so far, and anyway she could always throw him out.

'I'm quite good at throwing people out,' she finished. 'It makes me feel better.'

Not long after, following a blazing row with his landlord, Luke rang Tamara to find that her lodger had indeed just announced he was leaving, and Luke realized that God existed after all.

TAMARA LIVED IN a nineteenth-century block of warm glowing brickwork which had been owned by a housing association but no longer was, and it felt like happiness to Luke.

'This is it,' she said. 'This is your room.' She opened a door. 'Small, but, you know.'

'Perfect,' he said. 'Perfect.'

'I'm not around much, as you can imagine.'

'And I'm out in the evenings, of course.'

She smiled. 'When you're in work.'

'Oh, I'm getting a lot of offers, now.'

'Are you? You were a natural Hamlet.'

'Is that a compliment?'

'Of course.'

'I'll get my stuff.'

At the foot of the stairwell were two battered rucksacks, two suitcases and an old trunk, together with a number of boxes tied together with string.

'You'll never get all that in,' she said.

'You'll be surprised,' he said.

She helped him as best she could, until he lay dripping with sweat on his new bed. There was him, the luggage and the boxes, and the bed, and no room left over, but he squirrelled it away somehow.

'I don't know how you've done it,' said Tamara, later, about to go out for dinner.

'Practice,' said Luke.

'Who's that?' She pointed to a framed print of a young man lying on a bed before an open garret window. He was wearing bright blue breeches and white stockings, and a white shirt open across his chest. Beside him was a box of shredded paper. His hair was a mass of coppery red curls, his skin white, and his eyes were closed. On the windowsill stood what looked like a geranium.

'Ah. The marvellous boy. Thomas Chatterton.'

'He doesn't look very well.'

'He's dead. By his own hand, it's said, though not everyone agrees on that.'

'That would explain the pallor.'

He looked at her curiously. 'Do you really not know this painting? I thought everyone did.'

'Of course I know it. I just didn't know who he was. Are you going out or staying in?'

'I'm out. Not too late, though.'

'Anyone interesting?'

'A friend. What about you?'

'Business, not pleasure, as always.'

'On a Saturday night?'

She nodded. As she left he leaned out of the door of the flat and said, 'Hey.' She turned, halfway down the stairs.

'You look great, by the way. You look like Audrey Hepburn.'

She smiled. He could tell she was pleased. He liked making her smile.

'Juliette Binoche, too,' he called down the well, but she didn't bother to respond this time.

Her flat was furnished in grand style, now that he could look at it properly. There was a giant white sofa with big round cushions, and a white rug that covered most of the pale wooden floor. The dining table had a black marble surface and tapering chrome legs. Above the marble mantelpiece rose a mirror with a carved jade frame. The standard lamps were also black, with vanishingly thin silver stems. The walls were hung with abstractions that looked as if they may have been passed on by a relative who had collected them in the Sixties. Some were violent, some were lugubrious, but against such a minimal background they seemed perfectly at ease with each other. And indeed they had been given to Tamara by her mother, who had seen a thing or two in her life and was intent on seeing a few more, but among them she did not number these paintings, which belonged to another era and another husband. In the kitchen tiny spotlights were arranged on rails, and the steel surfaces gleamed. The bathroom was tiled white, and in the mirrored medicine chest Luke found boxes of sticking plasters and corn plasters, for Tamara had been a martyr to her feet since she was a child. Shamelessly, he progressed into her bedroom, half hoping to find it in chaos, or at least showing some signs of imperfection, but it was as magnificent – and as neat – as the rest, with a great gold-and-red chinese wardrobe against one wall and a double sleigh bed against the other. Tamara's was a world of smooth, lambent textures.

THAT EVENING HE met Angus in a bar in Old Compton Street. He didn't often get to see him, and they kissed a little shyly. Angus was wearing a loud green suit because he had a party to go on to, and Luke felt more than ever like a country cousin. Their lives had drawn apart over the years: Angus was a successful journalist now, for whom politics was an obsession. Luke found it incomprehensible. And Angus did insist, like all ambitious men in their late twenties, in talking about his work as if nothing else existed, until Luke realized that he would have had a uniquely privileged working knowledge of the intricacies of life at Westminster, had he been listening to a word. But nothing could interest him less than British politics, and he had the useful faculty of being able to look fascinated even if his thoughts were elsewhere. He observed his old friend as much as he heard him, and noted with concern the slight jowliness that was already beginning to affect his face, and the way his skin was coarser, some of it reddening a little over the cheekbones and round his neck but mostly paler and the pores more noticeable, like pricked pastry. Bags had appeared under his eyes like violet bruises. He was still a good-looking man, but the work and the drink were taking their toll. As usual, he showed little curiosity about Luke's life. What Angus liked to talk about was himself and the past, when they had been at school together, Angus because his parents were wealthy and it was a good school, and Luke because all masters' children enjoyed a free education there. That Luke was uncomfortable talking about Meniston was lost on Angus, who would reminisce about the other boys and the trouble they got into and the heroes and villains and the ungainly but terrifying headmaster and his silent wife and dutiful, oddball daughter, for whom Luke had once been Ariel in her production of *The Tempest*, and all the pantheon of teachers with their faults and occasional virtues. When they had these talks Angus seemed to have forgotten how close they had been, especially afterwards when they had lived and all too briefly slept together and Luke thought he had found himself and was happy for the first time. And Angus forgot, too, about Luke's ambivalent feelings about his father, so Luke would go quiet when Angus mentioned him and endure the agony of a subject he preferred to avoid – but Angus seldom lingered over things so it was soon over. This time Angus asked him directly how his father was, and Luke took a deep breath and said that he was well and that he was coming to London in a few months' time and would probably want to see him, then he changed the subject and Angus didn't seem to notice.

'I'm living with a beautiful woman,' Luke said.

'I always said you were secretly straight.'

'That's because you are. Stop projecting.'

'So how come?'

'Actually, I'm her lodger.'

He told Angus about Tamara, and for once his friend seemed interested in what he was saying.

'That name rings a bell.'

'She's very successful, I think.'

'She sounds like someone I should meet. Tamara de Lempicka, you say?'

'Yes. Who was she? I mean, I know the name.'

'Glamorous Russian artist, big on sexual ambiguity.'

'She is quite androgynous, I suppose, Tamara.'

'And you're just her lodger?'

Luke always blushed when teased.

'Angus, I've only just moved in, just today. But yes, I suppose I do think she's attractive. That's what you're implying, isn't it?'

'Good boy. And have you been looking after yourself?'

They both knew what he meant.

'Yes, I have,' said Luke, simply. And changed the subject again.

LIVING WITH TAMARA, Luke felt insubstantial, terrified of disturbing the beautiful surfaces. When Tam had friends round he joined in, however, playing the part of her bohemian lodger. It made him feel like a human goldfish, but Tam liked it, and he liked to please her. He was captivating, and captious, and he dressed more raffishly and down-at-heel than he usually did, and pretended to flirt with Tam in an adoring and hopeless way, which went down very well, especially as Tam affected not to notice. Her friends thought him charming, and thought them quite a double act, so that Tam would invite him to her dinners, even the important ones, because though he looked – in a clean way – as if he might have slept in a cardboard box, he behaved impeccably. He introduced an unusual flavour to her gatherings without ever being threatening or disturbing them. Tam was a labcoat-clad chemist of human relations, pristine and exact, adducing powders and distilling liquids in test tubes, clarifying and reducing and mixing and then warming them over a deftly handled flame. She liked to introduce chic people to political people, business people to beautiful people. She was expert at making connections, discerning mutual interests and being preternaturally aware of the tender electricity of touch and the swift currents of exchanged glances and the barely perceived pressure of palm or fingertip on someone else's arm. She sensed rather than saw shared confidences, and immediately divined enmities. She loved to read clothes and how they were worn: how they belied the wearer's age or revealed their attitudes and opinions, subtly referencing their affiliations to Oxford Street or Kensington, to Fifth

Avenue or Milan or Bondi Beach, to country or town, to revolution or establishment, old money or new, mind or spirit, values as style or style as values, to North, South, East or West, the arriving or the departing, in other words, to the endless gradations of human difference.

Then one early Saturday afternoon she got back to find someone she didn't quite recognize reclining on her sofa. One arm trailed listlessly to the floor, the legs were in pale blue jeans and he wore a white shirt. He seemed to be asleep.

She panicked and screamed. Immediately the person on the sofa opened his eyes and leaped to his feet.

'Sorry,' he said, running his hands through his bright red hair. 'Sorry.'

She stared at him.

'What have you *done*?'

He seemed bewildered for a few moments.

'What *have* you done?' she repeated.

He looked at himself stupidly in the mirror.

'Oh – my hair. I dyed it. What do you think?'

Her fury abated.

'I – thought you were someone else.' She began taking off her coat, then stopped. 'You were,' she said. 'You're the man in the painting, aren't you? The one who killed himself? You're weird, you really are.'

He didn't say anything.

Later, she said, 'I'm sorry. I think I overreacted.'

'That's all right.'

'I'm not sure it suits you, actually.'

'It doesn't need to.'

'Why did you do it, then? That's quite a virulent shade.'

'I'm having lunch with my dad tomorrow. He'll take me to his club. He always does.'

'Is it supposed to be a treat for him?'

'No.'

She was interested. He made her some coffee. When he handed her a cup he smiled thinly at her.

'Sorry again.'

She sat opposite him. The Harrods bags she had been carrying stayed by the door.

'Come on, then. Why does your dad get the shock treatment? Why have you shaved, by the way?'

'Hard to dye that bit.'

'So are you going to tell me?'

'I just want to see if he notices.'

'He'll find it hard not to.'

'You don't know my father.' He said this not in any self-pitying way, but as a statement of fact.

'I don't know my own very well, not as much as I'd like to,' she said. 'He travels,' she went on, in answer to his look. 'He always has.'

'Does your mum mind?'

'God, no. She's on her third marriage anyway. It's my dad I feel sorry for. I wish she would travel *more*.'

'That sounds bitter.'

'You don't know my mother.'

They smiled at each other. He felt like giving her another compliment. He felt like giving her a million compliments. He was, in fact, falling, quite helplessly, in love.

THAT WEEK, TAM's family were having a crisis, too, and Tam had been summoned to her mother's home by the river. Her mother was called Christine and her sister was called Bella and she was in trouble again. Bella had not been in trouble for quite some time, so it was probably overdue. Tam had thought that her sister's turbulent life had calmed down in the last few years, ever since she had found herself a second husband who, unlike the car mechanic from the local garage she had married secretly when she was eighteen, had a proper job at a merchant bank and had seemed very steady. They had bought a home in south London in a neighbourhood where everyone behaved as if they were ten or even twenty years older, and very few women distracted their waking hours with work. In this happy realm time passes in an unceasing stream of exercise classes and reading groups and charitable coffee mornings, and at least one dinner is given and attended every week. The common throngs with children and nannies, and organized football is played on Saturdays. Beefy young men fly kites in winter and extended familes play cricket and softball in the summer, and on Sundays after lunch and even church fathers are to be glimpsed asleep in armchairs with newspapers over their faces. Bella and Alan were happy there and Tam thought they would stay and have children and buy a place in the country and eventually move out and do all the things that Tam knew would never be for her. But they didn't rush to do these things and property prices had risen making it difficult to move so they decided to improve their house by building an extension, and then adding a conservatory, and they had had the builders in for months and months and it now appeared that there had been another reason for this.

'Run off with the *builder*?'

'Oh, I don't think he's a real builder, not the kind that does the brickwork and makes cement. Not that kind of builder.'

'What does he do, then? Loiter in houses he's supposed

to be doing up and make passes at his clients, apparently.'

'Well, I think he organizes everything and tells everyone what to do. There's nothing wrong with him, he sounds very nice, his name's Nicholas, he's just —'

'— not her husband.'

'And I'm afraid it doesn't seem to be he who made the advances, from what I can gather. You know what Bella is like.'

'Never satisfied, and no regarder of other people's happiness. The builder, Mum. Whichever way you cut it, it's not impressive. A power-drill thing, is it?'

'She was never ambitious like you, dear.' Christine was always defensive of her younger daughter.

'But this is taking unambitiousness several steps further than is, strictly speaking, necessary, don't you think?'

Her mother's own ambitions had brought her three husbands and a beautiful house by the river on Chiswick Mall, but she was careless about her children's behaviour. Tam had never understood what her mother wanted from her, but that she would fuss over Bella and take her side, that could be taken for granted. And that evening her mother fretted and admonished, and Bella sulked, and Tam wondered as she often did what went on in Bella's head.

'I don't know why you want me here, Mummy,' complained Bella. 'It's my life. I don't why I've come. And why is Maisy here?' She refused to call her sister Tamara, preferring the name she had used since childhood.

'I think it's important for families to keep close together at times like these,' her mother said, spooning pea soup into grey bowls.

'Is Freddie joining us? asked Tamara. Her stepfather was an erratic man.

'Alfredo is taking a class this evening,' replied Christine.

'I thought he usually did his life drawing here?'

'During the day he does. Not in the evenings, and certainly not this evening.' Family took precedence.

'I'm not going to change my mind, if this is what this is all about,' said Bella.

What this is all about, thought Tam, is a self-absorbed mother feeling temporary concern about her flakey younger daughter. Christine had been with Alfredo for five years, now. She must be getting restless herself.

'Of course that's not what it's all about, darling,' protested Christine. 'You know, I never thought Alan was *quite* right for you . . .'

'Oh, please,' said Tam.

'. . . perhaps a little insipid, but you seemed so happy together.'

Bella sulked on, but there was a change in her mood. She could tell she was being let off the hook.

'He got so boring, Mum. All my friends agree with me. He just wanted to go to art galleries and watch films and we never had any parties and he was never interested in having people round. And when I went to the health club I always had to go on my own, I just don't think we had *anything* in common.'

'You liked all that about him when you met him,' said Tam. 'I thought the whole point was he was supposed to be different. For a merchant banker.'

Bella scowled at her. She and her mother looked very alike: pearlescent highlighted hair and hazel eyes and pretty ears. Tam wondered where her father was now, and whether he knew about any of this. She wondered whether it would surprise him. He ought to know, she thought, and she said so.

'I'll tell him,' said Bella, and looked tragic.

'I don't think you should do that, dear; Tamara, do you think you . . . ?' Her voice trailed away.

'I don't see why I should.'

'Well, you're closer to your father, aren't you, he may take it better from you.'

'You will do it nicely, won't you, Maisy?' said Bella, anxiously. 'You won't make him hate me?'

'I don't think he'll be all that surprised to hear about it,' said Tam.

'You are spiteful, sometimes,' said Bella.

Tam raised her eyebrows. 'Thanks,' she said.

'Tell us all about Nicholas, dear,' said her mother, tactfully.

TAM WAS BAD-tempered for weeks, but this did not dilute Luke's growing feelings for her, and nothing could assuage his pain at her indifference to him. He tried to keep out of her way, wondering if he was destined to drift from one hostile domicile to another. Doors slammed, pans rattled, curt notes were left on the kitchen table. Tam was tightlipped most of the time and monosyllabic when she spoke, and that was when she was at home, which was seldom.

Luke was beginning to be possessed by his passion for Tamara in a way that shook him deeply, and he felt he was being swept away from himself and all that he knew about who he was. It seemed to be inflamed all the more by her absence. His love for her was partly defined by what was missing from his life when she was not there: the vitality, the unsquashability, the indomitable capriciousness of her. He admired, though he didn't altogether share, her ability to stay up all night and appear bright-eyed at dawn. He missed her raucousness and her jokes, her singing to herself in her thin soprano when she was happy and the way she would spend Sundays in bed reading. He loved the way she swore when she thought no one was listening. And he loved her silences, for when she seemed oblivious she was at her most concentrated, when some new idea or scheme had come to her and her mind was fully occupied with it. Oddly, he hated her absence, but when she was there, he treasured those moments when she was mentally absent, because then she was being most uniquely herself.

One day she announced she was giving a dinner party. She usually gave them with exhausting frequency, but she hadn't for a while, so Luke took it that she had resolved whatever it was.

'Anything special?' he asked.

She put down the Saturday-morning cafetiere. He recognized the inscrutable expression. How she looked at her most determined.

'Do you have any friends in politics?'

'There's Angus.' They had recently met, he knew.

'Invite him. Ask him to bring a friend.'

'Anyone?'

'Someone political. Macallister. Do you know Macallister?'

'Not really.'

'Angus will. Ask him.' She bent forward over a copy of the *Daily Mail*. Luke helped himself to a still warm croissant from the oven. He wondered what was going on.

'Who else is coming?'

'Never you mind.' Then she relented. 'My mother.'

'Your mother.'

'Right.'

'And?'

She was exasperated. 'Luke, this is *my* dinner.'

Luke went to lie on his bed and thought about how he loved her and how she would never know and looked at the pictures on his wall. This was not a life for someone his age. He had to get more serious. None of the auditions were getting him anywhere. There was a comedy part in a new play he had tried for, but comedy had never really been what he wanted to do. He could tell Tam didn't take him seriously, and doing comedy wasn't going to help. On the other hand, he did need to eat.

Dilemmas like these gave him a headache. Not ordinary ones, but ones that felt like they were unending, as if they were leaching all his vitality out of him. He was one big slab of desiccating meat located in a small room somewhere in north London, going nowhere. The worst of it was that he didn't really care about success, just about Tam.

So he told Angus about the dinner and asked him about Macallister.

'She's spreading her wings, isn't she?'

'You think?'

'That's what she said when we met. I thought she was quite interested in me, actually.'

'Why would she be interested in politics? Why would anyone, apart from you?'

'Perhaps it was just me, then.'

'Likely.'

'Thank you.'

'Well, you know I would think that. But Macallister. Tell me about him.'

'Archetypal newshound, knows everyone, hardboiled as they come, last of the finest, broke the mould when they made him, all that.'

'So, contacts?'

'It breaks my heart to say it, but yes, I think so. We are but flagstones on your Tamara's pavement to glory.'

Luke clicked his teeth. 'This thing when you met?'

'Art gallery opening. She likes art, doesn't she? So she told me.'

'She does.'

'She certainly laid on a lavish show.'

'Was it hers? She didn't say anything about it to me.'

'You must have been working.'

'I wish. But even so. We met in the National Gallery, you know.'

'You've told me. Several times.'

'What were you doing at this thing?'

'I was with someone who introduced us. She seemed to know all about me. Must have got it from you.'

'Not much more than a whisper. Sorry.'

'Now that does really impress me.'

Luke sighed.

'You do like her, don't you?' said Angus.

'Yes. Terribly. Too much. Far too much. It's driving me crazy. Literally.'

Angus decided not to tell him how he and Tam and a number of them had ended up at dinner afterwards, and how drunk they got. Or about the way she had looked at him that night.

Macallister eventually said he would come, and Tam's mood improved immediately. At the same time, Luke decided to take the part he was being offered in a new treatment of Goldsmith's *She Stoops to Conquer*. There were two aspects to the production that made it unusual for that theatre: it was a very traditional choice, and it was played straight. And Luke had to accept that he had a talent for eighteenth-century foppishness – reluctantly, because although he may not have been ambitious and may have been lacking in competitiveness, he knew that he should not be so quickly seduced by what came easily to him.

Some time before that strange and fateful dinner (Tam liked to plan well in advance), Luke discovered Angus and Tam had made friends, and things suddenly seemed to move frighteningly quickly. Angus didn't live far away and was able to come over often, and Luke could tell they thought he would be happy about this, though he knew Angus, in his heart of hearts, knew he wouldn't.

'You can't just come round here like this,' he said.

'Why not?'

'Well, you know. And there's you and me.'

'Luke, you've got to move on.' Angus hadn't the courage to say their affair had been a youthful indiscretion, but that's what he thought it was, now. For him, at least.

From then on, when the three of them were together, Luke felt he was doing all the hard work. Not making the running – that would put him in charge, and that's what he wasn't. He was the one in the middle, unsure if he was bringing them together or trying to force them apart. The more he felt he was separating them, the more guilty he felt and the more accommodating he tried to be. When they went shopping together he chattered endlessly to make sure Tam and Angus were having a good time – or was he trying to monopolize the conversation, so that neither could have a good time without him? He rattled on about the clothes they shopped for and advised unnecessarily on the menus when they stopped for lunch; Angus smiled affectionately at him, but Tam looked bored, though Tam could look bored at the best of times, it was a bit of a speciality of hers.

Angus, on the other hand, thought he was the one who was keeping them together. He could see, for all his natural insensitivity, exactly what Luke was feeling, how he watched out for Tam all the time and how Tam didn't seem to care. So when she snapped he soothed, and when she didn't pay attention he drew her round, and he took extra care to laugh at Luke's jokes, such as they were, and look at Tam expectantly. And she, because she liked him, tagged along with it, and Luke, because he liked him, gave him the benefit of the doubt, and chose not to see that Angus and Tam were becoming interested in each other.

THE CATERERS HAD been busy for hours when Luke got in. It was six-thirty, and they were getting their briefing. Set out neatly in rows on the table were twenty-four photographs. Luke recognized only two of them: Angus, and Tam's mother, Christine.

'And when this one comes in,' she was saying, pointing to the photograph next to her mother, 'I want you to make him feel like he's the most important person in the room.'

The short, burly Glaswegian, Edward, who always did Tam's dinners and with whom Luke sometimes exchanged exploratory glances, murmured in astonishment.

'You want us to treat Roderick Brennan like he's someone *special*?' he said. 'That'll take some doing.' His sideburns bristled and his shorn head seemed to steam in protest. 'He always thinks he's the most important person in the room, anyway. The guy's an arsehole. What have you got him here for?'

'Edward,' said Tamara. 'You are the caterer. Do the catering.'

'So I can't ask why you're so interested in him, then.'

'No. You can't. Now get my canapés moving and I want lots of those miniature hamburgers with zippy mustard stripes.'

She drove her staff like galley slaves, her eye on the perfect evening. Luke loved to see her strutting like a bird among her guests at these events, part martinet, part incorrigible flirt. Sometime he couldn't take his eyes off her feet, knowing that out of sight her toes were packed in corn plasters.

'Why your mother? I still don't get it,' he whispered.

'Why do I have to explain everything I do?' she cried. 'There's a letter for you by the way.'

Luke recognized his father's spidery handwriting.

Tamara glanced at him appraisingly.

'Are you coming dressed like that?'

RODERICK BRENNAN WAS a man of many bankruptcies, and a best-selling novelist. The novels followed the bankruptcies. He had a feline charm which neither men nor women could resist, he wore a light beige linen suit for preference, whatever the weather. The lines on his forehead were caused not by anxiety but by a considered appreciation of the finer things in life. His skill was to make whoever he was talking to feel that they were one of those finer things. His eyebrows were extravagantly thick and easily raised, in humour or disdain or both, his eyes had an expression of bland lasciviousness and were enhanced in their beauty by eyelids gently curving like small scimitars. His nose was long and fleshy with arching nostrils and a confident bridge, while the space between his nose and his lip, where the essence of the male personality resides, bore an ebullient moustache.

Bankruptcies must make a man attractive, for the more of them he had the more the young wives of London and the Home Counties threw themselves into his welcoming arms, and thereafter his welcoming bed. (The threat of vengeance from young husbands hung tantalizingly in the air about him, seeming only to add to his allure.) A man of his acquaintance and reputation was inevitably going to discover Tamara sooner or later; she had always fended off his attentions firmly but lightheartedly, so that he could never have an excuse for pretending to be hurt, and could always retain some small hope that she might relent. She had plans for him tonight.

Macallister and the editor of a national newspaper arrived within moments of each other, bursting into the room like a pair of comedians. One was almost twice the height of the other.

'Ye're not expecting me to break bread with this pile o' shite, are ye?' expostulated Macallister, and a bout of vaudeville backslapping ensued.

'Excuse my companion,' said the editor to Tam, bowing, then straightening to his full six foot six. 'We met for the first time on the stairs.'

'Oh, he always does this to me,' said Macallister. His leathery face cracked into a grin that was midway to a snarl. It was a face that bore seams where others had wrinkles: at sixty plus he looked older, his drinking having chiselled lines in his skin that perversely resembled the tiny cracks and miniature gullies that open in the earth after a long drought. Like many great drinkers his hair was beautifully preserved, and he cared for it meticulously. It was wiry in strength but silken in texture, and stood up like a well-groomed quiff, leaning slightly forward over his brow, while on either side it swept majestically over his ears like the bow wave of a mighty liner.

He was a small man and embarrassed about it. He dressed impeccably, and could never be faulted for elegance, at least before lunch, by any of the grandees whose society he enjoyed, and from whom he elicited so many low tales with which to skewer his enemies on the left. He could shoot his cuffs with the best of them, wore beautifully cut soft grey suits, bought his black brogues from Lobb and his ties in Jermyn Street, and regarded white collars worn on striped shirts as an abomination. He'd come to politics late in life: for years he was a doorstepping footslogger who went after stories like a stoat down a rabbit hole. He claimed to be a Gorbals boy, brought up in dismal wartime Glasgow, but it was Aberdeen he came from, apprenticed to a stonemason when he was sixteen, fleeing to the local paper when he was seventeen, willing to cover any story at any price to escape the world he was born into, and even, at times, to be ferociously, mawkishly loyal to it, so long as he no longer had to be part of it. He made his way by writing exactly what the newspaper's editor wanted to read, whichever newspaper he was working on at the time. When the local mayor was arrested on charges of embezzlement, Macallister slept the night outside the house of the accused in his battered Austin A4 having told a reporter from another newspaper that the mayor had been taken to hospital because of a heart condition that had deteriorated suddenly because of the stress, and collared the first interview for himself. He became obsessed with crime and hung around the courts like a ghost. When a prominent landowner was arrested for drowning his mistress in the river, and local opinion was of the view that he could not have done the deed and run home five miles over the heather in time for high tea, Macallister donned his running gear and tore over the hills to show that it could be done — especially if you had a possible murder conviction yapping at your heels. Sometimes he was over a case like a rash, so that trials became famous as *his* trials: he was always on the side of the white, ambitious, working-class male, or the housewife, or the police, but never the judges, or gays, or feminists. He saw himself as the assassin of privilege and reputation, and he drank when he won, and he drank when he lost.

At the sight of Brennan, Macallister's brow darkened, and when he saw that one of his least favourite women MPs was to be his companion for the evening it grew even darker. But Angus slipped a large scotch into his hand and said, 'Don't worry, Mac, I'll see you through,' and the old man seemed to relax.

'It's Mr Macallister to you, young man,' he said. 'Your health.' He took a sip from his glass and nodded in mock surprise. 'That's no' bad.'

'It's your favourite, I made sure they laid it on specially,' said Angus. 'Anyway, I always call you Mac, don't I? Everyone else does.'

'Aye, you do. They do.' He gave Angus a stony look over the rim of his glass as he took another sip. Angus wasn't sure whether he was being teased or chastised.

'Hello, Macallister.' The woman MP, loud and unafraid, strode up. The body language was atrocious.

'What the fuck are *those*?' cried Macallister, almost howling, pointing with outstretched finger at her shoes.

She shied as if she had been struck. Eyes swivelled to look at the long, pointed, bestriped creations on her feet. Macallister was a specialist in cheap shots.

'Prada by the looks of them,' said a voice, and there was Tamara looking and being bewitching. 'You *must* be the famous Macallister. I've heard such a lot about you.' She took him by the still-outstretched finger. 'There's someone I'm desperate for you to meet.'

Angus had no idea who it could be. He watched Tam out of the corner of his eye as he engaged the MP, whom he knew to be Sheila Smith, single with an adopted child, her constituency in the Midlands, he thought Coventry but wasn't sure, leftish without being unreliable, a great campaigner, unsurprisingly, for unmarried single mothers, but trying to develop a wider base by involving herself in overseas development.

'What does the PM really think about Mugabe?' he began. She was still flushed with anger, and he could tell she was in two minds about pursuing Macallister, but no politician can resist an invitation to air their views to a journalist.

Macallister, meanwhile, was shaking the hand of a man, even smaller than he, with a closely shaved head who was wearing faded jeans and a white Fred Perry T-shirt and who had a torso straight as an ironing board and biceps like bread loaves. A soft expression of awe had come into Macallister's eyes.

'Hey, you, Jimmy Liddle.' His voice sang the words. 'Ye're my hero, d'ye know that, I've watched every fight ye've been in.'

Jimmy Liddle, for his part, smiled. It was okay to be living with the editor of a fashion magazine, and it was far away from the Cardiff docklands he grew up in, but with Angela he didn't often meet people interested in what he did for a living.

'That Maximilian fight, ye were fucking brulliant, I've got

it on video and I watch it over and over, the way ye got intae him in the third round, I thought ye were goin' tae waste him there and then, you were unlucky wi' the refereein' I thought.'

She's amazing, thought Angus. Room full of the wrong people and she finds him his hero.

'An' the Anderson fight, my god he had you on the ropes then, eh? But ye were too good fer him, weren't ye? I thought ye must ha' been puttin' him on, were ye?'

Jimmy Liddle smiled his thin smile and nodded slowly and kept his small blue glittering eyes fixed on Macallister and lapped it up. He lapped it up all evening, for Tamara's placement set them side by side, demonstrating that she had planned it all along.

Angus was immersed in the plight of single mothers in Zimbabwe when they were joined by the editor, a man whom Angus had worshipped for years. Professionally or otherwise – and given their politics, it must surely have been otherwise – it seemed that Sheila Smith had too, for she ran her forefinger down the inside of his lapel kittenishly while chastising him gently about the standard of his op-ed pages. His height was enhanced by the excellent tailoring of his suit, and the heavy frames of his spectacles together with his full head of hair without a fleck of grey in it – there were rumours that he dyed it, but these were surely malicious – contributed to his superb condescension, against which the egos of his underlings broke in vain.

Only the presence of Roderick Brennan could cloud his polish.

'What's that man doing here?' he rumbled.

It seemed an odd question to Angus.

'I think Tam likes to bring interesting people together,' he said. 'She likes to hostess.'

The editor sighed percussively.

'Well, she's got a lot to learn about hostessing, then,' he said. 'He's one of the most dangerous men in London.'

'I know,' said Angus.

'Let us hope she's safe,' the editor went on. Angus followed his gaze. Roderick was deep in conversation with Christine. From the concentrated expression on his face, and the delighted one on hers, it didn't look as if she was. The editor snorted.

Yes, it was not simply what Roderick Brennan did to women that made his reputation, but what he did to the men who saw him do it.

'That's Tam's mother,' said Angus.

The editor bowed slightly, as if humbled by the thought.

'Christine and I are friends of old.'

'Can we just talk about me, now, please?' said Sheila Smith.

THE PLACEMENT WAS contrived so that Christine sat next to Roderick, and so besotted did they seem with each other that they barely spoke to anyone else, which nobody seemed to mind save the magisterial editor, whose looks of rebuke went ignored by all, including Tam, who never once glanced at her mother, but seemed to reserve a great deal of her attention for Angus, and so it was that everyone seemed to have someone to be fascinated by and to fascinate, even the editor, who found the MPs fawning upon him, every word, but who sparred loftily with Jimmy Liddle's partner, as editor to editor. Indeed, the only one who was for once in his idiosyncratic life disengaged from it all was Luke, who sat mute and abstracted – to Angus's consternation.

'Is he all right?' he asked Tam quietly. Her face was very close to his at that moment.

'Is who all right?'

'Luke. There's something wrong.'

She didn't want to know, but he kept coming back to it.

'Has something happened?'

They were establishing, maybe confirming, their intimacy, drawing each other's attention to the conversation as it twined and knotted around the table, observing where it was gathering momentum and where it was fracturing, where mutual interests were flickering into life and where they were faltering, evolving a shared perception with a tiny private patter of harmless running jokes at everyone else's expense.

Angus, knowing he was drawing closer than ever to Tam, wondered if Luke could see this and felt guilty, but not for long.

'Macallister seems happy, bless him.'

'I thought he'd like Jimmy.'

'How do you know him?'

'Apart from being famous, through Angela.'

'You'd think they were rather unusual.'

'You would, but she was so unbelievably unhappy with that poet and then she was a single mother and alone and desperate, I mean in *such* despair, and one day she saw Jim at someone's party, he was just there and covered in children and she melted.'

'Real love at real first sight?'

'It happens.'

Did she give him one almost missable glance, then? He wondered what it would be like to be with Tam, to meet each other somewhere, maybe on a tube station platform or a street or at a concert or some very ordinary place and be with her, drawn by her living, breathing, exciting self with her dark, sea-blue eyes and her thin, tactile shoulders and the soft, vulnerable vertebrae of her back and her aching feet. He thought of them both wearing good clothes and loving the same things in life like theatre and the river at low tide and the air in the streets late at night in the summer. He thought of being aware of each other's possibilities, of what they might become and what they might do together, of what they might give each other and learn from each other. Romance, really.

Whatever happened to that?

'A fashion magazine editor and a poet?'

'You might as well say, and a boxer? It all seems perfectly normal to me. No more unusual than you and Luke.'

'I'm worried about him. He has a predilection for self-harm. He has black moods sometimes. He's manic, really.'

'Suicide attempts?'

'A few.'

Tam remembered the dead man in the painting and Luke's grotesque impersonation.

'How close were you?'

'Very.' Angus felt an influx of loyal sentiment.

'Very? Really very?'

'Yes. Oh, yes.'

And with this he felt he had paid some dues that needed paying.

'It was some time ago, though.'

He looked at Roderick and Christine, and Tam watched him do it.

'Why did you . . .' he began.

'My business.' She laid her two left fingers on the back of his right hand.

The editor was in full flood on the subject of human relationships.

'Men want to marry their mothers. That's their tragedy. And women want to marry their fathers. That's theirs.'

'Where d'ye get garbage like that?' said Macallister, distracted for the first time from Jimmy Liddle and his boxing stories.

'Very Wilde,' said Brennan. His head tilted, in approval, to one side.

'It's the stupidest thing I've ever heard,' said Angela.

'I hate my father,' muttered Luke, to himself, but no one was listening.

'I *do* agree,' said Sheila Smith.

Christine looked concerned.

Jimmy Liddle said nothing.

Angus said, 'Is that true?'

And Tam said, 'It so isn't.'

During the mêlée that followed, Angus wondered whether it was second nature to editors of national newspapers to make comments of this nature. He concluded that it probably was. It took a certain kind of personality to pronounce with such authority and with such evident banality on a subject of such sensitivity. After that everyone had a lot to say and wanted to say it immediately.

'Like rats in a sack,' Angus said softly, but Tam was too embroiled to notice.

He watched the editor, tall and bony and supercilious, and saw a subtle air of conceit spread across his features, where the ghost of a smile was floating. He had comandeered the conversation, his instinct for the issues that divided and excited people as finely tuned to dinner parties as to matters of national importance. He was not one to go home in the evening, take a beer from the fridge and watch the football. He was what he was every minute of the day.

This was something Angus might learn from. It had to be twenty-four hours a day, seven days a week. He felt tired at the thought.

Angus looked at Macallister, who was beginning to be angry, because this was not his field at all, he was suspicious of it, he felt, like Angus, oppressed by the senior man's agility and finesse. Journalists journey, they inquire, they campaign, thought Angus. Editors judge, evaluate and opine. Life divides between the journeymen and the judges, the adventurers and the examiners. Angus considered which he should aspire to, and whether it was something he had any choice about.

And then Luke did his party piece.

That's what Tamara's mother Christine called it, for years after.

His party piece.

In those years after, Angus thought there were more appropriate ways of describing it.

The noise had just reached its zenith and was subsiding when Luke's voice, insubstantial and, to most of them there, unfamiliar, since he had said almost nothing all evening, said, 'If men want to marry their mothers, does that mean they want to divorce their fathers?'

Angus's ears were intent on Sheila Smith's lengthy, much-interrupted but essentially unstoppable discursion upon the weaknesses of her erstwhile partner and the relative and considerable merits of her father, and he was hoping for some newsworthy titbit to ferret away for use at a later date. But however she might fulminate, she knew exactly when to stop: no such thing was forthcoming, though she came teasingly close to it on several occasions. So Luke's voice came to him through a daze of concentration.

'I want to read you a letter I have just received from my

father,' he was saying. His voice had a metallic timbre. 'He is a senior master at a school. Very grand, it is. I went there, actually, the sons of teachers go free, and so did Angus, by the way, though his dad of course is just staggeringly rich. You'll all have heard of it, it's called Meniston, but that's not the point, the point is that the headmaster is, what, famous, in headmaster circles, anyway, and, what else, very tall and a little bit uncoordinated and really pretty terrifying if you were a kid there, and that, Angus and I have worked out, is probably an effect of this dysfunctional thing he has, he connects with people in odd ways, but he was really tough, too, and he gave that school something it needed which related to a vision it had lost, or so my dad always says, who used to think a lot of him, but it turns out this wonderful, weird headmaster fell in love with one of the boys, which, if you think about it, is really not wise, anyway my dad told me about this the other day and you know what I thought most of all when he told me?'

The wonder of it all was the hush. Angus thought: why is no one stopping him? Why am I not stopping him? But there was something about what Luke was doing that night that brought silence down upon them all. Some looked astonished, some looked worried, some looked thoughtful and all were mute.

'Now a headmaster really should not fall in love with a boy, let's be clear about that, let there be no misunderstanding. Countless numbers of boys have been in his care over the years, and we don't know, at least I don't know, whether he's ever done this before, fallen in love I mean, but Dad thinks he has, how he knows I don't know, because I really don't think my dad knows what love is.'

He hesitated. Every part of his body was animated: his

eyes shone, colour had rouged his cheekbones for the first time, Angus thought, in years, and he held the letter as if it were unbearably hot but he was physically incapable of letting go of it. He was intensely alive. Years of brooding and uncertainty seemed to have been resolved by some sort of decision that had taken place in the last few hours.

'It's not as if he doesn't have a family, of course he does, you probably can't get to be a headmaster at one of these schools unless you are, you know, heterosexual and have children and stuff and all that, though his wife was a pretty measly character and his daughter, he only had one child, was a nutcase, I always thought, she liked to think she knew a great deal about Shakespeare, but I reckoned her a sort of degraded tramp-steamer, you know, butting through the Channel on the mad March days, sort of determined and gritty but haunted and sad at heart and doing it all for form's sake and the look of the thing and not letting Daddy down. I suppose I wonder if he went for boys, well, not went but turned to, perhaps, is the right phrase, whether it was because his family are the way they are or because he is the way he is. But that's not the point of this, because there's been a complaint, and a letter has been found, and it's out in the open and the governors know about it, and why do they know? Because my father brought it to their attention, though he says he had to do it, and what he says is —'

He began to read.

'Dear Lucas — of course, he always calls me that, he's the only person who ever has, nobody else does, Dear Lucas, I thought I would bring you up to date on events since our delightful lunch in London — it was not delightful, no aspect of it was delightful, the food was atrocious and the people were worse — as I think I said to you the governors had to be informed and it was a protracted and embroiled matter — why doesn't he just say it was too difficult or something, or that he found his conscience kept rearing up in front of him in an inconvenient way, which would be more truthful, though I wonder whether my father's conscience is on duty with the regularity we might expect of it — entailing a great deal of delicacy and patience. I was aware that I had been entrusted with a most exacting task, but I found its execution a heavy burden, and I approached it with great reluctance. Nevertheless my duty was clear and I went to the governors with trepidation but determination nonetheless, and they have chosen me as their, as it were, emissary to the headmaster and I had my first interview with him yesterday. It will, I think, be either the first of many or the last time we speak. He was not happy to receive the news I had to break to him, and I was a little disconcerted for after I had told him the purpose of my visit he did nothing at all but stare at me. As you will recall he has a demeanour that can make the stoutest heart quail, and I feared some display of anger, but to my dismay I saw a tear fall upon his cheek and a strangely — what shall I say? — hapless air crept into his expression. At this moment I do not think he was considering the nature of his position at all. When I began to speak again after some considerable silence had passed between us he raised his hand and turned to the window, after which there was another silence and I began to feel the situation was becoming intolerable, even absurd. But eventually he turned back to me and to my astonishment was smiling with a sweetness which took me aback, and he asked, "So, Alex, what is it the governors wish me to do now?" He has never, ever, called me anything but Alexander or Rainsford, and I immediately felt we had broken new ground, and was even moved.

But something about his behaviour made me uncomfortable and I said to him, "You do realize, headmaster, the gravity of your position?" to which he replied with a slight smile, "Oh, yes, Alex, I realize the gravity." I then told him that we, or more properly the governors, were most anxious that none of this should ever come to the attention of the public, but that something would need to be done to pacify the boy's family, and that this would – and here I could hardly bring myself to speak – necessarily mean his departure. He asked me if I meant early retirement, and I said I feared I meant retirement earlier even than that, indeed within the year. For did he not see, I asked, that his position was now irrevocably compromised? Of course, I did not at any point press him upon whether this was an isolated instance, but I surmised from his manner that he knew this was not an aberration to be swept under the carpet as a moment of madness. He nodded slightly after I spoke, and said, "I was a fool, Alex, a fool." Then the fey mood left him and the old incisiveness returned. "You may tell the governors, Alexander, indeed I shall tell them myself, that I shall not acquiesce in this. Appeasement is not in my nature, and I am not going to allow this business to prevent me continuing as headmaster here." I may say I was astounded. I pointed out there had been a letter. He asked me if I had seen it. I said I had seen extracts in the letter from the boy's family. Extracts, he said, should not be taken out of context. I said they had seemed conclusive to me. He almost sneered at this, saying he was not at all surprised that I thought them conclusive. He said he would talk to the boy's family personally. I urged upon him the finality of the governors' views with, I confess, increasing anger on my part, indeed I was quite giddy with rage, but he was not to be gainsaid. He rose and showed me out and when he said goodbye called me Alexander again, but in a way I did not like, with a peculiar emphasis.

'And then he goes on, this is the main part, the real hypocrisy, listen. He says, Now, my dear Lucas, I feel both wretched and confounded, and I feel you are the only one I can turn to – He's never said anything like this to me before, never – I know that over the years, and especially since your poor mother died, we have not expressed our feelings towards each other in the way we might have done, but I have always treasured you and your presence in my life. Indeed, you are as precious to me as life itself, and I tried to say something about this the other day, but of course the circumstances were not quite right, and I am never good with words, not in matters of affection. I have always been proud of you and of the way you have taken your life in your own hands and made what you will of it – he hates what I do, hates it – and I have often felt that I should make more effort to show you my feelings and share my thoughts and that, though the years have not been easy, we could be friends as well as father and son. So I have taken it upon myself to write to you with my innermost anxieties, and I hope that you might do the same, so that in our correspondence, for we have not written to one another much, and I blame myself for that, we can communicate with each other more happily than hitherto. I should like this. I should like this more than anything. For, Lucas, though it takes me, I admit, some effort to write such things, you are my son and a very beloved one, though you may not think so, and though I may not often make this clear, and I shall always hold you in the very highest regard and – you can just feel the pain as he grips the pen here – love you from the bottom of my heart. From the bottom of his heart!' Luke began slowly to tear the letter into long strips. 'The man doesn't have a heart!'

For a long while they went on staring at Luke, except Angus, whose head had sunk into his hands. And for a long while, as he dropped each strip of paper onto the table in front of him, Luke stared defiantly back.

WHAT HAPPENED NEXT was that nothing happened. At least, nothing of consequence. Not then, nor for some time after. There were expressions of sympathy and astonishment, some clearing of throats and a half-hearted attempt to discuss the contents of the letter, but the tides of conversation swiftly rushed in to move them on and those who were becoming close became closer still and in days and months afterwards talked about it incessantly, and the newspapermen locked it away in their thoughts for future consideration and probable use, and some never talked about it at all, but it stayed with them the rest of their lives. And no one knew what Luke had been trying to do nor whether he had, in his own mind, succeeded.

As for Luke, in the weeks that followed he felt the pressures building up inside him had eased for a while, but they were soon being stoked again by what was happening between Tam and Angus, which he could sense almost in direct proportion to the efforts they made to avoid letting him see. And anyway he couldn't work out which one he felt more possessive about, and both Tam and Angus worried that something in Luke was going to snap, and Tam didn't want it happening anywhere near her.

ONE SUNDAY SHE came back to find the surfaces of her flat obliterated. Everywhere she looked there were strips of white paper: the sofas were draped with them, the tables were laid with them, they were strewn on the floor, they hung from the mantelpieces and the lamps. They were like tree moss, like well dressings. In her living room Luke was crouched, tearing out pieces of newspaper and laying them in a pile next to him. He was so absorbed he didn't hear her come in.

'Luke, what are you doing?' she asked at length.

He shook his head and didn't reply. She began to panic. It was time for an exit strategy.

She thought hard.

'Luke, have you been on the Millennium Wheel?'

He looked at her.

'You want to take me there? Just the two of us?'

She nodded.

He looked around the room at the bits of newspaper obscuring the definitions of everything.

'Do you like the effect?' he asked.

'No.'

'Not at all?'

'I hate it.'

'Ah. Then you would be wanting me to clear it all up.'

'Please.'

He handled each strip as if it were silk or lace.

'I've been wanting to go on that thing for months,' he said, 'ever since it opened. Have you ever seen it at night? Close to, I mean? They're like huge baubles, those glass ball things with the people in them. All the time the camera flashes are going off, so they look like tiny explosions of light high up in the darkness, as if they're sparkling.'

He stopped.

'I'm glad it's just us two.'

Tam drew a deep breath.

'Good,' she said.

He wondered whether to say any more.

'I'll be able to check out an idea I've had. Want to know what it is?'

He's like a child, she thought.

'Go ahead,' she said. She wandered through to her bedroom. The paper stirred about her as she went, curling round her ankles, fluttering at her from the pictures on the wall like outstretched hands.

'That was the effect I wanted,' he called after her.

There was no newspaper in her bedroom, but there was an indentation on her bed as if someone had been lying there.

Her skin prickled with apprehension.

'What was your idea, then?' she called back.

'I want to make those baubles into a theatre.'

When she returned the room was clear and Luke was grinning proudly. How his moods changed.

'A theatre.'

'Yes. Do two- or three-man playlets. Some that last one spin of the wheel, some several spins.'

'OK. I'll book it, and you can check it out.'

'Soon. Do it soon. Do you think it's a good idea?'

'Oh, it'll be soon. I don't know if it's a good idea. Maybe.'

The thought of having Tam to himself excited him for days. His head was full of ideas for plays he would write for his Millennium Wheel Theatre; in his mind the theatre existed already, and he imagined the way in which he would use the space, frowning over whether the plays should be tragic or comic or whether they could be little medieval mystery plays or should have something modern and surreal or satirical about them or should be about London and its history with reference to all the sights that could be seen from the top of the wheel. He could do the story of Guy Fawkes interspersed with contemporary political commentary and the audience could be looking down at Parliament at the same time.

He was surprised how quickly Tam organized it.

'They're like bees coming to alight on a flower to take its nectar,' he said, as they walked along the South Bank towards the wheel.

'I prefer baubles, like you said, or cacao pods, full of beans, like in geography lessons in school.'

'Or rugby balls, being set just right, so a player can get a really good kick at them.'

'Or giant eggs on some kind of Wallace and Gromit apparatus delivering them to the giant's breakfast table.'

Really, the two of them went together hand in glove, chattering like this, he thought, thinking maybe he might just take her hand and then maybe not, squinting sideways at her like he did when they first met, and thinking still how beautiful she was, but still not taking her hand, because that would be too crass and would spoil things, especially now she was with Angus, he was sure of that, though he didn't know absolutely, and so perhaps he was wrong, and if so . . .

As they stood in their bubble being hoisted up by the wheel and looking out over the river a light rain fell and speckled the glass so tiny shadows scattered across the floor. Wind-ripples hurried over the water below.

'Something I'm still wondering,' he said, 'is why did you invite your mother to that dinner?'

Not his business, thought Tam, but I'll tell him. Is he going to apologize? That would be something.

'I wanted to see what would happen,' she said.

'And what did happen?'

'Exactly what I thought would happen.'

'Well?'

'They fell –' she said this in a sing-song way to emphasize its inevitability '– into each other's arms.'

'The one she was sitting next to?'

'Roderick Brennan. Penniless Lothario. They fall for him every time. He has a perilous charm.' She pulled in her lips tightly against her teeth. 'One has to be very careful.' She looked up at him with trouble in her eyes.

'So you meant that to happen? Her and him? How do you mean, they fell into each other's arms? Are they – you know . . .'

'I didn't mean it to happen,' she said acidly, as if he had said something stupid. 'You can't make things happen. I just thought it might. And it did.'

'Does this fill you with happiness, Tamara?'

'Not really.'

'So why?'

She took her time replying. They could see right across London now.

'I wanted to prove something to myself. And to her. I wanted to show her something about life. Maybe that's not it. Maybe it is.'

'And is *she* filled with happiness?'

'Not altogether. Slightly more than is good for her, I think.'

'Does she know you know?'

'Oh, yes.'

'How?'

'She told me.'

'Why?'

'Because I asked.' She was looking impatient, rocking on

her heels. 'You think I'm weird, don't you? Well, I'm not. But you are.'

'I'm not weird.'

'Yes, you are. Bits of newspaper all over the place. That performance of yours at my dinner, which you've never said sorry for.'

'Sorry.'

'It's too late, Luke. I think it's time for you to move on. Go and stay with Angus or something.'

'But I can't, you know I can't. I don't want to go, I want to stay with you. I'm probably in love with you.'

'That's what's worrying me.'

'You want me to move out?'

'I want you to move out. I'm sorry, Luke, I really am. But it's not a case of wanting, really. We're getting on each other's nerves. I'm sure I'm getting on yours and I know you're getting on mine. In fact, I'm finding you impossible. I'm not going to give you any more justification, Luke, because I'll only make you unhappy, and I know you'll be unhappy anyway, so you've just got to go. Please. Don't quarrel with this. Accept it. Choose it.'

Luke had that feeling you have when you know there are emotions whirling around inside you, but you're not sure what they are yet. People call it numbness usually, and it's said that numbness comes after great pain, but it comes before too, though it's not quite that, it's more like a suspension, a waiting.

All the way down they stood either side of the bubble. Towards the end, he said, 'I'll move my stuff when I've found somewhere new.'

'No, you won't,' she said. 'It's all at Angus's. Or it will be soon. He's been packing your bags and those boxes. You're going to stay with him till you find somewhere. If you came back now you'd never go. And before you say anything, yes, he is your friend, and he does love you, but you're not the only person he loves, Luke, and you need to sort yourself out.'

He was too astonished to speak.

'Don't worry,' she said, kissing him. 'It'll be all right. We'll still be friends.'

He stood and watched her lose herself among the crowds.

FOR HERSELF, SHE felt that she had worked the whole thing very neatly. No room for recriminations, or second thoughts, or tantrums, or protestations and vacillations. He had become intolerable, and she had no need to tolerate him any more. The wheel had turned, and there was an end of it.

It appealed to her sense of theatre.

Floodwater

I have forgot much, Cynara! gone with the wind,
Flung roses, roses, riotously, with the throng,
Dancing, to put thy pale, lost lilies out of mind;
But I was desolate and sick of an old passion,
Yea, all the time, because the dance was long:
I have been faithful to thee, Cynara! in my fashion.

Ernest Dowson, *Non Sum Qualis Eram*

WHEN SPRING CAME the river could rise very fast, was famous for it. In those days, a lifetime away, the banks were easy to break, and the river churned them into mud and turned the fields into small lakes reflecting the ragged April clouds, and the cattle stood uncomplaining, the water reaching up to their haunches. The river swept on, and the weir which in summer was so pretty, the water dark and its bubbles spilling demurely over its rim, became a tea-coloured fury. Deborah, six years old in May, was never allowed to go near it then, and the noise of it kept her awake at night. When the river flooded the water covered the path and crept up the dry-stone wall and came through it and inched its way up the lawn, which took months to recover. So Deborah's father had the wall heightened and reinforced with concrete so it was much uglier but the river stayed on its own side, and Deborah could peer at it by clambering up some steps and watch the water rushing past and be amazed at its force. It was as if there were two different rivers altogether, the thoughtful, translucent one of summer and this one, opaque with mud and brutishly barrelling along.

Frank was her best friend, they played together all the time. He was younger than her, a February birthday, stocky and headstrong and prone to misadventure. He helped her escape the attentions of her four older sisters, who were always quarrelling and were the despair of their mother, though they were good as gold at the Friends' Meeting House when it mattered. Sometimes Deborah was their pet, sometimes their victim; she was spoiled and bullied and pummelled and stroked depending on who was being friendly to whom, so she felt like a rag doll taking part in one of their tea-parties, when all the family cutlery and crockery was raided and set out upon the dining-room table and the toys were sat around and fed cakes and biscuits. With Frank she was herself again.

His face came back to her in dreams, living and waking, for years after. He was not a beautiful boy, particularly, he was too pudgy for that, and he liked to show off his strength, picking up great branches in the wood that bordered the river a little way upstream and carrying them above his head while making his voice as deep as he could as if he were a circus strongman, which he liked to do because the circus had visited their nearby town recently and Frank's father had taken the two of them to see it. Frank's father ran the post office in the village, and he was built along the same lines as his son. Frank was an only child, and his dad liked to see him with Deborah, he needed company. He had big brown eyes with a surprised expression in them, and freckles all over his generous cheeks, and a mouth that was dwarfed by his face and his prominent chin, but when you looked closely you could see he had well-formed lips with no hint of meanness about them. His hair was dark brown and shaggy and no one seemed to make much effort to make it less so, and his clothes tended to be worn and patched but well-ironed, at least for the first hour or two after he put them on, and new holes were always making an appearance, especially after any expedition over the bridge and into the woods near his home a few hundred yards from Deborah's.

They had a house in the woods he built just for her, and it got bigger and bigger. 'Oh, I'm tired of this,' she would say, and he would add something to it to involve her again. Once he scrawled a sign in crayon – 'Debraland' – and put it in the cleft of a stick and set it in the soft ground outside this collection of lean-to branches they played under, pretending it was their home. He knew how to interest a girl, that one. He was forever scouting for more wood to add extensions. The tree he had set the home against had enormous branches almost as thick as the trunks of other, younger trees, and they splayed out parallel to the ground and close to it so they were easy to clamber on, and easy to build things round and over, too, and the house grew out along them the way a shanty town follows a railway line, and sometimes they let other children play there but mostly they didn't. There were fewer of them around in those days.

Then one day in spring when the floods were at their highest and the river was in spate Frank conceived a plan to raise a tarpaulin over part of the house to keep out the rain. His ambition had grown as he had, and there was a village of rooms and meeting places and eating places and a place for bicycles around the old tree, and now he wanted to keep it dry and snug in winter, and he needed a pole, a proper one, longer and more reliable than the branches and bits of cardboard that made up the walls and roof of the house that was now a village, and he knew where to get it, too. But when he did get it, from a building site on the edge of the village, it was too heavy for him, and he struggled down the path by the river, his face getting redder and redder like a plump tomato, and as he carried it over the bridge he passed where the railings ended and stumbled and the pole swung round and pitched him backwards into the speeding water and the pole struck him across his head as he went down and he never had a chance.

And so it was that Deborah, leaning over the wall at the bottom of the garden, saw, first as a confused heap and then suddenly clearly, her friend's body rolling slowly in the flood, and she saw then and remembered for ever his face just beneath the surface, almost peaceful, as if he were floating in his own dream, beginning to sink away from her as she reached out to him and almost fell herself.

Somewhere, a long way off, her mother was calling her in for lunch.

CHILDREN GET OVER things, adults say, usually when there's something they want them to get over. And children do, sort of: emotional traumas and broken arms and abuse, they have to, they wouldn't survive otherwise. So Deborah went on growing up, and the house in the woods was colonized by newcomers and gradually disappeared, and her sisters went on pummelling and teasing and bossing her, and there was no Frank to turn to, but others came along. After her sisters found out what had happened to Frank, and what she had seen, the bossing became kinder, more protective, but when she awoke screaming at nights sitting bolt upright in bed, her hair clinging to her perspiring face, they privately thought her mind had turned a little, and later put her wildness and her mood swings down to what happened by the river. In her dreams he would loom out of the darkness, the image rising like a fish to the surface, his face sinking away from her as she held out her hands to him, and all around her would be the dun rushing water. And her moods did change quickly, perhaps more quickly, after that, but maybe that's just the way she was. They raced swiftly through her like leaf-shadows in the woods in spring, like rivers carrying debris and flotsam. But in the Sixties in England this restlessness was a virtue, made her interesting, and she grew up pretty, with baby blue eyes and beach-blonde hair, and she couldn't wait to leave her sisters behind though they were dismayed when she left for London, and they wondered what was wrong with Taunton, and who likes cities? Deborah did: and she wore her hair long and tie-dyed her clothes as the zeitgeist and the fashions on the King's Road flickered like an old film reel from one thing to the newer next, and she was so much part of it that she became quite famous for a short while, though no one afterwards would remember what she had been famous for.

Why, therefore, her friends would ask, did she marry a soldier? Where did she find him, was it outside Chelsea army barracks some sunny day among the floating clouds of mari-juana, and did she think, this looks like a better life? And why this marriage thing? Puzzled, they drifted away, but Deborah was in love, and she found that love a constant, and her Christopher, her soldier, he was a constant, too, though his firmness of purpose did not preclude him from declaring his intention to leave the army and become a teacher, which Deborah's friends might have approved of, but by then she was forgotten by all save a few.

They did not meet outside any army barracks. Her oldest sister Belinda had come to town and whisked her off to the party of a friend of hers, and Deborah was amused to see her imperious ways in a city she thought she had made her own, and she felt secure, and different, and her own woman, and she thought it would be fun to be the odd one out among her sister's stuffy kind, and so, unsuspecting, she was caught unawares, ambushed by love, and naive where she had thought herself knowing. In this way, the sisters reclaimed her.

Quite what the rest of the party made of her we shall never know, for they were a stiff lot, not much given to inspecting their feelings. Even Deborah's sister thought them dull, and was amazed by her sister's choice of lover. The army had ironed out some of his natural awkwardnesses, but by no means all of them. He stood six feet five inches in his grey cotton socks, and his posture made no concession to his height; you could tell he was a proud man the moment you saw him. He had big, practical hands, and long feet, and though there was nothing apologetic about his demeanour there was a faint comedy to the way in which his limbs would express a life of their own, hands upsetting glasses, feet finding themselves under a carpet rather than on top of it and making him stumble. But he was always quick to recover, and first with an iron handshake, and when he did take you by the hand the whole of his personality was concentrated upon you, and you were dazzled and flattered and a little afraid. Perhaps it was partly vanity that led Deborah to see him as her perfect foil. Or perhaps it was simply that intensity of character, the zeal to succeed, that fascinated her, for she had no ambitions for herself at all. Then, before his eyebrows had become quite so full and intimidating or his jowls so plainly irascible, he was alight with plans for the future, and so giddy with his attentions was Deborah that she believed that his desire to leave the army and bring learning and love of learning to children was something to do with meeting her, and this was an endearing illusion he did nothing to fracture, for he believed he loved her, and perhaps he did, after his own fashion. She was a catch for any man.

They were married in the church in the village where she grew up. At that time religion had ceased to mean anything to her, and Christopher was scathing about alternative forms of belief, by which he meant Friends' Meeting Houses, and her mother was put out, but happy to have her daughter seeing sense for the first time, and Deborah returned home in triumph, with a small retinue of her remaining Chelsea friends to petrify the locals, and vice versa. She felt she had by now absorbed some of her new husband's certainties, and before the dinner began she took one of the wreaths of roses and lilies and sweet-smelling stocks and made her own way to the foot of the old garden and, climbing over the wall in her wedding dress, stood by the river, watching the eddies spin coldly among the stones. Then she threw the flowers in handfuls of petals, pink and white, out over the water, where they scattered and the river turned from black to white reflecting the handfuls bursting like bombs above it and settling on its many surfaces, and she thought she had done with that memory at last.

SHE DID NOT tell Christopher where she had been. The family, those who noticed her absence, were tactfully silent. They liked to see her happy and home. The sisters made much of Christopher, and flirted with his army friends, who were numerous, and whose presence filled the marquee and gave the event some backbone. They were raucous with each other and formal but winning with the other guests; you could tell these were men who were used to living closely together, there was a palpable camaraderie between them even as they made gallant sallies among the civilians. Deborah found it comforting. Never had she had so much attention lavished upon her, and as she passed among them she saw they were illuminated by her own flaming, joyful presence. As the scratches and dents in metal – old plates or salvers or candlesticks of pewter – seem to run in concentric rings when placed near a light, so the crowds around her organized themselves about Deborah, and each of them felt blessed by her slightest attention.

'To speak frankly,' said her mother quietly to an old friend of the family who she had not seen for some years, 'I am relieved. She was getting quite wild, and who knows what might have become of her. Belinda's reports beggared belief.' And she raised her gentle eyebrows to indicate that all of the sins of the cities of the plain were as nothing to the debauchery of London in the Sixties, in which her youngest daughter had evidently been deeply mired. Her friend's brows rose in unison, and she leaned forward eagerly to place her lips in close proximity to the matriarch. 'Pot?' she whispered with excited apprehension. 'At the very least,' came the response, to her delight.

There was one face among the many that seemed to elude Deborah, a face she was not ever to know well, but one which was to slip in and out of her life just as now it was somehow there and not there, disappearing into shadow, often looking at her with much interest, even kindness. It was a face that wanted to be liked, that smiled at her but then was not there when she looked again. The man seemed younger, less coarse, than the others. His eyes shone with a happiness that almost matched hers, but it seemed to come from an inner quality that had nothing to do with his surroundings. A faint sheen covered his brow. Perhaps he had been drinking more than the others. His hair was very pale, and his cheeks were boyish and round. She liked him. Also, she knew that he did not quite fit in. The more she noticed him the more he inspired a stab of regret in her, until she realized that he reminded her of what she had left behind, the world where she was not going to go again. He might be happy there, this man. He might even be happier.

When she asked Christopher about him, he said, 'Oh, that would be Jonathan. I felt I had to invite him. Might have been a mistake, but it's too late now.' She did not press him.

At first Christopher taught at a boys' prep school near Guildford, and Deborah was fascinated and appalled by it. In the dining room at lunchtime masters waged war on the animal nature of their charges, prowling the aisles between the tables with menace, as if they had long whips in their hands snaking along the floor behind them and were looking for excuses to send them curling and snapping over the heads of the boys if one of them raised his snout from the trough. And yet the boys were full of irrepressible spirit, brimming over with a vitality that was obviously offensive to the masters.

She herself was made guardedly welcome. It was assumed that she knew how to bake and cook and sew and type, and that she was eager to supply the needs of the school, however humdrum and however meagre her skills, at a moment's notice. Yet as much as she helped, she was never more than anonymous. Her views were never sought, and were ignored if she gave them.

Christopher, however, was already being lionized. When he taught, he brought a passion to bear that carried all before it. He knew every one of the boys in his classes as if he could see into their minds, and he had an uncanny understanding of their weaknesses and strengths, of just how much knowledge they were capable of absorbing and how to raise their interest at the right moment and how to build their confidence in themselves and to accelerate their ambitions and how to calm their worries and puncture their complacencies. He had the gift of dispelling dullness. The most mundane passage from Dickens, the finer points of the Wars of the Roses, the life cycle of the horned toad (to Christopher anything was teachable: it was knowing how to teach, rather than mastering the subject, which was the important thing), all became magically alive in his hands, and the most truculent and sleepy boys began to wake up and fall into line and absorb the subject, and the standards of any form he taught rose dramatically, and his colleagues looked on in wonder and with some jealousy, and his fame spread to other schools.

For herself, Deborah longed for a baby, more and more. It was not something she had thought about before meeting Christopher, not at all. But the more she felt Christopher's attention drawn unremittingly towards the boys and the affairs of school life, and the more she felt her personality being eroded by those affairs, the more she felt an obscure anger, and at the same time the desire for her own child grew stronger and more overpowering, and yet it was slow in coming, and the years began to go by, and it occurred to her if not to Christopher that something might be wrong with one or other of them, and the more she wanted to conceive the more of an issue it became, and their lovemaking, never more than perfunctory, became uneasy and troubled. Christopher treated sex as a regrettable necessity, but for Deborah there was increasing cause for regret and an ever urgent necessity. She saw her doctor frequently, she turned to natural remedies, she became obsessed with the phases of

the moon and her own biorythmical cycles, and still she did
secretarial work for the school, when there was an emergency and often when there wasn't, she looked after the
silverware on sports days, she ran the school bookshop and
the tuck shop, she cooked dinner for the other masters and
their wives when there was school business to be discussed,
and she learned to avoid venturing opinions but to chatter
inconsequentially to their wives about school gossip and
which boys' parents were exceptional, by which they invariably meant egregiously wealthy, and which comparatively
lacking in significance, by which they meant thought likely
to default on the fees. She found that she was allowed, indeed
expected, to discuss the merits of other masters but never
to speak disrespectfully of 'the head man', was certainly
required to consider the characters of other masters' wives
with particular attention to their contributions to the well-
being of school life (and thus she learned that her very place
in school society would depend on her own performance of
tuck shop duties, secretarial work, etc.), but never to worry
her head over the structure of the curriculum and whether it
sent boys on to their next school, which was almost inevitably
going to be a nearby public school, in any acceptable state of
readiness for that school or the world that lay beyond it, a
world that was becoming less and less recognizable to boys
reared in the rarified atmosphere of oppressive formality and
thinly disguised brutality that prevailed at the school.

The longing deepened. She would find herself gazing
distractedly at babies in prams, would linger in the mother
and baby section of the local department store, and when the
family got together and Christopher was cutting a dash with
her sisters, who were some of them well advanced with children and liked to show them off to each other, she would plead

with him to leave early, and in-between pleadings would be holding herself back from picking up her nieces and nephews and playing with them, knowing that the feelings swelling in her heart would threaten to drive her mad, and then giving in and cradling them in her arms, possessed and possessive, and then she would take herself off into other parts of the house or down the road to recover her equanimity, and go back after a while and plead again with her uncomprehending husband.

There was an episode. It didn't last long, though Christopher never let her forget it. One of the masters and his wife had a baby boy. They too had waited a long time, and there was elation among the staff. The christening was held at a church in the village where the new mother's parents lived, some ten miles from the school. It was a lavish celebration, and after the baby had taken one look at the priest's lugubrious brow and opened its mouth and bellowed as the baptismal water was tipped over its forehead, and the godparents and guests had made their way to a marquee in the garden and a great deal of champagne had been served, for the new grandmother, like the new mother, had been waiting a long time for this arrival and her generosity was as large as her gratitude, Deborah found herself holding the baby as it slept among its christening clothes, one small hand curled into a fist lying on top of the folds of linen, its eyes tight shut, occasionally opening its mouth with a bored frown to yawn. Deborah could not stop watching it, and the mother was happy to have her baby admired, and Deborah shook her head whenever anyone offered to take the burden from her, and she was still rapt when she heard Christopher calling. There had been an accident at the school – the deputy head had taken a fall while out riding, and the head man wanted some of them back urgently, for it was the Sunday before the end of term and it was a busy week.

Floodwater

The head man loved an emergency, he didn't get enough of them. Deborah walked in a dream up the stone-flagged path behind Christopher, who was deep in conversation with the happy father. They made a turn round the cottage, its white-washed walls bright in the hazy afternoon sunshine, and Christopher backed the car out. Both men clambered into the front, and Deborah got into the back, and the car was half a mile down the road before a small wail emanated from the back seat, growing louder and louder in the brief, shocked silence before Christopher punched the brake pedal with his foot. The two men turned to see Deborah, still holding the baby as tenderly as if it were her own, raise adoring eyes filled with despair and tears towards them.

'Deborah,' the baby's father said, slowly, 'you seem to be kidnapping my son.'

Light was made of it, as is the way in this stretch of English society, and as is the way what was said in private differed from the expressions of astonishment and jocular self-chastisement that greeted their return. For though it was clear to all, as the mother told everyone at school, that Deborah was a very strange, disturbed woman and that she had always thought she was odd and now she'd proved it, everyone was awkwardly aware that the baby had not been missed, and they were all busy in their own minds trying to establish who was to blame, apart from themselves.

Although it did nothing for her reputation, the kidnapping, as Christopher insisted on calling it, did something for Deborah's resolve. She knew she had to come to terms with her own feelings, and do it soon, and accept that if her body was not ready – or Christopher's, for that matter – then she would have to wait. And maybe it would never happen, and she would have to accept that, too. But the addiction, the obsession, had to be dealt with, or she would end up destroying herself. She sensed a darkness out there somewhere waiting for her, and she willed herself away from it, successfully this time.

So while the murmuring and the sidelong glances around her continued, Deborah confounded them by throwing herself wholeheartedly into school life. This did not mean more rewarding activities, for there were none. It meant more and more of them, office duty upon shop duty upon sister duty upon task upon task until she could barely think an independent thought, and she went to bed exhausted.

This went on for a good year, and then another, until people forgot or forgave her strangeness, as they saw it, and the background chatter was pity for her childlessness and admiration for her energetic and selfless devotion to the school. Then one day Christopher received a letter from a school in Dorset called the Hall, inviting him to apply for the post of housemaster. So excited was he that for a few months he was quite insatiable in bed, and whether it was because of the effect of advancement upon his libido, or because Deborah had long ceased to fret and was living a life of cow-like subservience to the greater good, without expecting to, she became expectant. Her body was flooded with joy, and her heart rose like a salmon from the river, and with the birth of Anna she forgot all her troubles and returned to her old self and didn't really fit in but cared less than she had and soon began longing for another child.

THE LITTLE GIRL had an extraordinary effect upon Christopher, more than Deborah could ever have imagined. When she was a baby he attended to her every need, rocking her to sleep, quarrelling over the amount of milk she was to be given and how warm it should be, going on shopping expeditions – a thing unheard of – to buy her clothes, and not only that but doing so on his own, and bringing back skirts and dresses and scarves and hats of impeccable taste. (He didn't change nappies, though. That would have been helpful.) He read to her at night and constructed an elaborate programme of appropriate books that would last until she reached university age and beyond. As she grew older he cooked for her, meals he took from a recipe book for toddlers about which he was annoyingly fussy. Anna received attention from Christopher of a kind and an intensity that he had never shown Deborah, and she felt unhappily that she was seeing for the first time how he was with his pupils, and she felt jealous of them, too. His insistence that only he knew the right way to care for Anna hurt her, but she did not have the will to confront him, and in truth what could she have expected, for he was domineering in all things, and this was an aspect of what she loved about him, or had once loved.

On the last day in February, 1974, Deborah got Christopher a little drunk. She hardly saw him nowadays, whether out of choice or not, and whether that choice was his or hers, was anyone's guess. They had shaped their lives at the school in a way that meant they rarely coincided in the same place, save for when something concerned Anna.

She wanted another child, though, and that is why she got him drinking. Things were going well for Christopher at the Hall, and he was in an expansive mood, and Anna, just over two years old, was enchanting, and Deborah cooked a bouillabaisse from a recipe she had mastered when she had holidayed in Provence, and she cooked it knowing that he would hardly notice the food but hoping he would appreciate her efforts. Almost everything she made had a dollop of alcohol in some form added to it, even the ice cream, and she reminded him of how they had talked of having another baby, which they had not, but she convinced him that they had and that he had simply been too busy to notice. He looked about him at the neatly tidied piles of children's books and toys.

'Did I?' he said. 'Did I?'

'We did,' she said, and smiled. He looked back at her and his face worked thinly as if it were endeavouring to assume an expression.

'I do like sex,' he said, the words breaking from his mouth percussively. 'I've been meaning to say.'

Later, after he had fertilized her with the minimum of preliminaries, she wondered who it was he actually liked to have sex with. It was not a new thought to her. But she had taken what she wanted. It might be as mechanical as a plantation worker cupping rubber, but she had what she needed. And this time it worked.

She nursed her pregnancy alone. There was no one to take any great interest in it, and she did not wish to tell anyone, until she was sure of it, except for Christopher, who shrugged. 'There will only be one child for me,' he said, looking through the window at Anna, who was playing in her Wendy house in the sunshine in the corner of the lawn. She thought, he actually said that. But she ignored the gulf that had grown between them, over which Anna was the only bridge. (Sometimes Deborah pondered what a heavy responsibility this was for her daughter.) She ignored it because of the new baby, and the happiness it brought her. She played the organ in the chapel for sheer pleasure as much as to show her face, and she took to walking, nothing too strenuous, with Anna by her side or carried on her back. On weekdays and weekends the pair of them would set out, with sandwiches and juices in Tupperware boxes and mugs, strolling slowly through the woods in April sunshine, dodging showers, and Deborah would talk to Anna about all the things they saw around them. She was talking to herself as much as to her daughter, who was too small to understand most of what she was saying, and when she described how clouds were made as they watched them from the brow of a hill, spreading across the sky like lumps of dough flat-bottomed on a baking tray to the horizon, she felt she was talking to the clouds themselves, naming and describing them and sharing herself with them. In the fields, where fat wet slices of soil glinted in the sunlight like sequins, she told Anna how grass grows from seed, at first pale and insignificant, straining through the earth, then stronger and greener, and how the calves grew fat on it and how the cows gave milk and how she, Anna, grew plump and sturdy drinking milk and particularly cream, which Anna had just discovered (together with sugar). And in the woods she told her how the sunshine became the leaves of the trees – 'Imagine, Anna, how sun and water become a great, knobbly oak. Something so big and tough and solid and so *there,* out of nothing but sun and water. And an acorn, of course. Just a little acorn turns into that.' They followed a stream together, carefully picking their way around a field – 'I think it's rye, Anna, but it might be wheat' – until it joined another, the water curling over itself, heaping over moss-wigged stones, and she told Anna how a river joins another joins another all the way to the sea, where all river journeys end, and then the water rises into the air with the heat of the sun and becomes a cloud and comes back over the land and turns to rain and becomes a river.

'And so it goes on around and around, Anna, very simply, very beautifully.'

THERE WAS A walk she loved that made its way down a valley and over a hill to three standing stones, and one Sunday in early May they took this path which started at a stile near the school. It was a relief to get out; it had rained constantly for a week, and Anna was fractious with being stuck indoors, and so for that matter was Deborah, standing at the window watching the rain sweeping in curtains towards her down the hills as the clouds grazed their tops and in the far distance sheep huddled with their lambs under trees in their first flush of green. She longed to escape. Christopher, too, was in an unusual mood, silent and distracted; more than once she had found mud on his shoes, and he was not a walker by nature. He had been sent a letter which agitated him, she had seen him reading it over and over when he thought she was pre-occupied with Anna, and she had half a mind to follow him, then thought better of it, and then the weather cleared, and she knew Christopher had disappeared again, and she was desperate to feel the clear air in her lungs and feel alive again, and perhaps she might catch sight of him and perhaps not, and perhaps she wanted to know what was going on and perhaps she didn't. She would see what she would see.

She set out with Anna along the path by a river swollen by the week's rain, and she followed its course for a mile or so before the path swung gradually up into woodland filled with unnameable scents released by the damp and warmed by the sun. She wondered about the sex of her child, wondered whether she minded herself whether it would be a girl or a boy, a sister or a brother for Anna, and she fell to thinking about names, and the image of her childhood friend came back to her, laboriously scrawling 'Debraland' on a rough-edged piece of cardboard with a purple crayon, proudly hauling branches over the woodland floor, squatting next to her when it rained and the cross-hatched branches that comprised the roof of their shelter were barely enough to keep them dry. If she had a boy, perhaps she would call him Frank. She squinted up to the top of the ridge and saw where the path disappeared over it. The sun flashed through the leaves and half-blinded her, but she could have sworn she saw something moving there, it could have been a man or an animal. There were wild deer that roamed these parts. She felt Anna stir at her back, where she had fallen asleep.

'Mummy,' she began to say.

'Shh,' said Deborah. She did not want whatever it was to know she was there, but as she squinted up through the trees again she could already see it had gone.

Deborah loosened Anna from her shoulders and unpacked the picnic she had prepared for them and gave her something to drink and watched the river hastening by at the foot of the hill, and then they began to climb the hill. She found she was trembling a little, either from fear or anticipation.

'One doesn't want to get too close,' she thought. 'You just never know, though I'm sure it's perfectly harmless.' Last year a young girl who had strayed from her walking party had been raped and murdered only ten miles away. 'Perhaps we should go back.' She peered along the path again. Anna pulled at her skirt. 'Come on, then.' She picked the child up and kissed her, manoeuvred her into the carrier and swung her up onto her back.

The path ran along the ridge, but it was hard to see beyond the wood which smothered the hill. The light was green and the atmosphere close. There was no wind. Underfoot the debris of the years had formed a thick mulch, and her feet made no sound. Anna was singing quietly to herself as she began falling asleep again, swayed by the rocking motion. She was a small girl, almost too small, and Deborah was hardly aware of her weight. At the end of the ridge the way was marked by another stile and it plunged downwards and round a great slab of rock that broke through the tree canopy and reared skywards, before entering a clearing where the dolmen had been standing for four thousand years since its old chieftain had been buried beneath it, perhaps before the woods came. The path hugged the base of the rock, which meant that Deborah was hidden from view until just before the clearing, and at that moment, before stepping out from behind it, she heard a man's voice, raised in exasperation.

'Didn't I go through enough for your sake?' it said. 'I don't need any. I don't need any more.'

The last sentence ended on a plaintive high note. She knew the voice, though she heard it less and less these days. It was Christopher's. She tried to step back, but found she could not move. Worse, her body was dragging her forward into view, unable to resist the temptation to see who he was talking to. Slowly she edged forward, scarcely breathing. Another man was talking, more softly. She saw him before she saw her husband, standing between herself and the stones which stood at shoulder height, perfectly symmetrical, perfectly immobile behind Christopher, who had his back to her, and a smaller, younger, blonder figure, one she recognized. On her back Anna shifted slightly. As she watched, Christopher raised his arm and stroked Jonathan's cheek. He had long fingers that swelled at the knuckles and ended in squared-off, slightly flattened fingertips. Sensible, not insensitive, authoritative fingers. Now they ran slowly over Jonathan's skin with wonderful tenderness, then slid round the back of his head and pulled him forward for a sudden kiss of a passion Deborah had never imagined possible in him. It seemed to her to endure for ever, but it can only have been for a few moments, after which Jonathan broke away with an impatient movement, and in doing so he turned his head a fraction and saw her. He smiled, a smile that was for Christopher, and for her. Something gave way within her, and she slipped behind the rock and back the way she had come, panicking, hardly able to think and oblivious of Anna until she was woken by Deborah's stumbling half run, half anguished stride and began to cry. She was wounded, not at the infidelity, which was a solution and an explanation, if an unwelcome one, but by the one thing she had seen that the other man possessed and she did not, had not for years, maybe never had done. She saw the love in Christopher.

When she reached home she began a whirlwind of tidying and washing, blotting out thought in the way that was so often her way of dealing with unhappiness. But she couldn't do it all the time, thoughts would happen, you couldn't stop them. So. Jonathan. What trouble had Christopher been in? She had never heard of anything, but she was always the last to know. Would Belinda know, would she tell her if she did? Maybe there was nothing in it, not enough for anyone to comment. Would she ever know? She must stop tormenting herself. Whatever it was belonged to the past, before they had even met one another, she and Christopher. And yet something was still happening, which meant there were more things about Christopher she did not know, things from the past that were important for her now, things she should have known, should have been able to see. If a truth belongs to the past and is still true in the present, that does, doesn't it, change everything in-between. Therefore I have been living a pretend life, a nothing life, a fabrication.

And yet, and yet. Was it that much of a surprise?

She ransacked his belongings, left nothing to chance, put everything back the way it was with extravagant care, found nothing. As they lay side by side in bed, her mind scoured the endless possibilities and consequences.

To Christopher, however, she said nothing. Invariably she made herself ill with worry, but she managed to hide it. And then she began to realize that she really was ill, that her stomach was in increasing pain, and that there was something altogether wrong, and it was to do with her baby, and not long afterwards Christopher came back to find her lying on the bed, her eyes open but unseeing, having sobbed herself nearly into unconsciousness, and the lavatory bowl full of blood. And even Christopher was moved to be understanding, and he took his grieving wife and his beloved daughter on holiday to Ireland, and they walked together along the sands of Galway, and the wind blew fiercely through Deborah's hair but there were new lines in her face and none of Christopher's late-coming kindness could do any good, nor would it ever.

SOMETIMES MENTAL ILLNESSES are never diagnosed, and so never treated. We don't recognize them in ourselves, and even if others can see them they don't tell us. The brain is so subtle and strong, it can turn in on itself and break apart with subtlety, too, so that no one can say, here is where it all started, here is where it went wrong, where the repair needed to be made. As Deborah sank into quietness, by unspoken consent neither she nor Christopher spoke to anyone of what had happened, and Christopher turned his attentions to his first loves, his boys and his ambitions and his daughter, and perhaps a part of him, an unconscious part to be charitable, was more than willing to accept a silent Deborah, perhaps that was what he had always wanted from her. Her listlessness was not openly sullen or resentful, but why should it be? If he noticed anything wrong he attributed it to the loss of their second baby, and all the ensuing complications which meant there would never be a brother or a sister for Anna. As for her, in some curious way she grew to replace Deborah in his affections, though his feelings for Anna were always far stronger than anything he had felt for Deborah, and Anna grew with the strength of those feelings, and became confident and learned to love the same things with the same intensity, becoming even a subject of some mockery when they moved to Meniston, where she was known as the head man's little lamb (and as is the way of these things the soubriquet 'Mary' was added to the roster of his nicknames) for the way she followed her father about, fluttering like a scrap of paper at his heels. She thought like her father and even talked like him, had a fussy and martial air to her, tolerated fools hardly at all and treated her mother with the same puzzled indifference as did he. And what are *you* doing here, they seemed to be saying. And what are *you* for?

AND SO THE years passed.

THEN ONE DAY Deborah found Jonathan standing outside the front door.

He was more tousled, slighter and frailer, and he had a

tired look. Patches of eczema had formed at the corners of his mouth and there was a scratch on his left cheek. But his smile was as brash and disarming as ever it was. He knew she knew what she knew.

'I'm looking for Christopher.' His voice had a surprisingly deep timbre to it. Deborah thought he might have a good singing voice.

'Yes,' she said. She returned his smile, couldn't help it. 'He'll be back soon. You can come in, if you like.' Wondering at herself, she showed him into the kitchen.

'Tea?'

'Wouldn't mind something stronger.'

'Not in the middle of the afternoon. It's tea or nothing for you,' she said. Now that she could inspect him more closely, she saw that his clothes were dirty and unkempt, the cord trousers frayed around the ankle and at the openings of the pockets, the check shirt pattern peeling away from his shirt collar showing the white beneath. He had no belt, and smelled of beer and manure.

'Did you ring?' she asked, putting the kettle on the gas ring. 'Perhaps I was out.'

'Oh, I rang, yes, but I didn't get a reply so I thought I would come anyway.'

'You could have left a message on the answering machine.'

He gave her a blank look. 'Answering machine?'

'Yes. Haven't you heard of them? Christopher loves his gadgets.'

He had the grace to look sheepish. 'All right, I didn't ring, but I couldn't use a telephone because if you really want to know I've been sleeping rough for a few days. I haven't had much luck recently.' He pulled a face, looked bewildered. 'In fact, I'm sort of hoping Christopher might give me a job.'

Floodwater

The rattle of a key sounded in the front door.

'Have you seen Anna? Is she here? I need to ask her advice about something,' came Christopher's voice a moment later. She could hear the thick whisper of his coat being taken off and hung on a curling branch of the hatstand. The keys clinked softly in its pocket as it swung.

'We have a visitor, Christopher,' she said, her voice indifferent.

'A visitor?' He sounded impatient, hurried. He had things on his mind.

Suddenly he was in the doorway, one instant a rushing, distracted, busy man, the next quite motionless, gazing uncomprehending at Jonathan. For a few moments nothing was said. Deborah stood with her hands clasped in front of her and looked at Christopher with her face deliberately devoid of expression, as if presenting Jonathan to him, as if innocent, as if not obscurely pleased by what this would do to Christopher.

Nothing was said. The two men looked at each other, and it seemed as if many things were passing between them, though neither opened his mouth.

Then, 'Jonathan,' said Christopher, quietly, and with a curious inclination of his head. 'I see you've met. Well.' He nodded fractionally, as if outlining a way forward to himself, then his forehead creased. 'Look at the state you're in,' he said. 'What have you been doing with yourself?'

And Jonathan smiled.

THE APPOINTMENT OF Jonathan Davies as part-time singing master and part-time English master was of no great consequence in a school as grand as Meniston, but it did not pass without comment, particularly from the full-time singing master and the head of the English department. But if there was one thing Jonathan possessed — and besides a fine baritone it was pretty much the only thing — it was charm. Washed and trimmed and darned and generally spruced, he possessed a winning manner that could persuade almost anyone to do almost anything for him — as his appointment proved. Those moved to remark the absence of any formal training at all — for such a lack is difficult to obscure and Jonathan's ready lies wore threadbare after a while — were nevertheless also moved to comment on how he lightened the heart. He did not hide his sexuality, neither did he express it openly, and for a public school in the early eighties this was considered not only acceptable but daring and liberal, and the more avant garde masters, keen to impress each other and the boys with their freedom of thought, made sure to cultivate him, and there were rewards, for he was wonderful company, and if the years showed that he had little or no talent for passing on the gifts of his voice to anyone else, and that his grasp of English literature was elementary and liable to remain so, most were inclined to overlook these minor failings.

Most, but not all.

Alex Rainsford was the closest Deborah came to having a friend. He was an unlikely one. He had come to the school as head of the English department not long after Jonathan, eager to make his mark, proud to be teaching at Meniston, passionate about literature. He had a sick wife called Lucy and a seven-year-old boy called Luke. A coil of dark hair fell over his brow, and he was always flinging his head back to try and clear his vision. It could have been an affectation, especially in an English master, but was not. The rest of him was hardly prepossessing; he looked like someone had taken hold of his head when small and pulled it and pummelled it so it looked like a battered potato. In his dark brown eyes lurked apprehension. A restless, ambitious man.

Jonathan and Alex were not destined to be close. Alex was at first bemused by him, then irritated, then quietly angry. He began asking colleagues how Jonathan had come to be at the school, and they said, oh, he's someone the headmaster discovered, not the world's best teacher but very popular, and only part-time. You need an odd bod here and there in a place like this, they said. But Alex detested favouritism, loathed incompetence, and most of all hated not being able to do anything about it. That Jonathan Davies was some sort of protected species was proved when after a year or two of putting up with his lateness and forgetfulness and – to be fair, an accurate assessment, this – his uncertain grasp of the subject, Alex took it upon himself to approach the head-master for some sort of elucidation, he was fobbed off.

'Jonathan?' said the headmaster. 'He adds a certain some-thing, doesn't he? Beautiful voice, you must have heard it.'

'I'm not sure that qualifies him . . .' Alex hesitated. He distrusted his own urgent exasperation.

'I think you'll find Jonathan brings us more than you give him – in my judgement – credit for, Alexander,' interrupted Christopher curtly, effectively ending the matter.

But Alex was not snubbed so easily. Time and again he returned to battle, sometimes bluntly, sometimes stealthily, but always to no avail, and his animosity came to include the headmaster, and he found that he was not alone in his im-patience and increasing suspicion. 'But they can't be lovers, can they?' these few reasoned with him. 'Perhaps once. Not now. And he's married and has a child. There can't be anything in that theory.' He agreed, but something had to explain the existence of Jonathan Davies.

At weekends the school liked to arrange things for the boys to do, or they degenerated into a torpor of watching old black-and-white B-movies on Sunday afternoons, crowded round the television on wooden chairs in smelly rows. A favourite outing was on the restored railway line that ran from over the county border up to the coast. This was popular especially with the younger boys, yet to develop their carapace of English public-school cynicism, and the old steam engines puffed cheerfully through the rolling Somerset countryside and past renovated stations with flowerbeds and cats and milkchurns to the sea. Christopher often came on these trips and Deborah and Anna came too, and when they reached the once-thronged resort at the end of the line the boys were allowed to go and spend their pocket money and the staff would walk on the mud-flats that stretched deep into the Bristol channel at low tide, picking their way over great reefs of rock ribboned in layers of sediment that had settled and hardened and buckled over the millions of years.

On one of these outings Deborah found herself walking with Alex along a smooth boom of perspiring mauve rock running parallel to the sea and edged by gullies of quiet water reflecting the sky. It was a good day for her, she had received a letter from Belinda promising a visit from the sisters. From time to time they did this; they worried about her and by now had formed a less than flattering opinion of Christopher. Husbands as a class were always fair game, but Christopher really did not help himself, and where once he had made an effort to be sociable he now retired to the fastness of his study and refused to put his head out of the door until he could be sure they had gone. Anna would be thrilled: an invasion of aunts meant presents and cousins and a lift in her mother's spirits. So there would be jokes at Christopher's expense, at which Deborah would pretend to look disapproving, pursing her lips and shaking her head, but the shimmy in her eye – such a rare sight – would give her away. And Anna, who was so reserved, so aloof, would allow herself to be teased by her cousins, would be unhappy unless she *was* teased, and they would teach her things like riding a two-wheel bicycle (which was long overdue), and would play long unruly games of rounders with her under the big oaks that lined the cricket pitch, and they would all set off on picnics with hampers stuffed with food and wine for the grown-ups and there would be dogs and mayhem. They travelled in cavalcade, the aunts and cousins. Belinda, who had married a successful fund manager whom she rarely saw and who had a flat in South Kensington, a manor house in Wiltshire and a lover who was the stable boy at a nearby farm, drove a Range Rover caked in mud. Mary, who had abandoned a thriving career in public relations to become a writer, drove a much-dented red Volkswagen that was ten years old and smelled like it. Tessa had married a farmer and had another mud-caked Range Rover, and Jo wasn't going to marry anyone and drove an old Mercedes sports car that she used to give Anna rides in at terrifying speed, pelting around the country roads and frightening the cattle. Since their father died and their mother had been immobilized by an arthritic hip, the sisters had descended more frequently on Meniston, taking it upon themselves to monitor the well-being – or lack of it – of their youngest sibling and sending detailed bulletins home.

So that day by the sea Deborah was more talkative than usual. She still retained something of the looks that had once bewitched London, though her skin was papery and crows' feet clustered tetchily at the corner of her eyes and her hair was unkempt and she had a tired air about her, even today.

'She looks as if a strong breeze would blow her into the sea and she wouldn't mind if it did,' thought Alex.

They went on talking all the way to the pier, where he bought her an ice cream. Some of the boys were there, casting appraising looks at them. Masters and their wives weren't supposed to fraternize as if they were normal human beings. They went on talking back to the railway station and back to school, and afterwards, whenever they met in a corridor or the path by the old school wall where were inscribed the names of those who died during the Great War and the Boer War and the Second World War, or after chapel or before assembly. She liked his earnestness, his clumsy seriousness, and he was intrigued by her quietness and her intensity and her feyness, and when the name of Jonathan Davies came up their thoughts drifted in the same direction, and he would drop by occasionally for tea at times when they both knew that Christopher would not be there, and over time some elements of the story of Jonathan and Christopher emerged, so far as she knew it, from Deborah, and Alex was enraged at the way she had been treated, she being so gentle and defenceless, and his sense of injustice and of her wronged innocence grew with his own frustrations.

Deborah was conscious of how Alex seemed to find reasons to be near her, thieving them out of the air with the same determination that brought him to her kitchen door for tea on Saturday afternoons. He was welcome: the fog that enveloped her and ate into her bones seemed to lift when he was there. She knew his wife was dying, thought it strange that he never spoke about her nor about his son, a sweet, thin, untidy boy. The school talked of Lucy in that knowing, sad, English way that never quite comes to the point but proceeds through hints and significant pauses, and perhaps (only perhaps) that is a good way to do it, whereby something terrible can be described by what is not said about it rather than what is. She had been in remission when they arrived at the school, but the cancer had recently returned in a more vigorous form than before, and just as people skirted it in conversation, so they set a kind of exclusion zone about Alex Rainsford, and he felt their distance, and it pained him, but there were a few, and Deborah was one, who ignored such niceties, and the warmth of their friendship helped him, and during Lucy's last days he did the best he could, fighting his own terror of the time that would follow, for he had loved her desperately, she was the most important thing in the world to him, and he had no idea how to tolerate his life once she had gone.

Deborah thought that his son would help him, but after Lucy's death she began to see a formality, an awkwardness, between them, which dismayed her. The boy was wilful, undemonstrative; there was some history there, some unhappiness. The truth was that Alex's love had been so much for Lucy that he had failed to pay much attention to his son – even his name was close to hers – and when the incalculable trauma of her death came upon them there was no thread to guide him back through the labyrinth to Luke; they were estranged, and only became more so, more perplexed by each other, as time went by. Lucy had been the object of their hearts' affections, and somehow they had forgotten to include each other.

And of course Alex's experience with Luke mirrored her own with Anna, and in the year or two after Lucy's death

Sacrifices

the realization of this truth drew them closer. Both had lost their children emotionally to their own partners, without comprehending how or why.

'There's an inversion about you and me,' she said to Alex after she had seen Christopher and Anna arguing hotly about which teacher training college she was going to attend in a year's time, knowing that the one opinion they would not be interested in would be hers. 'We have both been orphaned by our only children.'

Alex nodded slowly. 'I don't know what I'm going to do about Luke,' he said. 'He says he wants to be an actor, now.'

'He's far too young to say that.' Being with Alex she found the courage to express opinions, something she loved him for.

'Determined, though, even so.'

They were sitting at the kitchen table once more. He hadn't bothered to take his coat off.

'You know Jonathan has disappeared,' he continued.

She looked up. 'Disappeared?'

'Gone. Vanished. Just like that. Didn't say goodbye, where he was going, nothing. We checked his room, it's very small, must be the smallest in the single masters' block. The headmaster may have thought well of our funny little friend but he didn't extend his hospitality to accommodation. Anyway, it's been cleared out. Not a stitch left. Skedaddled. Gone.'

'I don't think either of us is going to shed a tear over that.'

'No.'

'Not a bad man, though, you know, everybody liked him.'

Alex took her hands in his, gripped them hard enough to make her wince and laugh.

'Deborah, you know what a humiliation he's been to you. You should never have had to endure it.'

She laughed more softly in embarrassment.

'Don't, Alex. You're so formal and grand about it. It's not that harmful. It happened long ago, no one knows about it except you and me. I just hope Jonathan's all right.'

Alex swore violently and got to his feet. 'Deborah, you are wonderful, but you are impossibly naive.'

'Why am I naive?'

'Do you really believe it was all over years ago, before you met? Think about what you saw.'

She sighed and rested her head on her hands. She knew it would begin to swim quite soon.

'I do. I do think about that. But does it matter? I'm sure there's nothing wrong.'

'Deborah, you are deluding yourself. I'm sorry, but you do need to know this. The school is — there have been rumours. About Christopher. About Jonathan. About . . . boys, too, if you must know. There. I've said it.'

He bit his lip hard. He hadn't meant to go this far.

'Why do I need to know?' she said, and he could tell she was on the brink of tears. 'I don't want to know.'

'You need to know because I love you, Deborah,' he said, unhappily. Did he mean to say this? Did he mean it? Perhaps he was simply justifying saying what he had said. How could he not mean it?

'Do you? How does that help me?'

He sat down again and looked at her foolishly.

'It doesn't, I suppose. Maybe it just helps me.'

He needed to take her hand again, but she moved it out of reach. He nodded slowly.

'Yes. It just helps me.'

*　*　*

Sacrifices

DEBORAH HAD ALWAYS known Anna would be a teacher, but now the time had come she didn't want her to go, wondered whether she would come back, half-wished she had chosen something different that would have shaken her loose from the world she grew up in. She missed her when she was away, the house was empty, she felt herself drifting, was surprised at how important Anna's presence had been, how it made her feel necessary.

When Anna returned after her first term Deborah sensed the change in her. She had a new confidence, as if she had been finding things out and liked what she found and didn't need to let anyone else in on it. She kept herself to herself a little more. Deborah didn't mind, but she could tell that Christopher did. Anna paid him less attention than he was used to, than he required of her. She seemed to have a tangible world of her own to live in. She laughed more frequently. Deborah felt pride, but Christopher became sullen with her. Christmas was never a good time for them but that year was the worst of all. Christopher snapped and tried to bait Anna, but Anna simply ignored him and chatted to Deborah instead. The ground seemed to float beneath Deborah's feet.

'She seems not quite herself, our daughter,' said Christopher.

'She's certainly more our daughter than she was.'

'How so?'

'You know she's always been Daddy's girl.'

'Don't be so foolish.' Christopher was long unused to Deborah holding, still less expressing, opinions.

She guessed immediately one of the reasons for her daughter's mood, but said nothing to Christopher, not even when Daniel Ellis first made his appearance at Meniston, like an angel advancing from clouds of brilliant gold (as it seemed to her). She loved the way he talked to her, making her feel like a whole human being after years, decades of neglect, loved how Anna had grown, how Christopher was distrustful. Whether he could see what was going on between Daniel and Anna she never found out, and when everything went wrong she wondered whether Anna would ever have found the strength to leave the company of her father, but if there were ever to be an opportunity this was it, and there would not be another one. And so she helped Anna deceive her father, and then she helped her tell him about the baby as she knew she must, and where she found the courage she did not know then or afterwards, and when the weakness of Daniel became clear she told herself that perhaps it was in some dreadful way for the best, he would never have been a reliable husband for Anna – but who needs reliability? Love will do, most of the time. More than do.

And the baby, that moment when it was taken away, that had death in it, all their deaths, and only Christopher could have known how she felt, must have known. It was another kidnapping, and another boy. All the longings and loss of the past came back, engulfing her, worse than what she had experienced before. Even though it was not her son but Anna's, the hope that Daniel had brought deepened the catastrophe, in her nightmares she saw him, tiny and hardly formed, and sometimes she was holding him in a car speeding away from a christening, and sometimes she was lying sightless on a bed, and sometimes he was a baby, and sometimes a boy sinking away from her into the depths of swift brown water, rising up to her and falling away, and this last image came back to her over and over and over as if it were returning to claim her at last, reproaching her for ever forgetting.

*   *   *

THE NINETIES WERE an undertain decade for the school, and it was not hard to see where the turbulence was coming from. Christopher was at its epicentre; he would have been headmaster for twenty-five years by the millennium, and the animosities and discontents of the years now found him less fierce in his rebuffs. People were talking ever more loudly and insistently about his retirement, though Christopher did not hear them. He appointed Alex Rainsford as deputy headmaster, blind to Alex's surreptitious stirring of resentment. For Alex knew from Deborah that Jonathan had returned, this time openly dissolute and openly demanding money. He seemed to have gone back to his old ways, or any rate the paths he had been on from which his time at Meniston had obviously been merely a long diversion. He was increasingly ragged and he stank. He would stay in the house only for few moments before the smell forced Deborah to push him out the back door, but he would not go before he had seen Christopher. At first the visits were infrequent, once or twice a year, but Jonathan was not one to let necessity wait upon good judgement, and he was becoming insistent and greedy. Still Christopher would not explain to Deborah what it was that gave Jonathan the hold he had over him. Evidently they had been lovers, so much she knew, and so much the school, too, seemed to surmise. Even Anna had heard the rumours, and was beginning to hear others, uglier ones she chose to ignore.

LUKE LEFT HIS father for London just as soon as he was able to, and the love between his father and Deborah deepened as they passed middle age, but it was never fulfilled in any way, and Alex continued to keep his burning sense of injustice alight on both their behalves, for his animus towards

Christopher did not diminish after Jonathan left, but
remained fierce for the sake of the woman he now loved.
She, for her part, was possessed by a sense of the losses
she and Alex had sustained in their lives, and so their pre-
occupations conjoined them and dominated their lives, and
when the foolishness of Christopher in his old age became
apparent, when he had been headmaster too long, when his
powers were waning and his wisdom in its dotage brought
scandal upon their heads, they had at least each other for
solace and for triumph. And then came the business about
the letter, and Christopher would have resisted Alex if it had
not become public knowledge, and when the press were on
to it, it was like a slow, anguished scream among hills when
the echoes widen out and rebound and crisscross each other
interminably and the tumult becomes unbearable, and
Chistopher took the only course open to him, the only one
offered, and when he retired there were some who were
surprised by how much he still entertained the world's
respect, for he had been thought a great man for many
decades, and most were willing to forgive, but resignation
and retirement were not the end of it, and Christopher found
his once proud reputation deteriorating as rumour piled upon
rumour, and old boys recollected, and some of it was true
and some malicious, but he was finally plunged into disgrace
and Anna watched with growing anxiety as his health began
to fail and age, which had seemed to leaved him untouched,
suddenly came upon him. He developed a limp and had to walk
with a stick, and great pouches formed under his eyes, and his
skin grew sallow and his hair whitened and liver spots appeared
on his scalp and he skulked in the grace-and-favour cottage
granted him and Deborah by the school and never emerged,
always denying any wrongdoing. Anna, who never doubted

him for a moment, would coax him out on walks to get him
to exercise, and he would talk of the past and what he had
hoped for the school and what he had achieved for it. They
would talk of their enemies and their suspicions, among them
Meadows the MP who had been so instrumental in publiciz-
ing the scandal, who had himself left his second wife quite
suddenly one morning without warning or reason given
before or after, but who still avoided opprobrium while
meticulously destroying Christopher.

'He's a cruel man, a very cruel man,' Christopher would
start, walking slowly, leaning on his black stick with its heavy
ivory handle, Anna walking quickly by his side, the river
sidling by. 'I don't think he cares about people, you know.
Someone told me about that first wife of his, she didn't stick
around long. And the second, who had his children, she was
a dunce, he simply used her, then dropped her when he found
something more interesting. Money, power. That's all he cares
about. The new wife is an heiress, I believe. A cruel man,
believe me. As we know.' His shoulders had become hunched,
concave with age and the constant anger in him. He had
become a smaller man. 'Alexander,' he would go on. 'He
never wished me well, though I was good enough to him.
By god, I was.' Now and then he would knock stones sharply
along the path in little spasms of frustration. He would never
criticize any of the boys, any of those who had come forward
with their tales of touching and proximity and sometimes
closer intimacies. Anna thought them liars, traitors to her
father's greatness, but she did not argue. The less said.
Sometimes she summoned her courage and asked about
Jonathan, and he would ignore her, but once he said, 'He's a
vagrant, now, I don't know where he is, keeps turning up
like a bad penny,' and laughed softly.

'Has he turned up recently, this bad penny?' She was eager to take him up on this, if he would talk.

'Yes. He seems to be around rather a lot at the moment. He doesn't come to the house, there are places we meet. He always wants money. I don't have much more I can give him.'

Places they met.

'Why do you give him money?' she asked.

He didn't reply. His faculties weren't what they were, he can't have meant to say this. She was alarmed. She could sense the trouble coming. Her father did not walk far afield, and never without her, and although her teaching duties made it difficult for her to watch over him all the time, she was reasonably sure that he was there, at home, seated in his armchair with the black walking stick that was his father's within reaching distance, seemingly a source of comfort to him; he would hold its ivory head and stroke it slowly, almost sensuously, with his thumb as they talked. He would be waiting for her to return and read to him, or play cards, or discuss the news of the day. He was hungry to hear what was happening at the school, what Alex Rainsford was doing now that he had charge of it, what changes he was introducing, who the new teachers were and where they had come from, how he had altered the school prospectus. Christopher was intensely aware of any nuance of alteration in the character of the school that his former deputy might take it into his head to devise, and would cluck like an old hen with disapproval as Anna talked. She was careful to interlace the good news – that nothing had changed – with anything that would upset him. 'That's no good, he'll never get away with that,' he would snap, and 'He simply doesn't understand, he never did. The man's a buffoon. What did I see in him?' He would cover his face with his hands, his long, mottled fingers pressing lightly against his eyelids, but what was done was done, there was no fight left in him, and no fight to win, he had lost everything. The pain was deep, and it was as deep for Anna, watching him, who felt every distress and joy of his as if it were her own. And somewhere out there was a man who needed her father, too, who was old now like him or getting there, and even more wretched, who might soon come calling.

HE CHOOSES HIS moment well, as he has done before. Deborah is away, making a tour of the sisters, a means of release that has become increasingly necessary and easy to do over recent years, as Christopher's troubles multiplied and he ceased even to notice his wife and the sisters called to her to come and see them, taking her away from the whole imbroglio, and she can be away for weeks and months, welcomed wherever she goes, her presence or absence no longer material to her husband's old school.

It has been raining seemingly for weeks, and the rivers are in spate. The water gets everywhere. Roads and paths dive under scurrying torrents of it, fields drown under it, bones seem to ache from it and souls weary of it. In the evenings Anna and Christopher sit together and listen to it rattling against the tiles, and it's cold, too, this March, and there's no let-up.

There is a knock on the front door, a faint one, then another, louder, more decided. Anna regards her father with deep apprehension, he is struggling to get to his feet by the fireplace where the new logs are spitting and snapping. 'I'll get it,' she says, jumping up, but he goes on struggling, he wants to be on his feet, standing. Outside Jonathan leans on one hand against the wall, breathing heavily, his battered overcoat drenched and dripping, what is left of his hair matted tight against his scalp. The light above the door throws everything into chiaroscuro, flinging heavy shadows across the garden and beyond into the woods, but the raindrops spark and dazzle in it. When Jonathan lifts his face to squint at her she steps back with the shock of his ravaged features, reddened by raw alcohol, coarsened by sleeping rough, covered with cuts and bruises from squabbles and collapses.

'Can I see Christopher?' His voice is still pure in tone, though a tremulous whisper.

'You'd better come in,' says Anna, echoing her mother those many years ago. This is not what she wants, though, far from it, but she knows her father would not allow her simply to shoo him away. She watches him import the concentrated wetness of the outside world into their warm living room. There is an extraordinary expression on her father's face as the decrepit figure stands swaying before him. It's an expression she will remember and return to over and over again, trying to detect and tease out its elements: alarm, of course, but surprisingly not horror, something of pity, but also fear, and anger, and a resolve.

They help Jonathan take his coat off, Anna boiling with fury and revulsion at this invasion of human wreckage reeking of putrefaction and living decay. Christopher sits him down but remains on his feet by the fireplace.

'Jonathan,' he says, deliberately, 'I have nothing left to give you.'

'You've said that before.'

'This time I mean it.'

'You've said that before, too.'

'Jonathan, you need help, but not from me. Not my kind of help, proper help. It's not too late for that. You're not as

239

old as you appear. You won't live much longer, though, unless you get that help.'

'I know, I know, I've heard this diatribe. But I want some money from you, Christopher, you always have before, and I need it very badly now.'

'I should never have given you that money. I have only helped turn you into what you are. I mean it.'

Jonathan stares at him, and a smile of derision curls over his blistered lips.

'You mean it, do you? You do, don't you?'

'Yes.'

Suddenly Jonathan rises to his feet, clutching the back of his chair to steady himself. When he speaks, his voice is hoarse with rage.

'Does she know?' he breathes, pointing wildly behind him at Anna. Confusion floods Christopher's face. 'I can tell she doesn't. We were lovers, darling,' he says, lightly, a glimpse of his old provocative airs. 'That's why' — he edges behind the chair as if in readiness — 'we had to leave the army. They found us, didn't they, entwined in one another's arms. Oh, it was hushed up. Nobody knew, nobody. But . . . I could go into more detail. Much more. Couldn't I, Christopher? Much more where that came from.'

A log cracks in the fire.

'Daddy, this is nothing. I don't care about this, it means nothing to me.' The words tumble out. Protect him. Save him from this.

Jonathan nods.

'We were lovers.' His eyes, bloodshot and exhausted, are fixed on Christopher. 'Lovers. And not just then.'

Anna wills away the implications, wills him to stop.

'I don't care,' she finds herself saying, hears the tonelessness in her voice, feels the years of her father's dominance and possession of her, knows she does not know him, all of him, after all, that something has always been hidden from her. She does not know the whole of him. This is what hurts, hurts badly. But she won't let Jonathan manipulate her father because of her.

'*You* don't care.' Jonathan's eyes never leave Christopher. '*You* don't care.' He stops, self-consciously after the effect, savouring his moment. Hatred rises in Anna, she feels its acid in her throat. 'But I can think of plenty of people who would. People like to know these things. And I would not have thought, my beloved Christopher,' his voice curdling with intimation, 'that your life, your reputation, what's left of it, could take a further battering. I rather think it would be a coup de grâce.'

Anna sees her father leaning backwards, his hands out behind him clutching at the wall, and she thinks, he's falling, he's fainting, and she starts towards him with a cry, fear for him extinguishing her own pain.

But he is not falling, he is reaching behind him and his fingers are feeling for something, and when they find it he raises up his black stick and turns it so the ivory head becomes a weapon, and Jonathan sees it coming, but is not quick enough, his body is incapable of swift movement, and the ivory strikes his head with a sound that echoes the logs in the fire, Anna thinks it is the fire, she cannot believe what she is seeing.

And Jonathan is falling, his legs are crumpling as he steps backwards and his foot catches against a table leg in this crowded little room, and as he falls his head, rolling from the first blow, strikes the corner of a small bookcase, all these tame domestic things are conspiring to bring his life to an end, but they are not enough. Jonathan has not lived the life he has to be overthrown by a blow and a fall. He has slept rough for years, suffered far harsher beatings, escaped greater threats. He has conned elderly gentlemen out of their life's savings for a swift handjob, sweet-talked his way onto high tables and captains' tables, kicked out teeth over a half bottle of gin. He rolls himself over so he can sit up, feels his head with a practised hand and examines the blood on it, then grasps the arm of a wooden chair and pulls himself to his feet. There is a new look on his face which suggests money is no longer what he is looking for. He sways, but he stays upright. His lips emit faint panting hisses as he tries to regain his breath, but Anna can tell he is going to try and move quickly when he can, and she looks at Christopher and sees the exhaustion on his face, and more than that, the doubt, the revulsion at what he has just tried to do, and alarm at the impending result of his failure to do it. He raises his stick again, but this time in both hands, defensively, across his body, anticipating Jonathan's onslaught. The eyes of both men never waver from each other's, there is knowledge there of something final. Yet when Jonathan finds the strength to move he can do no more than grasp the stick himself, and their hands rest beside each other, evenly matched, neither one able, perhaps not willing, to bring about a resolution.

In Anna, however, the rage is strong, and it's against Jonathan for what he has tried to do and what he will do if he is permitted, and it is against her father for being someone who has kept a part of himself secret, after she has given him her life and made him the sole source of her happiness, and it is against herself for allowing this to happen.

So when she flies at Jonathan there is no stopping her, she would bring down a fit man twice her height she is so full of anger and the strength it gives her, strength such as she never knew she had. She wrenches the walking stick from their hands and swings it like an axe, just as her father had, and again, and as Jonathan drops to his knees and the ivory head cracks home a third time, she is already mindful of the blood and she puts her hands under his arms and pulls him into the kitchen where the linoleum is more washable, and she checks his breathing and puts a plastic bag over his head and takes rope from the cupboard under the stairs and winds it round his neck so it closes round the mouth of the bag and pulls on it to drag him out of the back of the door into the garden and into one of the beds where the blood can be dug into the soil, and she checks his breathing again and sets her foot on his neck and pulls on the rope and goes on doing this until his breathing stops.

The rope is sticky and wet with blood and rain, everything is sticky, her hands are too, and she returns to the kitchen to wash them. On the floor there is a pool of blood, red like cherries, smeared towards the door where she has dragged him, and when she bends to wipe it up she finds she is trembling so violently she can't hold the cloth properly, it just sends the blood shooting sideways, and then she is sick on the floor like a dog, it's as if the anger is coming out of her mouth and afterwards she sinks into the corner and cries for what seems like a lifetime.

Outside in the garden, someone moans.

Anna's eyes snap open in terror, but also in a sort of wild hope. But it is not Jonathan, it is Christopher, on his knees and pawing the body of his dead, stinking lover of old, peering at his face through the rain in the light from the windows.

He too is crying, he is sobbing, mumbling.

'What has she done?' she hears him say. 'What has she done?'

What she does now is wash, clean, obliterate all traces as much as she can, meticulous and methodical as she always is, scrubbing and soaping. Her hatred has vanished now, she is void of all feeling.

They will need to rid themselves of Jonathan, and they have neither strength nor time for digging.

'The rivers are full,' says Christopher.

So they drag him to the car and wrap him in plastic bin bags to protect the seats and take him to a bridge and unbundle him from the bags and roll him over into the boisterous waters and send him on his way to the sea.

He might be found, washed up against a bank somewhere. They'll think he's a drunk who got into a fight. A vagrant who ended up as vagrants do. He may be too decomposed for them to tell how he died. And whatever happens, probably no one will know who he is.

AND LATER, SOME HOURS later, Christopher, broken, says to Anna, 'There is just one thing left I want you to help me with, my darling.'

AND ANNA IS willing to help him, and she does it for love, mostly.

Afterthought

. . . Rumour is a pipe
Blown by surmises, jealousies, conjectures,
And of so easy and so plain a stop
That the blunt monster with uncounted heads,
The still-discordant wavering multitude,
Can play upon it.

William Shakespeare, *Henry IV, Part 2*

Angus doesn't like funerals on principle, so he's sitting this one out on a bench outside the churchyard looking down the road that leads to the centre of the town. He leans forward with his elbows on his knee, crouched against the steady wind, occasionally shivering and pulling on his cigarette. He is thinking about Alex Rainsford and Christopher Hughes and Luke, and how no one had intended it to end up this way, but that makes you wonder what they did intend, and that's what he is thinking about when someone blocks out the sunlight and a voice asks, 'Are they burying Christopher Hughes here?' He says yes, but the man doesn't move, is looking around him as if searching for something. He seems distracted.

'Up there,' Angus points, being helpful.

Instead the man sits down next to him. He's quite a bit older than Angus, but he's in good shape, bearing up well, skin healthy, no excess fat. Not a man who indulges himself, thinks Angus, who does. He's wearing a dark brown suede jacket and dark blue jeans and his red hair is cut short. Neat, sober and responsible.

But for some reason not going up to the church.

The man sighs to himself and rests his head on his hand, his elbow on the armrest of the seat.

'The funeral's just started,' says Angus. Then, 'I don't like them much either.'

'It's not that,' the man says, 'I'm not interested in him. I'm happy he's dead.' He looks round at Angus. 'I suppose that's terrible.'

'Well, you obviously didn't like him much. Plenty didn't.'

'Did you know him?'

'Up to a point. I was at the school.'

'So was I.'

'When were you here?'

'A long time ago. I wasn't one of the boys. I was a teacher. Not for very long, as it turned out.'

'Fell out with the old man, did you?'

'Oh, yes.'

Angus nods. Easy to do.

'One of Meniston's walking wounded,' says Angus. He stretches out his hand. 'Angus.'

'Daniel.' Then, 'His daughter wrote to me, actually, asked me to come. Anna.' As he says her name he presses his thumb into his palm and looks away, squinting at the sun.

Angus wonders whether to pursue this, then decides not to.

'You'd better get going, then.'

They sit together for a while, then Daniel says, 'Right,' and gets to his feet. 'Good to meet you,' he says to Angus. The sun is behind him, so his face is in shadow. He turns to walk along the wall towards the gate, but what with the sunshine and the curve in the wall off to the right, Angus can't tell whether he goes in at the gate or not.